THE AQUATICS

THE AQUATICS

OSVALDE LEWAT

Translated by Maren Baudet-Lackner

COFFEE HOUSE PRESS
Minneapolis
2025

Cover design by Alban Fischer
Book design by Ann Sudmeier
Author photograph © Philippe Matsas

Originally published in French in 2021 by Éditions Les Escales, Paris, France as *Les Aquatiques.*

This work received support for excellence in publication and translation from Albertine Translation, a program created by Villa Albertine and funded by Albertine Foundation.

Coffee House Press books are available to the trade through our primary distributor, Consortium Book Sales & Distribution, cbsd.com or (800) 283-3572. For personal orders, catalogs, or other information, write to info@coffeehousepress.org.

Coffee House Press is a nonprofit literary publishing house. Support from private foundations, corporate giving programs, government programs, and generous individuals helps make the publication of our books possible. We gratefully acknowledge their support in detail in the back of this book.

LIBRARY OF CONGRESS CATALOGING-IN-PUBLICATION DATA

Names: Lewat, Osvalde, author. | Baudet-Lackner, Maren, translator.
Title: The aquatics / Osvalde Lewat; translated by Maren Baudet-Lackner.
Other titles: Aquatiques. English
Description: Minneapolis: Coffee House Press, 2025. | Originally published in French in 2021 by Éditions Les Escales, Paris, France as Les Aquatiques
Identifiers: LCCN 2025022633 (print) | LCCN 2025022634 (ebook) | ISBN 9781566897457 (paperback) | ISBN 9781566897464 (epub)
Subjects: LCGFT: Novels.
Classification: LCC PQ3989.3.L485 A8813 2025 (print) | LCC PQ3989.3.L485 (ebook) | DDC 843.92—dc23/eng/20250508
LC record available at https://lccn.loc.gov/2025022633
LC ebook record available at https://lccn.loc.gov/2025022634

PRINTED IN THE UNITED STATES

32 31 30 29 28 27 26 25 1 2 3 4 5 6 7 8

To Hélène Ngahane
My mother, the cornerstone.

To Luc, Lucie-Hélène and Raphaël
My rocks

Ah! If you loved me
What chance would you have to hate me?

—Tchicaya U Tam'si
Epitomé

Prologue

We buried Madeleine the first time twenty years ago. Somewhere in the middle of nowhere. The funeral was like her life—rushed, slapdash. She had lived in splendor and died at the age of thirty-nine, poor as Job. Her family found a small plot of land, not too expensive, not too nearby, where no one would claim the square yard beneath which she would be laid to rest. A farmer from Fènn, the city where she had grown up—a former classmate, and a jilted ex-lover people said—had taken pity on them. Without too much haggling, he had agreed to cede a meticulously measured scrap of land outside the village for a trifling sum.

Madeleine Lapteu was five feet and three inches tall. The coffin was five feet and seven inches long. Before she died, her waist measured thirty-eight inches. After the accident, after the hospital, she dropped quite a few; everyone who saw her agreed that she'd trimmed down dramatically. Since wood wasn't cheap, they calculated the width of the coffin for half of her waist at sixteen inches. Then there was the zinc, yet another expense. Though it was terribly costly, zinc was indispensable, and they got it at a good price. Everything had its price: the depth of the grave, the tiling of the walls, the slab that covered the tomb, the sand, the cement, the water, the gravel, the choir, the labor (that of the gravediggers, the criers, the gun-saluters, and the priest), the rented hunting rifle, and the ammunition. They kept to what was strictly necessary, the bare minimum. There was no room for waste.

At the end of the Mass, the coffin was sealed. Holy water sprinkled. The priest uttered his litanies, and they sang "Libera me." Sennke, Madeleine's younger daughter, mumbled her final goodbyes to her mother amid sobs, and the attendees were duly moved. The older daughter, Katmé, kept quiet. No tears. No nothing. Someone shook her shoulder and whispered, "Say goodbye to your mother, dear, say a few words, she can hear you, you know." A second voice joined in, "Treasure, everyone is watching, you didn't even cry, people will think you're not sad that your mama is dead, and you know she's waiting for you to say goodbye to make her way up to Heaven." A third voice hissed, "Say something, Katmé! What is wrong with this child? Didn't you love your mother? God will punish you if you don't speak up, so say something, for goodness' sake, we're about to bury her and you'll never see her again, you know!" Katmé's lips remained sealed. Innocent Patong, the girls' father, tried to slip a handful of dirt, which he had just scooped off the ground, into his pocket for some reason. A member of Madeleine's family twisted his arm to prevent this. Two shots were fired into the air, in line with the Fènn tradition for a middle-aged woman's funeral; they muffled the wailing of Mama Récia, Madeleine's only sister, who knew more than most about crying, mourning, and burials.

With Madeleine wedged inside, the coffin was trussed with raffia straps, and carried by four of Mama Récia's many sons, who took slow, even steps, in time to the psalms sung by the choir and the paid mourners, toward what they then believed would be her final resting place.

I will not wait to strive
For the bliss purported;
He who sets forth, who goes ahead
Will be rewarded.

While the attendees recited their final prayers and shed their final tears, the coffin rested for a few moments on wooden slats placed across the grave. Then, maneuvered by the four sons, it began its descent into the earth. Exactly fifty-two seconds after the operation began, the casket got stuck. The hole wasn't wide enough. The men persisted. The coffin was being difficult, refusing to budge. The choir sang fervently, at the top of its lungs:

Near the throne, the crown
Awaits the victor.
No truce! Rise up!
Said the Lord.

Let us be content to obey;
Don't hesitate, don't stray!
He who loses his way, loses his place
At the banquet in Heaven.

Mama Récia's sons, the villagers who had come to the funeral (it was an opportunity for entertainment and feasting like any other), the nimblest of the choir members, the few friends who had made the trip, and various other volunteers bold enough to overcome their distaste for the reddish Fènn earth that stuck to and stained their shoes and clothes—in sum, all the able-bodied men got to it, struggling to push the recalcitrant wooden box down to the bottom of the hole. There was a sound of shattering glass: The window in the coffin lid, designed to allow the mourners to see Madeleine's face until the end, had broken. Once the initial surprise wore off, they conceded defeat. It was time to face the facts. The casket wouldn't reach the bottom of the grave, and it couldn't be pulled out either. They would have to find jackhammers, shovels, and picks. They would have to dig. They would have to demolish. As Katmé and Sennke looked on in horror, the men smashed the cheap tile whose substantial width had been left out of the otherwise meticulous calculations conducted to determine the dimensions of the grave. The choir stopped singing. The hired mourners—whose laments were nearly impossible to silence when it came to earning their due—curled their fists around their mouths to signify their shock. Everyone was quiet as the men savagely widened the grave.

Funerals never come at a good time. Madeleine's came at a particularly bad one. For several weeks, students and a handful of politicians had been demanding that the Father of the Nation and President of the Republic end the single-party system, declare the country a democracy, call free elections, increase wages, put a stop to arbitrary arrests, and make university free for all—in short, they had issued a host of demands that some shrewd observers described as naïve. The Old Man, the Father of the Nation, had turned a deaf ear, provoking economic paralysis throughout the country. Even if the family could have afforded it, it still would have been impossible, in those troubled times, and on such short notice, to find a hardware store open in Fènn so they could retile and cement the grave. Since there were more dissidents in the region than in most other parts of the country, shopkeepers enthusiastically complied with the call to close their businesses on certain days of the week, like Saturday, the big market day.

Following some hasty confabulation, Madeleine was buried.

Madeleine was buried on a Saturday morning. A Saturday morning before noon. That Saturday morning, before noon, as soon as her mother was buried, Katmé decided to bury her mother's memory as well. She was thirteen years old.

PART ONE

1

I preferred to take Boulevard du Trente-Avril, a site of permanent chaos that lengthened my trip, rather than the shortest, most logical route, which inevitably led me past the soccer stadium, shops, playgrounds, and my childhood home. The only moving cars were the ones driving in the wrong direction. Some drivers, tired of waiting, danced bare-chested on the asphalt or on their hoods; taxi drivers honked or listened to the latest hits at full volume on their radios; street hawkers glued their faces to windows, peddling all sorts of food and wares; and motorcycles slalomed between the larger, trapped vehicles. I was headed to Samy's studio, a former carwash located on the outskirts of the Cité des Enseignants. The neighborhood where Sennke and I had lived with Madeleine. I spotted a police uniform in the distance and unlocked the RAV4. Perched on the running board, the open door under my arm, I gestured vigorously in his direction. When he reached me, he pinched the visor of his khaki beret between his thumb and index finger.

"Mama Prefect, God bless you. You're in a go-slow, oh! I beg your pardon. I'll clear the road for you, now now."

The prefectural badge on the windshield hadn't escaped his attention. I got back into the car and rolled down the window.

I usually refused to take advantage of the priority lane. Today, I needed to keep my arms and legs busy. Avoid potholes, taxis, and motorcycles slamming on their brakes without warning, pedestrians who cross without looking. To get the letter from the Fènn Town Hall out of my head, I had to keep my attention focused elsewhere.

"Abeg, Mama Prefect, save a brother."

"And who will save *me*?" I joked.

"Mama, Mama, times are tough . . . Your sister at home dey always on my back."

I took my purse from the passenger seat, pulled out a five-thousand franc bill, rolled it up in my fist, then palmed it to the officer. In no time, he had cleared a path. I jammed the key into the ignition.

The SUV bounced down the dirt alleyway that led to the studio. It was a far cry from the paved roads and air-conditioned streets of the Fleuve neighborhood where I lived with Tashun. This district, where the government once housed Ministry of Education employees, had grown dilapidated since it was sold off to private investors, but the rent was affordable. Impoverished, like most parts of the capital, the Cité des Enseignants wouldn't be able to avoid the status of "ghetto" much longer, despite the flowering flame trees that brightened the houses. Everywhere, families had moved into makeshift shelters cobbled together from sheet metal and wood. During the rainy season, their hovels turned into hovels on stilts. An expensive renovation to raise its foundation protected Samy's studio from the elements; high above it all, the veranda provided a stunning, unobstructed view of poverty and all its ills. Samy knew that I used to live nearby. I would have preferred he settle somewhere else, but he said the atmosphere stimulated his creativity. And he really did seem more prolific since he'd been working there. If the exhibition—his first solo show—was a success, he would finally be able to turn the page on the moldings he sold to tourists on the hunt for cheap souvenirs. I was eager to see his sculptures, his new work. I knew this wasn't the right time to mention the letter I had received. I also knew that I would mention it anyway. Who else could I talk to about it? Under different circumstances, regarding any other subject, I would have laughed as I showed him the obsequious, handwritten note the mayor of Fènn had added to the bottom of the page. *The prospect of serving His Excellency and Madam Excellency fills me with deferential joy.* My laugh, which Tashun always found inappropriate, would have slipped past my lips. But not this time. This letter didn't make me want to laugh at all.

"The activist artist in all his glory!" Samy exclaimed, pointing at four sculptures supported by wooden rods. Hollow cheeks, red eyes, dark circles. He clearly wasn't getting enough sleep. "This isn't the final scale, just maquettes," he continued. "It will be bigger, the height of a grown man. I'm doing ten on the same theme."

Four male figures stood before me, their long necks headless, two-thirds of their abdomens replaced by their heads lodged between their solar plexuses and belly buttons. The square heads overflowed on all sides to create love handles and sagging bellies. Bloody nostrils, mouths twisted in pain, eyes wide with the same despair found in Courbet's *The Desperate Man.* The faces of the four terracotta characters Samy had sculpted were vaguely familiar. I thought for a moment. The president and the three vice presidents.

"So?" he asked anxiously.

"You really want to put this on display?"

"There's more, not just sculptures," he said as he gestured toward the far end of the warehouse. "I'm still thinking about the title for the show, but I think I've got something. Come with me."

A rattan bookcase, volumes on sculpture and photography, old newspapers, a pile of drawing notebooks, and on top of them, a sheet of paper.

"Come sit here, you'll be more comfortable while you read," he urged as he pushed toward me the tall bamboo stool where he usually sat to draw and held out the piece of paper.

Ante Mortem. Before death. As I read, I grew uneasy. In Zambuena, people weren't arrested for expressing disagreement with the president or his party anymore. Samy had the right to sculpt and write what he wanted, to criticize whomever he chose. That was his role. The important thing was that he have no political ambitions, and since he didn't, there was nothing to fear. I only hoped that he wasn't lying to himself so deftly that he actually believed that choosing the right type of clay—sandstone, ceramic, porcelain, or kaolin—and obediently following the meticulous, thankless steps required to create a sculpture or a bas-relief would be enough to influence the status quo. He couldn't actually believe that a bold and powerful piece of art forged from nothing could force society to deviate from its fixed trajectory. An activist artist, fantastic! Tashun would be sure to choke on that. "Your friend is a constant thorn in my side!" I could already hear him bray.

A projector displayed an experimental film on the floor: overweight children devouring banknotes, laughing hysterically with each mouthful, while others looked on angrily, licking their lips. I made a mental note to ask Samy if the bills were real or from Zambony, our local version of Monopoly—in the video, they looked authentic. Against the wall, a plywood trestle bore a series of 24 x 32-inch black-and-white photographs. Bodies of children, teens, the elderly, men, and women. Bodies pieced together to create a two-headed, multi-sexed fresco. Was it in keeping with the times? Was it good? Beautiful? Modern? I didn't know what to think except that I was troubled by the combination of buttocks as old as Methuselah with a young man's head, a grandmother's withered breasts, children's legs, and sex organs of different sizes and types. Not to mention the obese little gluttons.

Last but not least, a series of photographs titled *The Aquatics* featured terrified faces emerging from wastewater and flooding, ID cards floating, women hoisting babies, lamps, or suitcases overhead, the swollen face of a drowned man. The images weren't new. Every year during the rainy season, the same ones, more or less, appeared on television screens and newspaper pages. But Samy's frame—rusted corrugated sheet metal, scrap metal, and papier mâché—and his juxtaposition of these cataclysmic images with pictures of carefree couples lying in a field of ripening corn with their children, amplified the radical despair that was bursting from every scene. My eyes were full. When had Samy had time to do all this? His anxiety was stifling.

"So?"

I didn't know where to start.

"If you don't like it, you can say so, Katmé!" he exclaimed with a reproachful look.

"Come on, don't get upset. It's just that . . . How can I put this . . . ? It's . . ." I despised my voice for jumping an octave without my consent.

I asked to see it all again, once, twice, three times. How I wish I had been able to declare with certainty, "I like this but not that." Samy believed that a lack of linguistic precision resulted from a lack of sincerity; he would ask me to find the words. What little I know about sculpture and the visual arts I owe to him. The library catalogue at the high school where we met was not so bold as to include the fine arts; and growing up with Mama Récia—whose fierce devotion to the Bible and the Eucharist limited all attempts to embrace other forms of creation—certainly never exposed me to Sow, Depara, or El Anatsui.

Samy slid down the wall to sit on the floor and extended his legs. A part of the image from the video projector reflected off his plastic mules. I sat down in his rocking chair, the sole comfortable seat in the room. Samy only sat in it when he wanted to "unlock" his creativity. I looked down at him and steeled myself to say whatever I thought as it came to me, no hesitation or overthinking. "Maybe there's too much to take in at once. It's very dense, Samy."

"It's my first solo show! It can't be ordinary!" Anger loomed in his voice. He made as though to stand, but stayed seated, gathering his knees beneath his chin for a moment before stretching them back out.

"Sculpture is your art, not the rest of this stuff!"

"It's all my art! Some of these photos are four years old. I recorded the video footage two years ago during a workshop with my students. I'm obese like the kids in the video, obese and overfull of everything I want to show people. Did you really think I had done all this in two months?"

"You should narrow your focus a bit, Samy. You'll suffocate people, otherwise. You should tone it down a little. Really, it's too much."

He stood up, sullen, and leaned back against the wall. The fat children burst into laughter on the hem of his pants. I left the rocking chair to stand across from the photos of the flooding again.

"You really don't like it, do you?" he asked, coming closer.

I frowned. "Their faces . . . It's too raw, Samy."

"What these people live through is raw! Not everyone is lucky enough to live in the Fleuve neighborhood. You're starting to worry me! Keuna says they're very good. The photos and everything else!"

"Keuna thinks it's very good, well that's great, I'm thrilled for you. When did I lose the right to say that it's not perfect?" I asked, my tone drier than I would have liked. Hearing him mention Keuna always annoyed me. "Your sculptures, your title—*Ante Mortem*—you're looking for trouble! It's like giving unripe plantain to a newborn. Your Keuna, who loves to go around playing White Lady all the time, how long has she even lived here? When Tashun sees this! Let's not forget that he's bankrolling it all!" As soon as the final words crossed my lips, I could taste ash in my mouth. You can't choke ash back down.

Samy let out a nervous laugh. "What was that? What did you say, Katmé?" His lips curled into a bitter line. I reached my hand out to him, full of regret. He recoiled. "Keuna says it will be a success. I'll pay you back. I swear I'll pay you back."

"Samy, that was stupid. I'm sorry."

His features hardened and he grasped his arms across his chest, his back to the wall once more. I tried to unclasp his arms, but he pushed me away. How could I have said such a thing? My tongue could be sharp and merciless, but never with Samy. It was the letter. The letter at the bottom of my purse. The letter and Tashun's extravagant plans. I needed to hurt someone. Samy was my unlucky victim.

"That was hateful," I said, pleading now. "Tashun doesn't even know about the money or the studio. Please . . . I'm sorry . . . What do I know? I go on and on, but I don't even know how to hold a drawing pencil properly! Samy . . ."

He turned his red eyes toward me. He was a nervous wreck. He was a nervous wreck and, though he called me his airport, the safest place for him to land, his better half, I hadn't noticed. As usual. He pushed off the wall and made his way to the far end of the studio, pulling aside the curtain that hid the small private space that he had set up for himself, and lay down on his wrought-iron bed.

I followed him and sat down on the edge of the mattress, on the Scottish wool blanket that covered the sheets and pillow. Oblique rays of sunshine entered through the studio's glass ceiling and shone on Samy's ashy skin, on his face ravaged by insomnia.

I took off my ballerina flats, crawled up the bed, and lay down next to him. I lifted his arm and slipped my head onto his shoulder.

"It's not even you, Kat," he finally said after a long silence. "It's not even you. Ety called and it didn't go well. The usual complaints. I'm never available, the studio takes up all my time, and so on. I sat in the rocking chair for an hour trying to get over our conversation. And as soon as I got up to get back to work, the Loon turned up. Come to see what I'm 'up to in this dump' since I haven't been home for a few days. As usual, she made it very clear that, at my age, it would be best to give up on such frivolities, that if I were a real artist, we would know by now. I could have killed her. I could have strangled her."

"You've known your mother for thirty-five years, Samy . . ." I had forbidden myself to call her the Loon, as he did. He often said that someday he would write a novel, and the first line would be: *This is how I became allergic to my mother.* "Your mother's not a bad person, you know. Maybe just not very smart . . ."

"I have my doubts about that. At a certain point, the line between stupidity and cruelty blurs. I resent her for it. Ignorance doesn't excuse her behavior. She's right, though. I'm a fake artist and a real failure. Just thinking about this show paralyzes my brain and fingers."

Samy had been turned down so many times that he'd lost all hope of ever having a major solo show until he met Keuna, the owner of the new Bubinga Project gallery. As far as his work went, Samy had heard it all: too ethnic, not authentic enough, too documentary, not realistic enough, too conceptual, not abstract enough, too political, not socially conscious enough, too unique, not original enough.

I took his hand and placed it on my chest. "I don't have the right training to understand your approach. I'm not a good judge, but my heart doesn't lie. Believe in yourself."

"I hope it goes somewhere this time, or I'll have no choice but to rot away in my art teacher's smock until retirement."

"Please, Samy, don't start down that road again . . ." I loosened my embrace and propped myself up on one elbow. "Now it's my turn to show you something," I said. I walked barefoot across the floor to retrieve my bag, which I had dropped at the foot of the rocking chair. Amid paperclips, menthol lip balm, a headwrap, and some crumpled papers, I found what I was looking for. "Tashun gave me this at the prefecture this morning. I know it's not an excuse. Let's just say that I've been a bit of a mess, too, since leaving his office."

Samy skimmed the letter. "What do you plan to do?" he asked, just as Tashun had a few hours earlier.

"First, go to Fènn and find out more. They don't say when the grave has to be moved. It's supposedly urgent but the tone is about as dry as a shipping report. Urgent in this country could mean tomorrow or ten years from now."

Muffled voices reached us from outside. Someone was knocking. Samy handed me the letter. As he made his way to the front door, I gathered my things, frustrated that our conversation had been cut short. I joined him and squinted; the sun was in our eyes. There were six children who looked to be about ten years old, each holding a terracotta vase.

"Uncle Samy, we've chosen our designs, and we prepared the patina like you told us," said the tallest boy.

"Customers prefer vases with enameled necks, Uncle Samy. They always sell best. Can you show us how to make them?" asked another, whose T-shirt collar gaped.

"I thought you never saw anyone. Your goddaughters will be jealous when they find out," I joked. Samy usually gave Axelle and Alix sculpting lessons twice a week, but he had put them on hold to prepare for the show.

"I know, but if I stop teaching these kids, their parents will kill me. It's a good thing they come interrupt me, actually. Otherwise, I'd never see the light of day." Samy called the time he spent with his young potters his *pro bono publico* work. The children, who lived with their parents in dilapidated public housing on the outskirts of the Cité des Enseignants, sold the objects they made with his help at the market, claiming they were the artistic creations of tetraplegics from the local disabled center.

"What's his name?" I asked, gesturing towards the youngest-looking boy.

"Him? Little Paul. Little but clever. Very clever. Clay no longer holds any secrets for him, isn't that right, Little Paul?"

By way of reply, the kid puffed up his chest and smiled shyly.

"And here you have Blaise, Kouankeu, Emmanuel, Paul—Big Paul, that is—and Chrysostome."

I plunged my hand into my bag and pulled out a stack of bills, which I handed to Little Paul. "You share with the others, all right?"

He nodded. "Thank you, Mama. You lift us up, Mama!"

As I expected, Samy shook his head and gave me a disapproving look. He pinched my earlobe. "Mbindi, you know this is bordering on pathological, right?"

He walked me to the bottom of the stairs where we were surrounded by his beds of African violets, his miracle babies. The barren soil just outside of the studio had yielded to the gentle persuasion of Samy's fingers. The intense purple of the little flowers, a surreal shade of indigo, stood out against the ochre floor and muddy water around them.

I shared Tashun's big idea with Samy. "Maybe if we talk to him together, he'll see that it makes no sense . . . You could tell him—"

"As if your husband has ever taken me seriously! He only asks my opinion when it doesn't matter. It would be pointless, and you know it as well as I do."

The boys watched us impatiently, eager for me to leave.

Samy hugged me and went back up the steps.

As I opened the car door, I heard him say behind me, "Mbindi! *Ab amicis honesta petamus.* One should only ask from a friend what he is capable of!" Providence doesn't give you a Latin teacher for a mother without consequence: Samy declaimed classical locutions with scandalous ease.

I turned around, raised my right hand, and joined the tips of my thumb and index finger, my other digits raised to the sky. Samy smiled.

As I brushed the fallen pink flame tree petals from the windshield and shooed away the stray dog who was urinating on my back tires, I wondered if Samy was alluding to my inability to gauge the quality of his work or to his inability to plead my cause to Tashun.

2

Axelle and Alix attempted to lift their father, who happily tumbled to the marble floor in a fit of laughter. I watched as the three of them climbed the spiral staircase to the bedrooms. The girls and I had finished dinner in the kitchen before Tashun got home. Now I was setting the table for him, in the official dining room. I liked having dinner in the kitchen with the twins when he was out. "You're teaching them it's normal to eat surrounded by burners, pots, and pans—I don't like it," Tashun would say, but I preferred the intimate setting of the rustic kitchen, with its unfinished rosewood furniture, whose bold aesthetic made up for its lack of comfort. The huge dining room had been designed during the colonial period to host the Governor General's receptions. The space was so vast, so grand, so clean, so beige, so ostentatiously well-decorated. The Ministry of Housing had paid a European interior designer quite handsomely to redesign it when the decision had been made to turn the building into the residence of the prefect of the capital.

The residence came with a dozen employees, including two chefs, but Tashun demanded that I prepare and serve his meals. "The quality of the meals served to the man of the house should not be dependent on the staff's mood," he would explain. When we met, I was in my last year of teachers' college and he was in his final year at the National School of Civil Service. Back then I couldn't have imagined that he would someday espouse such a reductive vision of the ideal woman without a hint of irony.

"Is it ready?" he asked from the doorway.

"Just a minute."

I placed the sautéed folong with shrimp and ripe plantain on the table.

Tashun was barefoot, his shirt half unbuttoned. He had shed his jacket and tie. Heaven only knew where I would find them later and have to pick them up.

He sat down and shoveled in a mouthful of folong. "It's lukewarm, Kat."

"Hang on, I'll heat it up a bit more."

"Never mind, it's fine."

He was waiting for me to insist. I insisted.

I put the pot back on the burner. The leafy greens began to simmer, steam rising into the air. Tashun liked his meals very hot. His dinner was nearly scalding when I placed it back on the table in front of him.

"Weren't you supposed to make topsi banana today?" he asked upon removing the cloche, as if he'd only just seen the meal for the first time.

"When I left the prefecture, I went to see Samuel. I didn't have time to make topsi banana," I said.

The list of dishes Tashun would eat was fairly short, except when he was entertaining guests. For breakfast in the morning, he had leftovers from the night before. "No bread, coffee, or tea, like white people," he would say. "I need a solid meal to keep me going all day."

Cooking for him took me two to three hours a day. Thank God Bambili, the maid who took care of the twins, sometimes helped me out, like today.

"When's the preview again?"

"Early March. Balbine has put it in your calendar. I should warn you, though, the stuff he's working on is a little political," I ventured.

"Won't be the first time."

"That's true," I conceded, convincing myself I wasn't lying, not exactly. Samy had taken things much further this time, but Tashun would see for himself soon enough.

"We live in a democracy. It's good for people like him to express dissenting opinions. With all of the pieces we already have, let's not buy anything though, okay?"

"Not buy anything?"

"Oh, all right, I suppose we will . . . But, you know, we're Samuel Pankeu's biggest collectors. If his work were any good, he'd sell to other people. We can't be his only customers."

"We're not his only customers! What are you talking about?"

"If you say so . . . I'll believe it when I see it. I'm not a complete idiot, you know."

Tashun shoveled bites into his mouth, chewed, and swallowed as he talked, as if afraid someone might snatch his plate. Over the course of our life together, I'd observed that his tendency to swiftly devour, ingest, and consume extended well beyond the realm of food.

Between two mouthfuls, he wanted to know if I'd thought about his suggestion from earlier that morning. "I have, Tashun. And it's a no."

He placed his knife back down on the tablecloth, followed by his fork. He sat up tall in his chair, inclined his torso toward me, and looked into my eyes. "Katmé, when you are the wife of the prefect of the capital, not to mention a future member of the Central Committee, your mother's funeral—even after twenty years in the ground—cannot be a mere detail in your schedule," he said, his voice betraying thinly veiled irritation. "This new funeral for your mother—my mother-in-law, in case you've forgotten—has come along at just the right time. It's a sign. Don't tell me you don't see it!"

He wanted to turn Madeleine's exhumation and reburial into a party event. "A new funeral with honor and dignity," he had crowed upon handing me the letter which explained that Madeleine's grave—located directly in the path of a highway that would soon link the Haut-Fènn region to Akriba—needed to be moved promptly or else be demolished. Honor and dignity—if you added peace, you got Zambuena's motto. Grotesque. Utterly grotesque. Elsewhere people fought to escape death; in Zambuena we spent our whole lives preparing for it. Celebrating the dead was more important than taking care of the living. Depending on the extent of wasteful extravagance displayed, you earned respect, admiration, or disdain. People worked hard and saved up to build an impressive house in their native village, ready and waiting for future periods of mourning. After Madeleine's death, I'd seen my father twice. The first time was at my grandmother's funeral. My father's mother, who'd lived her entire life completely broke, was granted a "come-see" funeral complete with "shut-it" pomp. A coffin with gilded grooves; a black, Zimbabwean marble mausoleum; champagne, wine, and beer; an outrageous amount of food; professional mourners, renowned traditional dance troupes, and conspicuously famous guests. Everyone had congratulated my father. That day something I'd struggled to grasp at Madeleine's interment became clear: a funeral could be a success or a failure. Despite the presence of my father, the wealthy businessman Innocent Patong, Madeleine's had been a complete failure.

Tashun, having finished his folong, was savoring the soursop sorbet. "You can't rush your mother's funeral," he added. "Makes it look like you're running away from something."

"Or maybe you're the one running toward something?" I ventured.

He shot me a wild glance. "Spare me the wit, okay? Flippancy doesn't put food on the table."

"Let me remind you that you wanted to be the sole breadwinner in this household. It was your decision."

"We can't keep coming back to this, damn it! Plenty of women would light candles in thanks and count their blessings to be the wife of the prefect of Akriba if they were in your shoes."

I felt hydrocephalic. My head full of dark, gelatinous soot. I had never returned to Madeleine's grave. Never brought her favorite meal, palm oil, salt, or even a pitcher of raffia wine. As far as I remember, Madeleine preferred red wine. But raffia wine is what you place on a grave in Haut-Fènn. I didn't dare imagine what sort of condition her grave was in, or what people and friends would think of me if they knew that I'd never visited, never fed, and never cleaned it. What *wouldn't* they say upon discovering the contrast between my neglect of Madeleine's grave—and the deceased herself, they'd rightfully assume—and the indecent party organized for her second funeral? No one would understand. Of course they wouldn't! I wouldn't understand myself. Tashun asked me to consider it from another angle, in another light, from a different perspective. He rarely threatened me, but it did happen from time to time; I would take offense and resist, but, in the end, I tended to give in. That's how things had worked between us since our wedding. That's how it had gone for my leave of absence from teaching to play Madam Prefect full time. If I gave in yet again, I'd be no different from my father who had used his mother's death to make himself look good. No. The more I thought about it, the more something inside me hardened.

"Uncle Ambroise thinks having a statement funeral for your mother is an excellent idea."

“You’ve already spoken to Uncle Ambroise about Madeleine’s funeral?” I asked flatly. “When? The letter only arrived this morning.”

“I see him every day, Kat. I paid him a visit at party headquarters before coming home. I certainly couldn’t keep it from him! He asked me to have you call him. Do it tomorrow, don’t waste any time. He and Djama have invited you to lunch at their house next week. He wants to help us, you know how he is. Djama will free up some time for you. You’ll need her.”

I could resist Tashun. But I couldn’t even dream of defying Uncle Ambroise, my husband’s all-powerful protector. We both knew it. Tashun’s father, who loved hunting wild game, had handed down the passion to his son. Back when the family was wealthy and Tashun’s father was still an envied and respected minister in the government, back before their social demotion, he would take time off during school vacations to teach his sons, Tashun and his brother Henri, to hunt. He taught them to handle rifles, make themselves useful in a hunting party, and flush out doe, boar, pangolins, porcupines, hares, snakes, and even crocodiles on occasion. Sometimes they would spend the night in the bush tracking game. Nostalgic Tashun often retold the stories of those memorable hunting trips with their father. The same trips had turned his brother Henri into a vegetarian and the chair of a beetle protection society. Later Henri got a job with the World Wildlife Fund, so he and his wife had moved to Kenya and then France, where they currently lived. Tashun had retained a fondness for warrior metaphors and an instinct for seizing the moment: Too early or too late and you miss your shot and go home empty-handed. If Uncle Ambroise was involved in Madeleine’s funeral, it had been decided. In brandishing that invitation to lunch and mentioning Ambroise’s wife, Djama—the president of the exclusive Friends of Zambuena Club or FZC—Tashun wasn’t threatening me with your everyday double-barreled hunting rifle; I was in the crosshairs of a revolving rifle. With six chambers. Any form of counterattack would be social and conjugal hara-kiri. I intended to live. I held people who committed suicide and those who died young, like Madeleine, in equal disdain. Life first, as long as possible. Tashun had sensed that this hand would be difficult to win, so he’d played a joker.

Once the surprise had worn off, I considered getting angry. On principle. I decided against it. To be honest, I never actually thought I could defeat Tashun; at least now I wouldn't be wasting my energy. Uncle Ambroise would help me save face. I would have lunch with them and receive my orders. I was perfectly lucid: Uncle Ambroise didn't make suggestions or recommendations. He gave orders. My husband took after his accommodating, epicurean father, who died not long after our wedding, less than he took after this distant uncle and godfather who opportunistically reentered Tashun's life after he had helped the president's party regain control of the provincial town hall where he was deputy prefect. From that moment on, his godfather, who had eight daughters, became a fixture in our lives and made it clear that he saw Tashun as the son destiny had refused him. Harsh beneath his friendly exterior, Uncle Ambroise was a sly, bald, pot-bellied childhood friend of the president and a member of his inner circle. He was the gatekeeper, a *deus ex machina* for anyone who hoped to reach the highest echelon in any field in Zambuena. Every time our paths crossed, I couldn't help but shudder at the thought that Tashun, who aped his mentor—he'd adopted his felt hat, speech mannerisms, and many of his gestures—might soon become a full-on caricature. Like Uncle Ambroise, Tashun was far from tall, and he was losing his hair. Since he'd become prefect, his belly had grown rounder and the hair at his temples had begun to gray. At thirty-four, with his plump, baby face and eyes that were old beyond his years, my husband looked like a young man who had somehow snuck into the world of senior citizens.

A familiar feeling in my underwear caught my attention. Whenever Tashun hassled or taunted me until I wearily capitulated, my body would still refuse to surrender. A vain clamor of protest would rise up from my cramping pelvis and sticky underwear. A statement funeral for Madeleine was a calculated move. Why was I surprised? I felt a thin, viscous stream snake its way down my leg. I left the table and rushed to the bathroom. Uncle Ambroise's arrival in our lives had freed a new Tashun from his chrysalis. Not so new, actually. I could still see the look of disbelief on Samy's clean-shaven face the day I'd told him I was getting married. "You're going to marry him? Him?! Are you kidding?

Don't do it because of some silly Catholic notion; you don't have to marry someone just because you 'did it' with him."

After using forceps to help me deliver the girls, the doctor had announced I would be unable to have any more children. No boy for Tashun, who claimed he'd come to terms with it, turning down offers from the many women eager to give him an heir. "God gives us our children," he would always say. "He decided we would have two girls, so we have two girls." I gathered he used condoms with the others. Since I couldn't get pregnant, I didn't watch the calendar too closely; but somewhere, in a distant corner of my mind, I knew that the reddish fluid that had stained my underwear and was now forming a small pool on the speckled bathroom tile was around ten days early. I plunged my hand into the basket where I kept my pads.

Tomorrow I'll call Uncle Ambroise.

3

Still swathed in darkness, the room exhaled the scent of the night. The space next to me was dry. Tashun generally left early to arrive at the prefecture before his staff. I felt around for the cord to the mahogany lamp on my nightstand. My hand came up empty. The cord got tangled up behind the bedside table every night. A lot of good it did me to have a light within arm's reach. I got out of bed, knelt, and slipped my fingers into the tiny gap between the nightstand and the wall to give the cord a yank. The lamp toppled over, landing without a sound on the thick carpet. They'd thought of everything at the residence, except a multiway light switch on my side of the bed. Oh well, I'd make do in the dark; maybe I'd stub my toe on a chair or get my feet tangled up in the clothes Tashun had probably left strewn across the carpet. He invariably shed his things as he perambulated through the house. Hat in the living room, keys in the fruit basket, tie on the sofa, shoes in the family room, underwear on the bathroom tile, watch on the girls' nightstand when he put them to bed, socks abandoned on the kitchen counter. I picked them up. The one time I dared to call him out, he said that at least *he* left his things around his own house, unlike so many of his friends, who left them elsewhere. I kept my mouth shut after that. It was a compelling argument in Zambuena. About a year after our wedding, Djonbap informed me that Tashun "didn't go straight home" after work. I stormed into his office. "Who told you that?" he shouted, furious to see me burst in during his workday and make a scene that could have waited until evening. "Who told you that?" he barked, twisting my arm behind my back. Swayed by the pain, I betrayed my coworker at the high school. "Djonbap, huh?" I nodded, begging him to let go of my arm; it felt as though a host of thin blades were piercing my shoulder. "So Djonbap told you I don't come straight home when I leave the office . . . But did she tell you that I fucked her too?" So I started picking up his things. When I got tired of it, Bambili took over.

I confronted my curtains, full of determination. As a result of disproportionate effort on my part, the traverse rod and hooks eventually stirred, and a piece of sky appeared. That would do. Motto, our valet, would laugh to hear that I had once again failed to open the curtains properly. He seemed to be the only one who knew their secrets.

I made my way to Axelle and Alix's room. The twins could have each had their own bedroom—the house had seven—but they didn't want to be separated. In the morning, before waking them up, I would lean over their beds and study their sleeping faces, so full of hope and joy. I would savor the moment and remind myself that none of it would have been possible without Tashun. Without his ferocious talent for seizing the present and his passion for shaping the future. Attentive, reliable, alive, and reassuring, he always kept a close eye on our well-being, if not my happiness. He was our foundation, our rock. A rock with prominent sharp edges.

I opened the drapes, which were simpler here: a rod and rings. All I had to do was push them aside. Sunlight stole through the slits in the shutters, projecting the shadow of the leaves on the giant Senegal mahogany in the courtyard onto the wall.

"Axelle, Alix, wake up! *Moïndjamoto,* it's time!" School started at eight o'clock at Saint-Christophe.

The twins groaned from beneath the covers. Alix's head emerged first. "No, no. It's not time to get up yet. You're such a cruel mother."

Axelle joined in, "Cruel and—"

"A cruel and heartless mother!" we all said in unison, before cracking up.

Once the girls were in the shower, I set out to find Motto. I found him in the staff room adjoining the kitchen, where he was eating drop doughnuts and cassava porridge. I mentioned the recalcitrant curtains and, as expected, he smiled, revealing his diastema—the gap between his teeth. His childlike smile always put me in a good mood. So I turned a blind eye to his hunched posture, craggy face, and slow, halting gait, which betrayed his status as a clandestine retiree, a defiant retiree who, like so many others, had fudged his date of birth to keep from finding himself out of work and broke, unable to feed his family, who depended on his salary. Back in the bedroom, he explained once again—in vain, I know, said the impish look in his eyes—how to subdue the tobacco-brown burlap curtains. Without wasting a moment, he handily opened the curtains, pushing them all the way to the corners of the sliding glass doors which opened out onto the garden, dotted with flowers and Samy's sculptures.

I thanked the valet warmly.

After a year living there, I still couldn't get used to having a valet. In fact, what *had* I gotten used to? Certainly not watching my home become a hive of activity from the first rays of dawn. I had a steward, four gardeners, two menservants, two cooks, day- and night-shift guards, a pool boy, and Bambili, whom I'd hired right after our wedding. Discreet, predictable, and reliable, Bambili sometimes served as an able intermediary between the employees and me.

For nearly a year, I'd started my days shut up in the small office with the steward to "oversee the residence's affairs" and "set the priorities for the day." The number of bars of soap in the closet, the cartons of milk to be purchased, the menus for upcoming official meals, the suspension of this or that employee, a salary advance for another, the stock of hard liquor in the bar and of wine in the cellar, the mops in need of replacement, and the butter, honey, and cheese to be ordered. Grocery lists wormed their way into my dreams. How I missed my students! The din of the classroom, the roughhousing before and after class, their questions, whether sophisticated or absurd, the fights, the kids who needed my encouragement and those who needed a firm hand, the smell of chalk, the way it squeaked on the board, the small talk with other teachers at the end of the day, the practical lessons in cooking, sewing, and embroidery. The boys often complained, "Miss, these classes won't ever be useful to us, we men aren't made for the kitchen or sewing—we'll have wives!" But their eyes sparkled with joy when they managed to prepare a dish, mend a pair of pants, knit a sweater, embroider a flower on a napkin, or sew a child's dress. "Miss, my mother will be so impressed," they'd say. As for the girls, I helped them to make sense of their menstrual cycles and listened attentively as they shared their secrets, fears, and all the emotional turmoil of their first loves. Maybe it wasn't math or history, but I missed it all the same. So what if everyone called the home economics teachers Professor Good Sauce; I had been useful to my students. That much I knew for certain. In my class, they learned things they would use far more often than philosophy.

I parked in an alley perpendicular to the walls of Saint-Christophe's courtyard. The girls didn't want me to walk them to their classroom anymore. That suited me just fine. It meant I was spared appeals from teachers, parents, and priests. The school constantly requesting the presence of the prefect and his wife at various Masses: ordinations, communions, and celebrations of saints. Even during the eucharistic frenzy I'd been subjected to when I lived with Mama Récia, I hadn't been to church this much. Axelle and Alix got out of the car. As soon as their silhouettes—in matching yellow, button-up, short-sleeve shirts, brown skirts, and backpacks—disappeared around the corner, I moved the car to a spot across from the school entrance on the main street so I could watch them walk through the gate.

A band of street children recognized the RAV4 and ran over. I rolled down the window a bit and slipped them a few bills. They howled with joy. Others, who had been begging farther down the street and hadn't noticed the car, rushed to join the excitement. There were more and more of them, knocking on the glass with their little hands. I watched as they walked away, then started the car and headed to Mama Récia's. Though we were the daughters of Innocent Patong, Sennke and I had escaped becoming beggars after Madeleine's death thanks not to him but to my aunt. Full of determination and obstinacy, I had worked hard to erase Madeleine's memory and replace her with Mama Récia. A widow, she was raising her twelve children alone. Her polygamous husband—who had also up and died—had left her with nine children to look after and triplets in her belly. Twelve children. All living. I knew that Mama Récia wouldn't hesitate to become the mother of fourteen. Sennke and I went to live with her. And it had worked. It still worked. Life hadn't spared my aunt its difficulties; a keen sense of opportunity paired with boundless energy kept her spine vertical. Blind faith and love for her sister who had died too soon had strengthened her natural inclination to praise suffering and exalt family duty. Mama Récia had no time for frivolities. She wasn't tender, sentimental, or affectionate like Madeleine; she was alive. Alive. That was the main thing. I don't worship dilapidated graves out in the Haut-Fènn bush; I worship people with warm flesh and blood, like Mama Récia, Tashun, Axelle and Alix, Samy, and . . . Sennke, my little sister who ran off to join the Redemptoristine nuns.

The sun shone bright and hot when I stopped the car in front of Mama Récia's gate. She ought to be home from church by now. She always attended the 5:30 a.m. Mass. Then she prayed the rosary and walked the Stations of the Cross. Two hours of morning prayers. Her knees were covered in callouses as a result. She lived with two of her children, both unemployed and single. Despite the fact that my aunt had twelve children in total, most of whom had achieved varying degrees of success, Tashun covered all of her expenses and gave her a monthly allowance, which was nonetheless "never enough" and always increasing. "Our monthly tax," Tashun often grumbled.

Clutching a large missel under her arm in a posture anyone with less experience would find uncomfortable, Mama Récia hugged me. "God has brought you to me, praise be to Jesus!" she exclaimed before taking a step back. "You've lost more weight, haven't you?"

"Mama, it's only been three days since we saw each other! How could I have lost weight in three days with everything we eat at the prefecture?"

Informing Mama Récia that Madeleine was going to be exhumed was an ordeal. The letter from the town hall drew her focus momentarily. My aunt had watched many family members die in her arms—her father from tuberculosis, her mother from a heart attack, and her only brother from malaria—and had an approach to grief that forced admiration in those so inclined. Her reflexes kicked in and she immediately began enumerating the highlights of the deceased's life, which I had already heard ad nauseum. She detailed how she had saved young Madeleine from the polygamous marriage her father had arranged and how proud she had been to see her sister succeed and become the "Katmé," the "evolved one": the white woman of the family. Then there was the arrival of Innocent Patong who upended her life; her expensive lifestyle, the tragic car accident, the ruinous hospital stay when Madeleine was already ruined, her death three days later, the absurd mourning period with two coffins, two dresses, two hearses, two caterers, and two cameramen, and finally the shameful burial in a grave that was too narrow. Her maternal and paternal families had failed to confer; there were two of everything. Mama Récia spoke in a strong, dry, almost masculine voice, all while massaging her calves. Women of my aunt's generation massaged their calves when misfortune struck. They would knead and massage up and down, as if there lay the epicenter of the pain to be extracted. A true expert when it came to weeping and laments, Mama Récia emptied herself of both memories and mucous. My aunt's nose contained an infinite stock. The blades of the old ceiling fan seemed to creak in time to her sobs. Even the red cushions on the rattan furniture, the bubinga coffee table, and the shiny tile floor seemed to be in tears. I knew what I had to do. I put my arm around her shoulders, then used my free hand to take a tissue from my bag and wipe the snot dripping from her nostrils. My own eyes remained dry. There was precious little I could do about that.

"How do you keep from crying about your mother?" Mama Récia would ask later in a tone laced with distrust. My answer was always the same: "You're my mother." And my aunt would smile her magnanimous smile—proof that I had provided her preferred answer. Thank God I'd only had to put in a call to the mother superior of Sennke's convent to inform her. Sister Marie of Divine Providence would arrive a week before the ceremony. Perfect. I would have struggled to survive a second melodramatic session spent excavating the past.

Once she'd emptied her box of memories, Mama Récia blew her nose for the umpteenth time, then shouted toward the hallway, "Tanga, Sokjou, where are you? Come here! Katmé has news. Where are you, children? We have to call the family, we have to get together." While we waited for the fifty-five and forty-five-year-old children to appear, I realized that this was how I like my aunt best—in action.

If he was surprised to get a phone call from his daughter, and then to see her turn up at his home the same day after twelve years of silence, Innocent Patong did not show it. The last time I'd seen my father was in the months preceding my wedding. I'd gone to the headquarters of his cocoa export company. I had wanted him to walk me down the aisle, and, though I didn't really believe he'd agree, I had hoped he'd help pay for the wedding.

"What ethnic group does your fiancé belong to, and what does he do for a living?" he'd asked with his eyes half shut as he puffed on a thick Cohiba.

"He's a student," I replied. I failed to specify that he was a student at the Civil Administration School, which may have made a difference in my father's eyes.

"He's a student? And you're going to get married? Misery loves company, I suppose," he'd mumbled as he exhaled a cloud of cigar smoke.

He wasn't sure he'd be able to make it; he had some health issues, medical appointments in Europe. I insisted: Tashun and I would find a date that worked for him.

"I'll meet your student, there's no rush," he replied. "Don't change anything for me. I'll try to be there."

When I contacted him a second time, he said that he was truly sorry, but he couldn't come, his health was worsening. Two days after our wedding, Tashun showed me a photo in the national daily *The Voice of Zambuena.* My father had attended a traditional ceremony organized by Haut-Fènn dignitaries in Akriba. He'd been in town the day of my wedding.

My new last name—Abbia—sparked an enthusiastic outpouring unlike anything he'd expressed before. "You're the wife of Prefect Abbia? You? The prefect of the capital? I knew his father back in the day!" Madeleine was being exhumed? A new funeral? Of course I could count on him! Now that we'd found one another again, he wasn't about to let me disappear. He wanted to get to know his son-in-law and his granddaughters, we'd wasted enough time already. My father lived in a port city five hours from the capital and had all the trappings of a man who'd achieved success. That is, of course, if you consider several houses, several cars, several well-stocked bank accounts, and several mistresses to be proof of success. After the country secured independence in the late sixties, he was one of the first "native" planters to own cocoa and coffee plantations and to export his harvests on the international market, wherever demand was strongest and the price highest. Years later, he also became a major shareholder in horse-race betting operator Zambuena Pari-Mutuel.

On the way home, I struggled to stamp out the atoms of pride that, despite my best efforts, had spread to every corner of my brain, rejoicing in the idea that this man—a man who exuded superiority, a man who was admired, feared, and envied, a man who was still handsome at his age—was my father. But as I drifted off that night, I realized something: During the two hours we had spent together, he hadn't asked about his second daughter, Sennke, a single time.

4

Tashun wasn't alone in his office. "Mr. Aleksandre Fortès," he said as the visitor stood up and shook my hand. He was tall. Much taller than Samy. I couldn't help but think of my father, who stood six foot six. Black abacost buttoned up to his chin, short, curly hair, relatively light skin. Mixed race, no doubt. He must have been what, forty-five? Maybe fifty, but no more. Tashun suggested we convene in the green sitting area and asked Balbine to bring us coffee.

"Mr. Fortès, call me Tashun. Let's drop the formalities between us, all right, Aleksandre?"

The man spared us a reply and instead curled his lips into a forced grin that he tried to pass off as a smile. I noticed a scar, which must have once been a harelip. For Tashun to suggest using first names, the man had to be an expatriate.

"Darling, Mr. Fortès is one of the deputy directors of Mival, the company responsible for building the highway that will link Akriba to Fènn," Tashun explained. "He's responsible for corporate social responsibility, CSR manager, I think you say?"

Fortès nodded.

Tashun suggested that since the town hall had sent a letter to inform them that his mother-in-law's grave had to be moved as soon as possible, it must be because it was near the beginning of the highway's path.

"That's likely," Fortès conceded, turning his head slightly in my direction.

"We plan to host a sizable ceremony," Tashun said, gleefully emphasizing the word *sizable.* "My mother-in-law must be exhumed as late as possible to ensure we have time to build a house in Fènn and organize a beautiful funeral. Your CEO suggested you would be our point man."

"Me? Your point man?" Fortès asked. He repeated "point man" the same way he would have said factotum, errand boy, or lackey. Though he was shocked to learn that his CEO had thought of him for this insulting role, he didn't let it show; his face remained stolid. "We at

Mival can provide information on an ad hoc basis. There's no need for a . . . point man. But contacting the families impacted by the demolitions is the responsibility of the Fènn town hall."

He spoke at a leisurely pace. He was taking his time. The contrast between his speech pattern and that of my husband, the verbal machine gun, made me smile to myself.

I noted that Aleksandre Fortès didn't deign to look me in the eyes. He kept his lids low, his gaze focused on his camel suede Derbies or on Tashun. It would have made no difference if I had disappeared, if I had never entered the room, never sat down on the sofa on the opposite side of the glass coffee table from his armchair.

I looked up from his Derbies and glanced around my husband's office. Tashun had kept the décor inherited from his predecessor. The lacquered wooden table with sculpted bronze elephant leg feet, the heavy amaranth curtains which swallowed the daylight, the white strip light, the green, tufted leather sofa and armchairs set out around a glass coffee table and separated from the rest of the room by huge, fake, white flowers in huge, cheap Chinese vases.

Balbine discreetly cleared her throat to signal her return. She carried a tray topped with cups and spoons. She placed a cup across from each of us, turned around, bowed slightly, and left the room as quickly as her imposing size allowed.

"My mother-in-law's funeral will be attended by members of the government and the Central Committee. I'll need to know, as the work progresses, exactly what to expect from the local population. People are going to be evicted, and that's never popular, even when you find room for them elsewhere. There will be much gnashing of teeth and discontent to manage. Haut-Fènn is a peculiar region, disastrously managed by the opposition and its bedridden governor. It was the national government who handed this roadbuilding project to your company," Tashun continued.

"We won a call for tenders put out by the European Union!" Fortès protested.

Tashun continued as though he hadn't been interrupted. "It's one of the president's star initiatives for this seven-year term. We have elections on the horizon, so I can't risk being poorly received by the locals.

It would be a real nuisance for me, as well as for your company. We know Mival would like to secure more public works projects here in Zambuena. And we'll need someone to manage the highway once it's finished . . . If I wanted the sort of information provided by a town hall employee, I would have asked my secretary to handle it. You understand, I can't bury my mother-in-law too hastily; we need time to build the house and arrange everything for the ceremony."

Fortès gave Tashun a cold look. "Mr. Prefect," he said, his lips pursed, "Mival has a contractual obligation to the European Union, which is funding the highway. The demolitions calendar was extremely difficult to schedule and simply cannot be revised to accommodate the individual needs of the people impacted. That would upend our plans and jeopardize timely completion of the project. What's more, I'm not authorized to negotiate demolition moratoriums. You'll have to take it up with the CEO."

As a silent spectator no one encouraged to speak, I vigorously stirred my coffee. They hadn't touched theirs. I was seething. Why had Tashun asked me to drop everything and meet him at his office?

Tashun appeared to be considering what Fortès had said. "I see," he finally replied. "I'll be in touch with your CEO then." He must have remembered that, despite the government's messaging on the topic, the European Union was, in fact, funding the work. Should Mival refuse his request, Tashun would be unable to force the company to adopt a demolition calendar that suited him on his own. He picked up his cup, downed his coffee in a single gulp, and abruptly returned it to the table. Then, in a tone of forced cheer, he said, "You won't be able to say *this* falls outside your purview. My wife is putting together a social initiative in Fènn, a structural project, something useful for the local community. I'm certain you can help us with that, can't you?"

I held my breath. A social initiative in Fènn? A structural project? What was he talking about? What was he going to come up with this time?

"What kind of project?" I heard.

Fortès studied my face, his impassive eyes on mine. Green eyes. Cat eyes. "Impenetrable, unfathomable eyes, sorcerer's eyes," my grandmother from Fènn had always said. I hate cat eyes. My brain froze. Tashun covered for me, blathering on, beating around the bush as he did so well. Then, as if the idea had only just popped into his head, he invited Fortès to dinner at our house the same night. With excessive courtesy, Fortès declined the invitation. He had a long-standing engagement.

Once Aleksandre Fortès had left, Tashun groaned. "We'll see about that calendar! We should have given the contract to the Chinese. They're more pragmatic than the French. Not even a real white man either! Did you see the color of his skin? And all dressed up like Mobutu! Only the leopard-skin hat and the cane were missing. What a jackass. Hasn't anyone told him the abacost's gone out of style?"

I was fuming. "Do you mind telling me why you asked me here? What's all this about a social initiative in Fènn? And you just announce it like that, without even mentioning it to me beforehand?"

"Calm down, it just came out!"

"It just 'came out'? You made me look like an idiot!"

"Come, come, you'll see him again in Fènn. You'll have plenty of time to display your intelligence. That's what you're after isn't it? You want people to know Mama Prefect is more than just a window dressing. You can go now, I have work to do."

As usual, his biting tone left me mute. I swallowed my rage.

As he walked me to the door, he asked casually, "What's Samuel's brother's name again? The one who teaches at the university in Haut-Fènn?"

"You mean Kizito?"

"Yes, that's it. Kizito. How is dear Kizito Pankeu?"

"Well, I suppose," I replied cautiously.

"Is he still running the journal that eclipsed the one published by the University of Haut-Fènn?"

"Yes, of course. Why?"

"Just curious."

"As if you don't already know the answer . . ."

He gave me a mocking look and fiddled with the door. "Think about the social initiative. It would be a good idea to found something there. We need ties to Haut-Fènn. You never know."

As I dozed in the back seat next to Samy, who was fast asleep, my olfactory memory noted—despite the closed windows—that we had entered the Haut-Fènn province. Back at the residence, there was the heady fragrance of ylang-ylang, which grew in the garden, and the wild daisies which grew around the house. There were lilies, whose meticulousness and reluctance to open up to others reminded me of my own character; there was torch ginger, crane flowers, yellow sweetbriar, and even a handful of roses in an unusual bluish hue which would only bloom with encouragement from Samy's patient hand, aided by Alix and Axelle. I love flowers, the magic of their colors and scents, the solitude of their company, but none of them—not one—made me feel as dizzy as the woody fragrance that was currently subjugating my nose. As a little girl, during the long, two-month school vacation, the smell of thin-needled pines wafting through the air had always enveloped and dazed me long before I reached my grandmother's embrace. A blend of promise and despair, the scent of spruce kindled feelings of lightheartedness, unpredictability, and audacity—the hallmarks of childhood. I opened my eyes and pushed the button on the car door; the window slid down. Along the winding mountain road, the narrow, treacherous, two-lane highway, a line of proud spruce—the pine trees of the good years, the pine trees from before Madeleine's death—flashed by at full speed. I smiled, pressing my forehead into the top arch of the car door and resting my chin on the edge of the window, my nose in the wind, my eyelids fighting against the valley breeze.

Through the morning mist, I glimpsed the staggered peaks of Haut-Fènn's mountain chain, the raffia plantations, the green hillsides dotted with vegetable fields and jagged strips of forest. Bested by a swell of contradictory emotions, I laughed at the sentimentalism which had taken me by surprise. I laughed without any sort of premonition or intuition. I laughed without understanding that this suffocatingly sweet moment would resurface in my mind like a soothing balm a few months later, an antidote for my contracting horizons. The cool air woke Samy, who cleared his throat and rubbed his arms. "You're nuts, roll up the window!"

"Do you smell that?"

"What? The pine? It smells like something out of a spray bottle, doesn't it? It's going to give me a headache. Quick, roll up the window or we'll catch a chill."

Samy was wearing a short-sleeved cotton shirt, though I'd warned him that it would be cooler in Haut-Fènn. We'd left at four o'clock in the morning to avoid the traffic jams on the bridge leaving Akriba. For days neither one of us had slept much. For me, the thought of returning to Fènn had turned me into an insomniac; for him, it was the hard bed in the studio where he'd been spending his nights. Samy dozed off as soon as Célestin loaded his suitcase into the trunk. I closed my eyes but never managed to fall asleep. Now and again I opened them to make sure Célestin was awake and to point out tufts of grass on the road, in case he hadn't noticed them, as well as other drivers who'd broken down, cars parked on the median, and turns in the road.

I took a deep breath and rolled up the window.

Samy yawned. "Are we there yet?" he asked.

"In Haut-Fènn, yes," I replied. "Célestin, how long until we reach the town hall?"

"Forty minutes, Madam."

"The last time I took this road, it wasn't paved. It was for my grandmother's funeral. Did you ever ride in one of those old buses?"

Samy said no.

"You know, the ones with the horrible wooden seats. The other passengers would talk your ear off during the whole trip. There were always clucking hens underfoot, not to mention the driver's music, chop breaks on the side of the road, and peeing in the bush. One time there was a fat lady who didn't even bother to move away from the group or hide behind a tree; everyone could see her. She leaned forward, spread her legs, balanced on the balls of her feet, heels lifted, picked up her skirt, displayed her shriveled, cellulite-ridden butt for all to see, and then peed and peed and peed. She must have drunk at least three liters of water, it was unreal. I've forgotten almost everything about my bus trips, but I'll never forget that! That woman with her butt and the piss that just kept flowing on and on. It was awful!"

Samy rubbed his eyes, struggling to keep them open. "How do you know they were hens?"

"What?"

"You said there were hens clucking beneath your feet. How did you know they were hens and not roosters?"

"Because *I* can tell the difference between a hen and a rooster, sir! They were hens, not roosters. You're the city boy. I still haven't forgotten the day they asked you to kill that rooster at your house," I said with a laugh.

"Oh God!" Samuel said, laughing in turn. "Not that, please don't remind me."

"The poor rooster!"

"Poor me!"

Samy curled up against the door. Just a few minutes later, he was fast asleep once more. The sight filled me with affection. He had agreed to come with me to Fènn even though the opening date for his show was just around the corner. To persuade him to leave his studio behind for a few days, I suggested throwing in a visit to Kizito . . . but with or without Kizito, Samy would have come. I know it. We have the sort of immediate, direct, natural, and slightly abrupt relationship in which affection takes root and flourishes with no need for ornamentation. We have been known to disagree on incidentals. But where it really matters, we're of the same mind, we protect one another.

We met in our last year of high school. One day at lunch, as I was finishing my philosophy homework for the following period, he sat down next to me. He was skinny with very dark skin—charcoal black, we used to say at school—and thinning hair. He was wearing a striped suit and a tie. I glanced at him distractedly, still writing. "I've come to offer you my friendship," he'd declared in a solemn tone. My pen remained suspended midair. I had vaguely noticed that this Samuel Pankeu never raised his hand in class and spent quite a lot of time collecting his thoughts whenever a teacher asked him a question. I'd wondered more than once whether this was because he was shy or because he was actually a little dumb. Was he hitting on me? I could only see the side of his face. Heat rash had formed constellations on his cheek. Thin lips, hooked nose. Maybe he wasn't Bantu? I told myself I'd be sure to get a better look once he went back to where he'd been sitting.

"I'm not like the other boys," he said.

"You want us to make a solemn declaration of our friendship? Do we slice our wrists and mix our blood afterward?" I asked sarcastically.

"You say hello whenever you walk past me."

I did? I hadn't paid attention; it must have been pretty perfunctory, if it was true.

"You take the same way home as me. Can we walk together?" he asked.

I sighed. It seemed I wouldn't be finishing my homework before class started. I studied his profile for a moment. "Where did you go to school before?"

"Boarding school."

"Did they make you wear that suit and tie?"

"We had to dress nicely. It's important to dress nicely," he said with a seriousness that made me snort.

"Which boarding school?"

He swept his hand through the air dismissively as if to say, no matter. Then he added, "My mother teaches here."

"Really? What subject?"

"Latin. Mrs. Pankeu."

He craned his neck to get a better look at the homework I was doing.

Mrs. Félicie Pankeu. Five foot one by five foot one, hairy chin, never stingy with bad grades. The students called her *Qui bene amat bene castigat.* The Latin equivalent of "spare the rod and spoil the child." I'd had her in seventh grade. Short, round, and sweaty. The physical antithesis of her son: thin, tall, and crisp. He must take after his father. I wondered again if he might be a little slow. He was obviously reading my homework.

"You omitted the *N* and the *J* in Hountondji, and your reasoning in this paragraph," he said as he placed his index finger on the page, "contradicts your argument in the preceding paragraph."

I reread what I had written. "I don't think so."

"It does. Here and here."

After class, he joined the group of students with whom Sennke and I walked home. He let me into his exuberant, utterly unique world where he was a painter, photographer, writer, philosopher, professor, dancer, sculptor, and musician by turns. School, church, and my many cousins, all Mama Récia's children, shopping, cooking, praying—my days would have been dull and my exposure to culture limited if not for the books I checked out of the library and the film club I led at school with a few classmates. Our eclectic lineup included Westerns, kung fu films, and Bollywood melodramas. When Samy joined, he introduced us to new names as well: Dreyer, Ozu, Kieslowski, and the Hollywood classics. His father, who was a tax inspector and wanted Samy to become a banker, happened to be a cinephile. Beneath the unfashionable suits Samy wore—despite other kids' jeering—he hid a vibrant, colorful mind. I didn't have as much to share. I'd told him my secret, the thing I considered most interesting about myself. "Mama Récia, the woman whose house I live in, she isn't my real mother. My real mother's dead." Then I had started shaking. That's the only time I ever remember shaking when talking about Madeleine after her death. Samuel put his lips on my forehead. He would do that often in the coming years, devouring the first sign of melancholy as soon as it appeared on my face.

A speed bump rocked the jeep. We were coming up on some tollbooths. A swarm of street hawkers descended on the car. Célestin rolled down the window and flashed the badge that exempted the prefecture vehicle from paying the five-hundred-franc fee the other drivers had to hand over.

The booth operator sucked his teeth. "Big man, big woman, oh. Go on through," he said as he raised the barricade. "The ones who can pay never do."

The car passed through, followed by the hawkers.

"Nice Papa, Nice Mama, look here! Look at me! Pretty Mama, buy from me!"

Célestin parked on the side of the road. I woke Samy and lowered the windows. The peddlers slipped their wares inside the car, jostling before our eyes braised plantains, safous, groundnuts, kola nuts, and cassava bread. Overwhelmed, Samy and I tried in vain to raise the windows. Célestin, whose colleagues at the prefecture had nicknamed him Bao, for baobab, or sometimes Longueur, a common moniker for tall people in Zambuena, unfolded his six-foot frame and dispersed the throng. I noticed a young woman, still a girl really, who was balancing a colorful enamel dish overflowing with boiled groundnuts on her head. In her upturned palm, suspended at cheek level, she carried a plate full of half-ripe plantains and safous baked in hot ash. She came closer. I felt the plantain, checked the color of the safous' skin to make sure they weren't sour.

"How much?" I asked.

"A hundred francs for the plantain, Mama, fifty for the rest."

"Will you give me a deal if I buy it all?"

"You've got to be kidding me, you're haggling?" Samy scolded.

"I'll take off fifty francs, Mama."

"Sold. Two plantains and five plums for four hundred francs."

I noticed the girl was about to use some crumpled, old paper bearing the name of a cement company. "No, no, not that! Here, here, use this," I urged, holding out a copy of *The Voice of Zambuena* that had been left in the car. "Never put food in paper that has been in contact with cement," I explained as I paid and cracked open the car door. "Célestin, do you want anything?"

Célestin turned to face me and shook his head. "No thank you, Madam, if I eat, I'll fall asleep."

"I'd like some bitter kola," Samy said.

"Bitter kola! Bitter kola!" Célestin shouted.

New hawkers swarmed the car and the girl moved on. Samy bought ten bags of the aphrodisiacal nuts.

"Oh, looks like you have big plans for tonight!" I whistled.

"You have a dirty mind, Kat," he replied as he removed the rubber band from the bag and peeled a nut's brown wrapper to reveal its pale flesh. "I'm bracing my stomach for whatever sad black broth they'll make me choke down in your village. I'd hate to get sick before my show, you know."

"Black broth!" I teased. "Who, besides you, even uses that term anymore? I seriously doubt the mayor of Fènn will serve Mama Prefect broth, though. He seems to be particularly keen to help us. He's taken the day off for me."

"When you're the wife of the prefect of the capital, everyone is *particularly* keen, Mbindi!"

"Tashun met with him and seems to like him. He claims the man is a member of the respectable opposition. I'm not certain what that means coming from him, but we'll soon see this respectable opposition for ourselves."

"If you ask me, it'll be rather plump, with weak bones."

As I bit into the buttery flesh of a safou, an idea popped into my head. I poked my head outside. "Célestin, can you find the girl from earlier, please?"

The driver walked off. A few minutes later, he came back with a group of young girls, all carrying trays on their heads. I recognized the one.

"What's your name?" I asked.

"Jasmine."

"Jasmine? Here, Jasmine of Haut-Fènn, this is for you." I placed my closed fist in the palm of her hand. Catching on, she curled her own hand into a fist in mine. With a broad smile and gleeful eyes, Jasmine unleashed a litany of thanks and benedictions, then ran off. I had just enough time to watch her open her fist to check how much she'd received before she disappeared from view.

Célestin turned the key in the ignition.

"Why didn't you just buy what she was selling at the price she set?" Samy asked. "She didn't need your charity."

"That money will keep her family going for at least a month."

"And after that? Will you come back? You're like a Saint Bernard with your collar barrel full of money. You can't help but palm a bill to anyone who has less than you—there's something desperate about it. Truly desperate."

"I'm re-establishing the balance between haves and have-nots," I replied while carefully removing the skin from a safou. I popped it into my mouth.

"And balance can be reached by handing out bills in the street?"

"Among other things."

"Why don't you ask Tashun to put the issue on the agenda for the next big central committee meeting," Samy said mockingly. "Instead of redistributing wealth among APM apparatchiks, they can give it to the people."

"Samuel!" I objected, nudging him as I raised my chin toward Célestin, who continued driving in silence.

"I can't believe you won't taste these Haut-Fènn safous, they're the best in the country."

"You know not much interests me in the morning besides puff-puff and beans . . ." Samy grumbled.

"Your puff-puff and beans are in the trunk. Bambili made the doughnuts dripping with oil, just the way you like them, and the beans are so hot they'll kill you."

"Bambili made puff-puff and beans for me? Really?"

"Mm-hm . . . She showed me the container and beamed, 'This is for Mr. Samy.' You never believe me, but she has a crush on you. She got up at three o'clock in the morning to put it in the car herself to be sure I wouldn't forget."

"Ah, my beloved Bambili! I'll invite her to my show!"

"Seriously?" I balked, stifling a laugh. Then I turned to Célestin, who'd just stopped behind a heavily loaded logging truck which had clearly broken down. "Could we please park somewhere less dangerous? I hate these trucks."

He backed up to increase the distance between the truck and the jeep. I was still worried though, since logs regularly came loose and flattened any vehicles whose bad luck had placed them nearby.

"Can we go around?"

"There's no way past, Madam," Célestin replied. "We'll just have to wait. The logging truck is taking up the whole road. See for yourself."

I craned my neck. The huge vehicle was parked right in the middle of the road, blocking the way.

"We can't stay here, we could end up in pieces," said Samy. "Look, let's go wait over there," he urged, pointing toward a dirt access road two hundred yards back on the right. He got out and began asking the line of drivers who had slammed on their brakes behind us to back up.

Sitting beside me on a boulder, Samy was savoring his puff-puff and beans from a glass bowl. The wind was keeping the sun tolerable.

At some distance from the main road, the path led to four abandoned, partially collapsed mudbrick houses. Also fearing an accident, other vehicles had joined us in the makeshift parking lot. Célestin was smoking with his back against the car.

"Why does the thought of me inviting your maid make you laugh?" Samuel asked.

"Samy," I scolded, kissing my teeth. "Don't goad me. Bambili will be thrilled.

"People will be disappointed when they realize the pottery salesman only *fancied* himself an artist," he replied, putting down his bowl. He took his head in his hands. "I'm so, so stupid to have accepted this show! It reeks of failure! I can smell it, believe me!"

"The self-flagellation of Samuel Pankeu. I was starting to miss it."

"*Samuel Pankeu, would-be artist,* how does that sound?"

"It sounds dumb."

Movement in the crowd drew our attention. People were heading back to their cars. Célestin made his way over, "It's moving again, Madam."

We'd lost twenty minutes or so, but we wouldn't be late, there would still be time to spare. The jeep roared to life.

"I'll come by the studio when we get home," I said. "Have things changed much?"

"I'm not sure it's a good idea for you to come by . . ."

"What are you talking about, Samy?" I asked, searching his eyes.

He looked away, outside, gluing his forehead to the window. "I'm so scared that sometimes I wake up and all I want to do is destroy it all, then dissolve my body in lye."

There was so much tension and discouragement in his voice. I took his hand, which he surrendered without turning to face me. "You really don't want me to come, Samy? Listen, I'll just stop by and take a look, I won't say a word. Not a single word. I swear." I touched the tip of my index finger to my thumb and raised my three other fingers skyward.

"No, Kat. It's a no," he resolved, his tone dry. He pulled his hand away. "Try to understand! I just can't bear to hear you say I've messed up. It's too late now."

"You're serious, aren't you? You really want me to see your show for the first time at the preview?" I asked, eyes wide.

"Just before, when we hang everything. Put yourself in my shoes. I know it's hard for you, but if you're on my side, please try to understand."

I ruminated for a few minutes, then asked, "What about Keuna? Is she allowed to visit?"

"That's not the same and you know it."

"I can't believe this! Keuna can visit the studio whenever she likes, but not me!" I let out a bitter laugh.

"You're not the only one. Ety is just as furious as you are that I won't let him see the final version before the show."

"Ety and I are getting the same treatment. Great, I feel so much better."

"Don't talk like that, Mbindi, please don't talk like that. He went nuts when he found out I was coming with you to Fènn. We haven't seen each other in a week. I worked nonstop to free up these two days for you. He thinks I don't love him anymore. You know what he said to me? 'Artists have muses, but all you see in me is an Achilles tendon.' That's what he dropped on me yesterday. What can I say to that? Then he said, '*Amare et sapere vix deo conceditur:* Even a god finds it hard to love and be wise at the same time.' He's learning Latin to impress me, and goodness has he succeeded. As if I didn't know how to love. As if anyone could struggle all day with clay like I do and stay wise. You and Ety should understand me better."

"Keuna can come to the studio. *She* can see you work. Not me. Not Ety. Wow!"

"Mbindi, Keuna is a gallery owner. She wants to sell pieces and make a name for herself, she wants to make a name for me. The expectations are clear with her. It's different with you and Ety, it's like looking at myself in a mirror or hearing echoes inside my head. Keuna's outside of me. You would see me in the cruel light of day, and I don't want that. If you criticize my work again, I won't finish. I know it. And if you come to the gallery, you won't be able to help yourself. We both know that."

"I hope Miss Cigarillo knows how lucky she is."

"You can't call her that! Keuna's not the person you think she is."
"I can't, huh? Really? I think you'll just have to get used to it."

Keuna. Samy had introduced us in the sandy courtyard at her gallery, Bubinga Project. Four thousand light-filled square feet on the ground floor of a four-story apartment building. Keuna lived on the fourth floor with her son. A German family occupied the other two floors. Keuna was short and had a buzz cut. Her belly button was on display above tight jeans, a belt buckle featuring intertwined serpent heads, and combat boots dotted with lapel pins. A cigarette protruded from her lips as she waved distractedly in my direction. I disapproved of the commission—fifty-five percent—she planned to charge on the sale of Samy's works, and I told her as much. Keuna riposted that it was better to have forty-five percent of something than a hundred percent of nothing at all, her annoyance showcasing the speed bumps that were her lower eyelids. Samy got upset; money had always been secondary for him. He didn't want us pestering him with tax collector concerns. Shopkeeper squabbles reminded him of the Loon—and that was unbearable. The fact that he refused to take my side and called his mother the Loon in front of that . . . that Lilliputian with all the allure of tainted whisky or a smuggled Cohiba, when I was the one footing the bill, it set me off and I threatened to leave.

Samy went inside to properly space the pieces in the gallery. Still smoking her cigarillo, Keuna stated the obvious, "You don't like me very much, do you, Katmé?" She stamped out the butt under the heavy wooden heel of her boot. "To be honest, I don't like you either. So we're even. Let's have for one another . . . a healthy dislike. We don't have to enjoy each other's company to ensure the success of Samy's show. He told me what you said about his pieces. You know, when an artist really has something to say, to show, they don't pussyfoot around. These days, an artist who uses only one medium is monolingual—in other words, stillborn. Now it's all about interdisciplinarity and multiplicity. Sam is in step with the times. He's original, rooted in a place, and open to the world all at once. His interdisciplinary approach enriches each piece to create a whole; nothing is isolated. His robust sculptures, the unprecedented confidence they exude with their heads where their bellies should be, their faltering first steps, a cross between totemic figures and mythological creatures; his uncompromising, comprehensive photographs, that's what people expect from an artist like him. No offense, but I'm not sure you really understand Sam's work."

I granted her a smile dripping with disdainful tolerance and replied, "Who do you think you are? You think inheriting a nice space from your parents makes you the curator of the century? You're using Samuel to put on your first big exhibition. Why are you so sure of yourself? Tell him I'll be waiting for him in the car. I'll see the inside of your gallery another time—that is if I agree to set foot here again!"

Keuna slipped her fingers into her beltloops and yanked her jeans up, but the gesture did nothing to reduce the square of skin exposed to the breeze. As if taking the heavens as her witness, she leaned back and burst into a booming laugh. The insolence of this woman, who was likely my age, was captivating. It made me want to steal it and run off with it tucked under my arm.

Samy was distraught. He was certain that Keuna and I were made to be friends, that it was just a bad first impression. It was silly, we had to get together again. No, Keuna hadn't meant what she'd said, no, I shouldn't take it like that. And I hadn't said only nice things either, and it was true that he didn't want to talk about money before the preview—it was bad luck. To appease Samy, who was miserable at the thought that things might be irreconcilable between me and the woman who held the keys to his immediate future as an artist, I invited them both to lunch at the residence. We spoke about our children (she had a son named Xavier), the rut the country was in, the administration's inertia, civil servants, and coconut democracy. Nothing terribly original, but we all enjoyed the conversation since we shared similar opinions on the topics, which could only be discussed in the company of trustworthy interlocutors. Toward the end of the meal, I concluded, in a rather exalted tone, "What we need in this country is a revolution. A real revolution!"

Keuna paused for a moment with her fork in midair, then mockingly replied, "When you eat with four pieces of silverware on either side of your plate, you don't rise up in revolution, Mrs. Abbia!"

The jab still haunted me . . .

The jeep pulled into the courtyard at the Fènn town hall. "Samy," I said wearily, "sometimes you ask too much of me."

"I know, Mbindi. All too well," he replied, his eyes full of gratitude and tenderness. He came closer and kissed me on the forehead. "You're the only person in the world who would agree to fund an exhibition without even seeing it first. I know how lucky I am, I know how lucky I am to have you, Mbindi."

5

The Fènn town hall cut the village in half. The colonial building, located across from the market near the main street, was clad in dried mud that made it look as though it had been fully submerged in some garnet liquid. As soon as we got out of the car, peddlers selling polyester material made in China—perfect reproductions of local cotton fabrics—hurried over. A young man from the townhall's security team, who was wearing a neon vest over his shirt, brandished a palm-fiber broom in their direction, and the hawkers backed off, hurling insults, calling him a green dog and a boastful maggot. It must have been a frequent occurrence. Samy's amused eyes met mine. The last time we'd heard someone called a boastful maggot, we were still in high school.

It was market day and the hubbub—roosters crowing in raffia cages, women roasting plantains and safous over hot coals, and stationery vendors selling stamps, blank forms, official documents, office supplies and a wide range of trinkets—pervaded the square in front of the town hall. At some distance from the rest, behind a newspaper stand immediately adjacent to the townhall steps, there was a stand selling kola nuts, small no be sick, and menthol. Behind it, an old man in khaki shorts, sneakers, and a long-sleeved T-shirt sat reading the paper, completely indifferent to the din around him—the mayor's father, the young man informed us.

Inside the town hall, the reddish earth covered the walls, floor, and windows. Spiderwebs clung to the ceiling, and bird nests sat atop the cornices, giving the building an abandoned feel. In a corner, wrapped in decorations, sat a Christmas tree emitting a carol. It was early February. I walked over to the tree and brushed my fingers over its dry needles, which fell to the floor. I sniffed the tree—it was real. When I'd performed the same test at Uncle Ambroise and Djama's house, I ended up with grease on my fingers. In a house where everything gleamed—armchairs, curtains, rugs, trinkets, plates, and silverware—the tall, green tree had escaped the gilt and was covered instead in a layer of fake snow. While waiting for my hosts to make their appearance, I had rolled the needles between my fingers; the fragrant oil that had been sprayed all over the tree stung my nostrils.

"Convincing, isn't it?" Djama had asked. "Do you like it? I'll give you the address." She came closer, looking resplendent in an elegant, beaded tulle caftan, her head held high. "You don't have to clean it, it doesn't lose its needles, and you can reuse it several years in a row. Convenient and cost-effective." She paused and looked deep into my eyes, "It's a real statement, don't you think?"

Plastic dusted with fake snow. I'd mumbled whatever came to mind. Snow. In a city where the temperature never dropped below seventy-five degrees. Ever since Djama had secured a solid foothold in my life and intimated that Tashun's appointment as prefect of the capital was the result of a sustained battle in which she herself had participated, I had discovered that her daily life was all about convenience, cost-effectiveness and . . . making statements. A term Tashun had recently added to his vocabulary.

Samuel had guessed wrong. The mayor, Edouard Limu, was all skin and bones. With his angular features and prominent cheek bones, he was quite unlike the affected old man I had imagined upon reading the letter. I even saw a slight resemblance to Tashun, though Limu was thinner and more courteous. He shot furtive glances at us from behind his sun-drenched, paperwork-laden desk. I introduced Samy as my brother, making clear that his "same father, same mother brother" was Kizito Pankeu. "I imagine you've heard of him?"

"Around here everyone has heard of him," Edouard Limu replied, his voice dripping with insinuations.

Kizito, who was ten years older than Samuel, was a law professor. He had founded *Counterpoint*, a journal known for its rigorous analyses and incisive articles, as well as for its caustic critiques of the government, which were sometimes picked up by the national press and academic publications abroad. It had come to overshadow the university's own journal. Kizito had been an adjunct for ten years—his political stance had caused his career to stagnate.

Edouard Limu was displeased to learn that Sennke would not be cosigning the documents authorizing the exhumation, since she would be arriving only a few days before the ceremony. The town hall had recently dealt with several cases of identity theft, grave desecration, and pillaging of human remains. Just two days earlier, they had caught a group of women leaving the cemetery with a wheelbarrow full of bones. Limu called Tashun to make sure he had his blessing to break the rules, then sent his secretary to the archives to make copies.

"Could we invite Kizito Pankeu to tonight's dinner?" I asked with a quick glance at Samy.

The mayor's eyes darted back and forth between us. The wife of the prefect of the capital, a member of the president's party, was asking him to invite Kizito Pankeu, of the opposition, to dinner. The logic escaped him, and his reticence was obvious. Her Excellency Madam Prefect didn't realize how complex the situation was in the province.

"It's important to us," I insisted. With his faint resemblance to Tashun and the powdery deference he sprinkled over me, Edouard Limu made me want to sneeze. It didn't surprise me much that a mayor from the leading opposition party, the Union of Progressive Forces or UPF, was reluctant to receive Kizito Pankeu and had taken the day off to help the wife of the prefect of Akriba find a plot of land to build her family's future house. He was undoubtedly planning to campaign for the president's party in the next elections. Just your everyday turncoat.

The secretary brought the documents for me to sign and asked me to verify that they matched the originals. Madeleine's thirty-nine years on earth condensed into three certificates. Birth. Death. Burial. Since I couldn't bring myself to examine the pieces of paper, Samuel took them from me and carefully checked them against the originals. He noticed a coincidence. Madeleine had been born on the twenty-ninth of December—the same date Axelle and Alix were born years later. He pointed it out to me. I shuddered. For ten years, since the twins had come into my life, the twenty-ninth of December had been the day the dazzling, mauve flowers of the jacaranda had bloomed in my heart. Nothing else.

The mayor wanted to know when I would like to pay my respects. When I didn't understand, he added, "to your mother, at her grave."

As unbelievable as it may seem, I hadn't thought for a second that this first trip to Fènn might involve a visit to Madeleine's grave. I couldn't just turn up, without having made any preparations, without . . . I replied that there was no rush, I'd go another time. I remembered a distant place, overgrown; it would take up too much time for such a short stay, the priority for this first trip was to sign the official documents and find a plot of land at the top of a hill, a place to build the house, the vault.

Limu caught himself, but not before I saw a flash of shock in his racoon eyes. His father ran a newspaper stand just outside the townhall; I guessed they rarely left one another's side. "We can go tomorrow, Madam Excellency, in fact—"

"I said no! Another time! And for God's sake, stop calling me Madam Excellency, all right? My name is Katmé Abbia."

Samy intervened. "Come on, Kat, we can find the time tomorrow and—"

"That's enough, Samuel, okay?"

A mother who left like a thief in the night, leaving Sennke and I, eleven and thirteen, with no rampart against the rough days ahead, did not deserve my time. It was cowardice to take off like that, with no warning, to get into a shouting match with our father because he'd fucked yet another of her childhood friends, to get into her car and speed through the dark night, hurtling into a truck that was also moving too fast, to be dragged along the road, to have grooves cut into her back, her arms and legs scraped up, her clothes in tatters, her face miraculously intact, to survive, then learn that she'd be paralyzed for life—but what did that matter! She was alive, she was lucid, she spoke to Katmé, to Sennke, to the owner of the wandering cock, to everyone! But then to have internal bleeding go undetected by the doctors, to simply up and die one morning, a Sunday morning, at eleven o'clock, three days after the accident, three days after the fight with our father, when everything indicated she would make it; yes, that was cowardice. And twenty years later, nothing changed, no matter how you look at the way she snuck off. It's inelegant, spiteful even. When you love your children, you don't leave. Period. You support them as they make their way through life. You wipe away their tears, tend their wounds, scold them, spoil them, congratulate them, punish them, encourage them, tame, shape, and educate them, berate them, chide them, whatever you like, but you don't just split! I felt my throat tighten. Madeleine had become to me a distant relative buried far away. When I introduced Mama Récia, I naturally referred to her as "my mother." That Saturday, out in the bush, after we had shattered the tiles and slid the coffin to the bottom of the grave, I had zipped up my pain. I was not about to unleash it all now simply because the Fènn town hall had sent a letter and Tashun had gotten carried away. Now more than ever, Mama Récia was life, and the other, ephemeral one was death. I would not make a show of a grief I no longer felt, a loss I had healed, to feed my husband's professional fantasies and live up to the expectations of those around me. And Samuel knew it! Whenever someone mentioned Madeleine, it annoyed me that I was expected to display my suffering—eternal regret, as memorial plaques always say. No one wants to come off as a monster, so I would always put on the customary mask and let people offer their condolences. For what? I could have slapped them! At the same time, how could I openly say, with the world watching, that I'd decided to devote myself to the living? "Let the dead bury the dead," may have been the only sentence I hadn't rejected from the Judeo-Christian dogma I'd been force-fed by Mama Récia, whose approach to religion was rather like that of the crusaders.

Samy gave me an angry look. "Whatever you say," he grumbled. Under his breath, for me alone, he added, "*Abundans cautela non nocet,* abundant caution does no harm."

At dinner, Kizito, who was accustomed to orating in noisy lecture halls, used his voice to drown out the drone of the television which devoured half the mayor's living room wall. He made everyone laugh by telling a story I'd heard a hundred times, the story of a former university classmate who had become a judge and always said that he liked it when both parties gave him the same amount of money—that way he could deliver a fair ruling. Kizito invariably concluded his anecdotes about the deleterious state of the university and the country with the same maxim: "Our unbridled race toward the Middle Ages continues." To sate the table's curiosity about how our friendship began, Samy and I relived memories from our high school years, the film club, Bollywood, and kung fu followed by art and essays, literature, and new African authors. I had to wait until the end of dinner to mention the charity to support young, unmarried mothers which Tashun and I planned to open. The mayor, his wife and most of his team, the deputy prefect, and Aleksandre Fortès—I hadn't expected him to be there—listened without interrupting me. No one commented or raised any objections, not even Kizito, who nonetheless shot me several peculiar glances. The group's silence made me feel like I'd uttered a load of nonsense.

My impression was confirmed the following day in the office of Mival's CSR manager, Fortès, who was supposed to help me refine the idea. "This isn't the capital," he said bluntly. "Here people get married first and have children second." He explained that when someone jumped the gun, the pregnancy was "evacuated", or, if the mother gave birth, the baby most often ended up in a septic tank or at the bottom of the lake. Young women preferred such extreme measures to bringing shame upon their families and the community. The number of women who were brave enough to deliver and keep a child without a husband was so small that it would be counterproductive to open a charity that would stigmatize them. Fortès had spoken without interruption, his eyes fixed on mine. Swallowing my humiliation, I thanked him for his "invaluable insight." I could explain why, at dinner the night before, the mayor, his wife and team, and the deputy prefect hadn't challenged me: They hadn't dared. And it made sense that Kizito hadn't wanted to point out the stupidity of my plan. But Fortès? He had only opened his mouth to answer questions put to him about the progress of work on the highway, to concede or laugh at Kizito's statements, or to discuss sculpture, art, and Samy's upcoming show. He hadn't spoken a word to me. He knew nothing about me, and the little he had gleaned was hardly flattering. He saw Tashun and me as inconstant opportunists. Thanks to Uncle Ambroise, we had secured a deferral for the demolition of Madeleine's grave. Mival had upended its calendar for us. That had to have stuck in Fortès's throat. Sure, Tashun hadn't properly considered his idea for a center for single mothers. He'd thought: woman, young, child, vulnerability—all the prerequisites were there. But Fortès's arrogance, his condescension? How long had he been living in Haut-Fènn? How dare he speak to me like that—my umbilical cord is buried in this village, my parents were born here and grew up here, my childhood and story are indissociable from this region. He'd spoken to me as though I were a foreigner motivated exclusively by prosaic calculations. To be honest, I didn't fully understand why Tashun had come up with this idea of founding a charity either. Yet another one of his epiphanies. As for me, cowardly as I often was and weary of rebellion, I'd followed his orders. But still. Tashun was right to call him a jackass. Loathsome cat eyes, harelip scar, a forehead as square as his jawline—nature was rarely wrong, he was wholly unattractive.

Had Fortès, who was wearing a dark teal abacost, realized how harsh he'd been? Had he suddenly remembered that I was the wife of a man who could impact the outcome of the project he was working on? Had he decided it was time for me to see a softer side of his personality? Whatever the reason, in a friendlier tone that clashed with his icy gaze, he declared, "If you're truly invested in improving the lives of the people here, tell me how I can help and I'll do it. Nothing else matters. I'm in no position to judge your reasons." Now he was feeling magnanimous. I'd had enough. My voice was biting, my words sharp. What did I say exactly? The only thing I remember is finishing my salvo with, "and I'm out."

While I steadied my breathing, a hesitant new glint appeared in Fortès's eyes, an ironic, eloquent glint. I had just come to life for him. I could clearly see the inner shift underway inside him. The dam of prejudices wedged in his small mind was yielding to my first assault. Strangely, I was not pleased. And that ridiculous "and I'm out," which I had borrowed from Tashun, the former big game hunter. With an invisible shrug of my shoulders, I told myself that no matter how hard you try to maintain them, the locks that fasten your inner stopper in place eventually come loose, exposing a few cracks.

I had planned to buy the plot of land the mayor had showed us, but while studying the cadastral survey, I realized that lingering litigation would block the sale. Edouard Limu hadn't bothered to check on the plot's legal standing before introducing me to its owner. It hadn't occurred to him that someone might try to cheat him, the mayor of Fènn. He was one of those people who are convinced that their title will protect them not only from everyday misfortunes, but also from routine flimflam. The owner protested, swore on the lives of his children, there had been a mistake, an honest man like him. Then he proffered violent insults, took God as his witness, cursed us, climbed atop his motorcycle, revved the engine, and took off in a cloud of noise and bitter smoke from the exhaust pipe. Limu roughly loosened his tie. Without conferring, Samy and I burst into laughter simultaneously. We kept trying to compose ourselves, but every time our eyes met, our hilarity redoubled. The mayor was dabbing at his forehead; his retinue was unsure what to do. How could they understand that the dishonest, foul-mouthed salesman was a specimen I no longer had the opportunity to encounter? He'd dared to attack the mayor and me without the slightest hesitation, without fear of possible reprisal. I felt something akin to pride for the man's hilarious effrontery. He had momentarily freed me from my status as an untouchable mummy, a status in which I'd been trapped for the past year as the wife of the prefect of the capital. But in the fit of mad laughter convulsing Samy's body and my own, I could also hear the echo of cheap diversion.

We began looking for a new plot of land. Nothing met Tashun's specifications: at the top of a hill with a view of the valley, the mountains, or the village. In Fènn, people bought land, they didn't sell it. The owners of vacant lots turned down my offers. When it was suggested, I refused to visit the Montagne neighborhood. My father had built a house there, the house where Sennke and I had spent our vacations with our grandmother before Madeleine died. I remembered a huge photo of the President attached to the main gate along with a sign bearing the party's initials. When the opposition movement began, around the time Madeleine died, my father had let student protestors and the leaders of illegal parties use his company's premises for free. A harsh audit had brought him back in line. He joined the Allied Patriots Movement or APM, fastened a party pin to his lapel, and, with the zeal of a recent convert, crusaded against "the government's detractors." His ties to the party in power tempered the enthusiasm of the tax inspectors and his business prospered. Though my father was retired now—his sons managed his affairs—my name, the one I bore before marrying Tashun, continued to be associated with those who had helped the president's party to withstand pressure from the opposition during the time the whole country remembered as *the ember years.* The parties who refused to join the presidential majority remained bit players even today.

After a long day of fruitless searching, Samy and I had dinner at the Zimanto Inn, where we were staying. The temperature had dropped. I had lent Samy a cardigan, but his arms stuck out of the sleeves, inviting jokes from the waiters. The red neon lights paired with sensual zouk-love to make the dining room feel more like a brothel. Movement at the door drew our attention. Fortès, in a full white abacost, came in with a group of people in coveralls. They sat down in the farthest corner of the room, diagonally across from our table. Before I could suggest we keep a low profile, Samy waved at Fortès, who stood back up and left his party to come shake our hands. The mayor had mentioned the disaster with the owner of the plot. "I live in the Tam-Tam neighborhood," he said. "My landlord owns another house, not far from mine, four hundred yards away, to be exact. It's two stories, unfinished. It's for sale, along with the surrounding eucalyptus grove. There's a pond between the two houses. It's a pretty nice place. If you don't find anything tomorrow and you're not opposed to eucalyptus or water, come have a look."

The next day, Samy and I explored the Tam-Tam neighborhood and the eucalyptus grove.

PART TWO

6

Djama made her entrance at the lunch hosted by the FZC, or Friends of Zambuena Club, followed, as usual, by a young woman trailing ten feet behind with her purse. She also jogged Djama's memory and finished her sentences whenever her boss pointed at her or raised her chin her general direction. The young woman was a part of the pomp which accompanied Uncle Ambroise's wife wherever she went, just like her sophisticated wardrobe, iridescent silk satin scarves, monogrammed high heels, the armed soldier sitting next to her driver in the Bentley, her princess-cut diamond solitaire, platinum wedding band adorned with baguette-cut diamonds, gold bracelets laden with rubies, sapphires, and emeralds, and huge earrings featuring imitation gemstones—because earrings are easy to lose, you know. Though she had eight daughters and was in her late sixties, Djama was still svelte and had not a single wrinkle on her face. She was beautiful and she knew it. Her husband's position endowed her with power and influence, and she knew that too. She was hemiplegic on her own, half-finished; she needed multiple third parties to extend and complete her existence—she needed others. She had high expectations for the people she set her sights on, and she made it difficult to cut the ties that bound them to her, unless of course she had decided it was time to sever them. Intrigued at first, then enthralled, Katmé had fallen under Djama's sway. Her feelings for the older woman were a blend of admiration, fear, exasperation, and disbelief. In her presence, Katmé regressed, becoming a little girl eager to please, acquiesce, and concede. When she was in the same room with Djama, Katmé was all compliments, no sharp edges. Afterward, she always felt drained, exhausted from so much silent snickering. Under the watchful eye of her cunning new friend, Katmé had birthed a version of herself that horrified her. During their teen years, when Sennke lost her nerve with a boy she liked, she would say, "It's because he's walking through my brain." That was exactly it. Djama was walking through Katmé's brain. Even though everything about the woman got under her skin.

She wondered when she would truly begin to hate her.

Maybe today.

Definitely today.

The luncheon was taking place in the home of the newly appointed Deputy Chief of Staff to the President. Madam DepChief, previously known as Ameline, was putting her hostess skills to the test by welcoming the FZC for the first time. In line with an unspoken rule, the previous Madam DepChief had stopped coming to events the same day her husband was stripped of his functions. There was actually only one unspoken rule: the husband's position. Around thirty women had gathered in the opulent living room whose glass lateral wall overlooked the black waters of the Zambuena River. There were ambassadors' wives, ministers' wives, the wives of CEOs of public companies, and those of influential party members. Elegant, subdued, and sweet-smelling. Katmé still couldn't wrap her head around the fact that these women—herself included—had become mere offshoots of their husbands, and all with a smile on their lips.

The sunlight got the best of the thin cotton veil stretched across the vast sliding glass doors; the glasses sparkled in its rays. Hindered by long, straight, navy-blue skirts, the waitresses took small, careful steps as they offered the guests champagne and "exotic" fruit juices, though they were all made from local fruits. The air conditioner kept the room cool, in stark contrast to the temperature outside—over a hundred degrees.

The women had lunch together every Friday. No one was under any sort of *obligation,* of course. But absences had to be explained and justified with a comprehensive apology both before and after the missed date. Weaving a credible lie took just as much out of Katmé as attending the never-ending luncheons, so all things considered, she preferred to make roll call every Friday at noon. Did none of them secretly harbor indignation about wasting their time on such trivialities? Spending hours of their lives they would never get back on stupid quilting, headwrap tying, and vegetarian samosa tasting workshops?

As usual, small groups had formed. Katmé listened as Djama's words launched the troop of women around her into a fit of laughter.

As usual, a dozen women had thronged to her side. She fiddled with the foot of her champagne glass as she narrated her grandchildren's latest exploits. Commonplace kid things, really, more deserving of a smile than a laugh. But Ambroise Béma's wife was telling these stories, so they were innately funnier. The hearty laughter continued.

Outfitted like the butler, in gloves and livery, each of the waiters carried a platter of savory canapes in one hand and in the other a pile of linen napkins so thin that Katmé was afraid she might rip hers while wiping her mouth. She would have been hard pressed to say exactly what she was feasting on, but she was definitely gobbling it up. Eating was the only thing she'd found that could stave off the terrifying boredom which otherwise overwhelmed her at every FZC luncheon. The setting, people, and conversations sometimes seemed so unreal that she had to relate them all to Samuel to convince herself she hadn't imagined the whole thing.

An unpleasant shiver had made the hair on the back of her neck bristle when the butler's ceremonious voice had announced the arrival of "Madam Secretary-General of the Allied Patriots Movement." She suspected she knew why Djama had come. Despite her role as the Club's vice-president, Uncle Ambroise's wife always skipped the lunches which were followed by what she called "adventures in squalor." After the meal, the FZC would make its way to Vita House Orphanage to distribute donations to the children. "I've got nothing against the outings the white women organize, but this country is more than prisons, orphanages, and shantytowns. Don't the tourist attractions and landscapes deserve their attention as well?" Djama had once confided in Katmé. An adventure in squalor. Yet here was Djama. Slender and stately in her ultramarine brocade dress and matching scarf, a pleasant scent in her wake and a reserved smile on her lips. She had gone to the trouble to discuss just one thing, Katmé thought as she shot a biting glance her way.

Samuel's show . . .

A source of disagreement between them.

Gertrud, the Swedish ambassador's wife, who had hosted the event the previous week, had suggested taking the kids from Vita House to see Samuel's show—unable to properly pronounce his name, she invariably called him *Pankoo.* Katmé had watched Djama's thick fingers tighten around her fork. The figure of a Masai, but the hands of a lumberjack. "Excellent idea!" the Japanese ambassador's wife, Kihiko, had exclaimed enthusiastically. "Samuel Pankeu is wonderful, just wonderful! He's inspiring! So inspiring!" Slightly skeptical interjections had been heard here and there, but since dessert had been served and banana flambé doused in aged rum deserved to be savored in peace, they had postponed the decision until their "next gathering."

Today, in other words.

A month earlier, Katmé had called Djama during a fitting for yet another caftan at her tailor Grand Moké's shop. Samy had just dropped off copies of the exhibition catalogue. Djama had promised to stop by as soon as she was finished. If anyone could give the show a leg up, it was her, her friends, and her address book. Katmé had urged Samuel and Keuna to host a preview for Djama and Tashun's guests, to flatter them and make them feel like they were even more valued than the vernissage guests. Katmé would give Djama invitations and catalogues to help her convince her entourage.

When Djama turned up with her purse-carrier-memory-jogger in tow, she flipped carefully through the catalogue, read the texts, lingered on several images, ran her thumb along the spine of the book, and asked, "This Samuel, Samuel Pankeu, shares a last name with that man at the University of Haut-Fènn. They're not related, are they?" Without waiting for an answer, she continued. "Tell me, why is it that artists who were born here, who grew up here among us, who thrive here alongside us, free from restrictions and impediments, why is it they bite the hand that feeds them? It's because elsewhere people tell them, 'to succeed, you have to criticize your country, otherwise you'll never sell your work abroad or be invited to our fairs.' I hear our artists are getting more and more exposure in Asia. Who knows why. My guess is it's a Trojan horse of sorts, but that's another other story. Ambroise and I went to Moncton in nineteen . . ."

Djama pointed at her assistant who finished her sentence. "Ninety-nine."

"Yes, in nineteen ninety-nine, we attended the . . ."

Same interaction. "Francophonie Summit," the young woman completed.

"Yes, the Francophonie Summit. The Boss asked Ambroise to represent him and he invited me along too. There were some surprising countries there, like Albania. They accepted Albania as a member. Do they even speak French in Albania? But that's another story. There was a contemporary art fair for artists from member countries. We happened upon the work of a filmmaker from Zambuena who was living in Canada as a political refugee. In his apocalyptic video installation, he claimed he'd fled because he was persecuted for his ideas. Honestly, Ambroise and I would have doubled over in laughter if we hadn't been worried the heads of the other delegations would see us as the henchman of a country who had persecuted the so-called artist and forced him to emigrate. You know what he called it?" she asked, raising her chin toward her assistant again.

"Pandemonium," she answered.

"Yes, *Pandemonium.* The so-called capital of hell. Right here. In the country where you and I live. His political refugee claim was bogus, we didn't believe it for a second. But he managed to fool the Canadians and get a permanent resident card, so good for him. He even had the gall to argue with us when we expressed our outrage about the image he was painting of our country for the world. 'Zambuena is hell,' he said. 'Canada may not be heaven, but at least it's close.' We're here in hell while in Canada he's in the anteroom to heaven. Lovely, isn't it? You see, your Pankeu is doing the exact same thing with this show. Taking pictures of poor people and their hardships, using art as a pretext to aestheticize their misfortune, selling it like vulgar merchandise. Where's the conviction in that? Where's the social conscience? It seems your pal slipped his shame to the dog," Djama concluded, waving the catalogue in Katmé's face. "Did you really think I would back this? That I'd get my name anywhere near this pompous mess? Have you even read this?"

Djama opened the catalogue, chose a page at random, and began reading aloud. *"With this unique expression of profound unbelonging, a happy refusal to choose between abstraction and documentation, between concepts and facts, and ideas and matter, artist Samuel Pankeu has sculpted a gray elegy on an antipoetic, ahistorical world, resistant to the usual narrative. His pieces embody the present and disclose the past, then counteract one another by moving in identical but opposite directions before finally coming together to land boldly in the very heart of inscrutability.* What a farce! *Ante Mortem: Trance-Versal Therapies.* Catchy title," she scathed, tossing the catalogue onto the table. "The millipede only gets lost if it walks alone, as my father always said. You're the daughter of a man to whom the party owes a great deal, you were born with his name, before your husband's. If it's quality artists you're after, people we respect, you need only ask. We'll find some."

Usually, when she was with Djama, Katmé blathered on and on. The less she had to say, the more came out. A steady flow of words to dispel the feeling that she was hollow inside—"utter emptity" as Samy put it—which latched onto her every time they were together. But that day it was as though a form of verbal tetanus had struck. She swallowed the words that stung her throat until she felt nauseous, somehow managing to withstand the spears Djama kept driving into her heart, again and again. Katmé imagined her impaled. A stake rammed into her body just below the sternum and exiting through her mouth, muzzling her for all eternity. In a pinch, tape would do. She'd wrap it around her Brazilian weave, her forehead, eyebrows, lashes, nose, ears, and mouth, pausing at the mouth to add a few extra layers, checking that they were good and tight. That would finally shut Djama up. Such a bitch. A secret-French-passport-toting bitch. A bitch whose children and grandchildren all had dual nationality because "you never know . . . things could go to hell here someday . . . You and Tashun should consider doing the same for the girls. When they turn fifteen, send them to a boarding school in France. By eighteen, they'll be citizens." A bitch who boasted about her plastic Christmas tree dusted with fake snow and gleaned her "art" from Ikea and the like during her trips to Europe.

"And maybe no one told you, but I know the gallery owner, Keuna Bubinga! She used to work at the French Embassy, until they got rid of her. She was a member of the FZC—accepting her was an accident, madness really! We got rid of her too! She'd been sponsored by that idiot ambassador's wife, *intuitu personae,* which made it hard to say no. Madness! That stuck-up diva, whom we'd graciously accepted though she isn't even married, thought she was the only one of us with a properly functioning brain. Nothing was ever good enough for her, she always had to put in her two cents. After a while, we kicked her out, you know why?"

Katmé had heard the story. Tickets to the FZC's charity gala cost as much as a hundred grams of saffron. Keuna had bought two that year. The other "friends" were certain that she'd be attending with a date, that she was *finally* going to introduce them to her partner. Instead, Keuna didn't show. What was worse, they'd found her panicked cleaning lady in an eccentric dress sitting at the American ambassador's table. And her driver, in a green suit, green shirt, and green tie, at another, elbow to elbow with the Minister of Justice.

"Keuna," Djama continued her harangue, "gave her gala invitations—a gala from which deputy ministers and CEOs were turned away because they left it too late—to her cleaning lady and driver!"

The FZC had called an extraordinary general meeting. Instead of offering her humble apologies as expected, Keuna had disdainfully maintained that she didn't see what the problem was. The FZC sold tickets; she had bought them, and given the price she'd paid, what she did with them and who she gave them to was none of their business. Her maid and her driver were still people, until proven otherwise.

"And now you want me to support a show organized by that bald little minx? She made fools of us all."

Katmé bit her lower lip to keep from bursting into laughter. It was so gratifying to learn that you could be inadvertently avenged. That's exactly what Keuna had done; she'd preemptively exacted revenge for Samy and her. While hanging the exhibition, Keuna and Katmé had come to see one another in a new light. A pleasant surprise. The "healthy dislike" Keuna had suggested the first time they met had been the basis of their fraught relationship up until that point. But that afternoon they were reborn in each other's eyes, and Keuna had declared that the days of "healthy dislike" were behind them. Their simultaneous moments of worry and relief, their consensus on the direction the scenography should take, and their shared affection for Samy, who was deep in the throes of anxiety, meant Katmé hadn't needed to wait for the formal declaration ending hostilities to begin to admit to herself that this Keuna, with her rough manners, boyish figure, and a mouth that could make anyone feel like a prude, this Keuna who had so thoroughly annoyed her, was actually all right. The fact that those conformist caryatids had allowed the gallery owner to join the FZC would always remain a mystery to Katmé, a mystery as impenetrable as black holes and the laws of quantum physics.

Since the words Katmé could have said, the words she *should* have said, had remained lodged somewhere between her sternum and her solar plexus, refusing to budge, refusing to advance in an even line like brave little soldiers in the army of verbal retaliation, it was the cheerful arrival of Axelle and Alix—not the stake or the tape—that had signed the armistice and ended Djama's verbal assault on Samuel. The twins had flung open the doors and thrown themselves into Grandma Djama's arms. With her palms resting on her lap in the blue sitting room, where a photo of the Mother of the Nation surrounded by the FZC had pride of place on the sideboard, every inch of Katmé's five-foot-seven frame was the picture of equanimity. Astounded by her own cravenness, she had taken refuge in the silence while watching her daughters cuddle up to Uncle Ambroise's wife.

Madam DepChief returned from the kitchens and extended both arms, palms up, toward the butler, who announced that the buffet was open. The waiters cleared the glasses, champagne flutes, and canapes. The waitresses formed a guard of honor for the *wives* to walk through on their way to the vanilla-scented dining room. Two long, rectangular tables, elaborately set with fine cloths and flower centerpieces, stood in the middle of the room, perpendicular to the glorious buffet where kitchen staff stood at the ready.

They had been standing thus far, and now it seemed no one had informed the new Madam DepChief that she would need to have a chair ready for Djama's attendant. The hostess always placed a chair in advance to ensure she'd be able to maintain eye contact with her boss while remaining separate from the rest of the group. When Djama saw that the young woman she'd never deigned to introduce and whose name had always remained a mystery had nowhere to sit, she raised an eyebrow. Madam MinHealth tried to intervene, but Djama's icy glare stopped her in her tracks. Ameline eventually realized there was a problem. Mortified, she asked the butler to bring an extra chair. Katmé helped her to find the most strategic place for it: far from the buffet, far from the tables, and far from *them,* but still in Djama's line of sight. Then everyone pretended not to notice the panicked inflections in Ameline's voice while she begged Djama to forgive her "unforgivable oversight" or the way she touched the older woman's hand and swore that it would "never happen again."

Katmé was hungry.

As they ate, the women exclaimed that everything was "very good" and "remarkably well prepared."

Gabrielle, the American, clinked her fork against a glass and raised her voice over the chatting. "Friends, when we take the kids to visit Bubinga Project, can we ask the artist to lead a workshop for them?" she asked in heavily accented French.

With her brown hair, crescent-shaped eyebrows, heavily lined lids, and the fake mole tattooed on her chin in henna, Gabrielle seemed to think she was Gloria Swanson in *Sunset Boulevard.* The FZC's African members still hadn't forgiven her for inviting them to a funeral for her Alapaha Blue Blood Bulldog. Katmé thought it was entirely possible she'd offed the dog herself just so she could display his body fireside, draped beneath a floral, wool shawl with black fringe—like Nora Desmond's chimpanzee.

"That's an excellent idea," said Aline, who was Belgian. "Bubinga Project is more than big enough. I'm sure Keuna will be happy to lend us one of the rooms in her gallery for an afternoon. Madam Prefect, what do you think? Could you ask them? Now that the preview is behind them, maybe they have a bit more free time?"

Katmé chewed her sanga—cassava leaves and fresh corn cooked in palm nut juice. She pointed to her full mouth, gesturing to Aline, who was sitting at the end of the table while Katmé was in the middle, to wait for her to finish. Thirty pairs of eyes, including Djama's, were now trained on her. She chewed slowly, swallowed, and meticulously wiped the corners of her mouth. "Of course," she said, casting her gaze toward Djama, who was sitting across from her and a few chairs down. Their eyes clashed.

"And maybe the kids can also make something too," said Gabrielle. "A little piece of art, something simple, easy, a souvenir, you know what I mean," she said in her signature blend of approximate French and English. "What do you think? It could be great."

Djama spoke up. "Now, now, dear friends, I don't believe we've reached a formal decision as to whether or not the FZC will even take the children to visit that man's show."

The waiters impassively filled wine and water glasses, provided salt here, and passed the pepper there. Katmé felt her expression darken as if storm clouds were gathering. How would she ever work up the courage to put Djama in her place and tell her what she really thought? This was Uncle Ambroise's wife, a woman in whose good graces she had to remain—at least on the surface. A woman to whom she felt increasingly indebted.

Elevated to the status of "grief godmother" by Tashun, Djama provided immediate answers and efficient solutions for the kinds of preoccupations that had always been the focus of her life while Katmé looked on, a complete novice. Godmother at a baptism, communion, or wedding, sure; she was often asked to serve in such a capacity herself—it was never free, either, always ended up costing her a fortune. But grief godmother? Tashun never ran out of bright ideas. Djama didn't pay for anything though, she only offered advice. Funeral home, caterer, criers, decorator, invitations, protocol, streamlining costs—she shared her experience generously. The work to be done on the unfinished two-story home they'd bought in Fènn had become the source of recurring arguments between Katmé and Tashun, at least until Djama got involved. Enchanted by the view of the village and the church steeple from the top of the hill and the charm of the pond and the eucalyptus grove at the edge of the property—the perfect place to plant pine trees, she'd thought—Katmé had been undeterred by the overwrought architecture, bizarre layout, and exorbitant cost of renovations required to create a livable floor plan. From the patio, you stepped directly into a vast kitchen, spanning about six hundred square feet, which you had to walk through to get to any of the other rooms in the house. Its four doors led to the only bathroom—an updated take on the Turkish bath—as well as to the dining room, living room, and hallway to the bedrooms. The bedrooms were austere. Taking their inspiration from monastic cells, they were devoid of anything that might distract from sleep. Stark and small, with just enough room for a bed and a table, nothing to excite the eyes, everything to encourage rest. Vamy Kounkeu, the seller's village real estate agent, had provided explanations that amused her and Samy. The bizarre, utterly unique nature of the future acquisition had stirred their imaginations. Katmé was certain it would be easy for a contractor to make the space more coherent while maintaining its quirky character. The first one had pocketed a substantial advance and quit after two weeks. The second, an architect recommended by Aleksandre Fortès, had suggested bulldozing the place. Katmé had refused. The third, the mayor's nephew, had demolished one wing, and then run out of ideas. One night when they were having dinner at Uncle Ambroise and Djama's house, Tashun had brought up the disaster. Djama had done what she always did so well: she gently scolded Katmé, then made a call. The son of a friend of hers was an architect who worked wonders. Télésphore Zambo had visited the site, and wonders he had wrought indeed.

"You're a miracle worker," Katmé had exclaimed, overwhelmed with gratitude.

"Miracles are my lot in life, Madam," he had replied with a twinkle in his eye.

He drew up several different blueprints for the vault, so Katmé could choose her favorite. Djama, who was always pragmatic, presented a recent model: her own. Well, hers and Uncle Ambroise's. Death certainly wouldn't catch them by surprise. They'd planned it all out, everything including the invitations to one or the other's funeral, four years after the death and burial.

"You have to handle everything yourself, you see. It brings shame on your family if you don't. A funeral is the grand finale of a life, after all. You don't want people laughing at you." *A funeral is the grand finale of a life.* Djama was one of those people who believed she would live on, even in death.

Mélanie, the French wife of the CEO of the national chocolate company, tapped her fork against her glass, imitating Gabrielle. She had once asked Katmé if violence was innate in Black people (two of her employees had fought over a woman, and then there were all the wars, of course, all the armed conflicts . . .), but this time she said, "Have you heard about the show? It's a runaway success. I've been back several times and there are red dots everywhere. Almost everything has sold. And there's a new article about Samuel Pankeu in the papers every day. It would be an honor for the FZC to have him run a workshop for the children from Vita House.

"The problem is that we don't all have the same take," Djama replied in a tone so sour she could have just bitten into a slice of lemon.

The problem, Katmé thought as she took the ramekin of hot pepper the waiter was handing her, is that Djama doesn't waste her time on "anti-government newspapers." *The Voice of Zambuena,* the government's official mouthpiece, was enough for her. It had written:

The artist's deliberately fallacious interpretation of sensitive historical situations is problematic. How can sculpture, photography, and dance shed light on a topic historians themselves have been unable to untangle without controversy. This show is proof that extravagance and alternate truths do not amount to talent. Do we live in a dictatorship as Samuel Pankeu suggests? A strange stance from an artist whose work has never been muzzled and whose exhibition received official authorization. Let's concede that our country expresses and has expressed at particular moments in its history a certain degree of authority. Who can blame us? Has any major power ever become so without authority? Authority is what keeps the world turning.

"The show is an epiphenomenon, nothing more!" exclaimed Madam MinCulture, who was wholly indifferent to social niceties and diplomacy. She was repeating her husband, the government's spokesman and Minister of Culture, who had declared on national television, "That man's show is an epiphenomenon, nothing more."

"We may not all agree on the message, but the artist's work is of incredible quality; that much is undeniable," chimed in Khadidiatou, the Senegalese ambassador's wife. "If I had the means, I would have bought a sculpture at the preview."

"Me too, without a second thought!" added Mélanie.

Katmé watched as the two women at the neighboring table exchanged looks of support. Aleksandre Fortès had told Samuel and her that the night of the preview, a woman wearing blue lipstick and a pagne tied like a pharaonic headdress—the description matched Khadidiatou—had exclaimed, "*Eyway!* That's a lot, isn't it?" upon seeing the prices for the pieces.

"You can buy whatever you like, but why should I mobilize the state's property for such disrespectful nonsense?" asked Madam MinTransportation, who had had no such scruples when she requisitioned a bus for family gatherings back in her village or for other FZC outings.

"Sorry, but what does respect have to do with art?" Gabrielle asked in English. She was so surprised she hadn't even bothered with French.

"Where you're from, you've lost all your values, so maybe nothing," replied Djama. "But here, you can't attack collective memory with such careless disdain. The man is not only distorting reality, he's falsifying history. And his photos of the so-called Aquatics, why doesn't he explain that the neighborhood is called Les Flamboyants and that it was precisely that: flamboyant? Why doesn't he explain that the residents are the ones who turned it into a heap of unsanitary shacks? It used to be full of nice houses built by the National Real Estate Company for middle managers."

Katmé was nervously poking the tines of her fork into the cotton and lace tablecloth, making tiny holes. Keeping her mouth shut was taking its toll. The other women—the ones who always went dumb when touchy subjects came up—ate or discussed their children, next postings, the latest films out in Europe, and highly recommended new businesses in Akriba. The ones who were following the debate turned their heads left and then right, again and again, as if they were sitting in the stands of a tennis court. Others craned their necks, adjusted their position, and listened closely to ensure they didn't miss a word of what was going on at the next table. Katmé focused her gaze outside. Through the blinds on the windows overlooking the garden, she caught glimpses of plumeria, torch ginger, birds of paradise, and parrot plants which disappeared and reappeared as the sheer curtain danced in the breeze. If she spoke up, Djama would never forgive her for challenging her in front of the white women. She'd made her show of bravery when Uncle Ambroise, alerted by his wife, urged her not to minimize the possible political repercussions of the exhibition and to keep her distance from this insult to the Father of the Nation—and when Tashun ordered her "to steer clear of that gallery, period." She had gotten involved in the scenography and helped hang the works. And on the day of the preview, she'd worked as an assistant to Keuna and Samuel, answering visitors' questions, sharing insights to help them understand the pieces, and handling sales. Today at the FZC she could keep quiet without shame. Samy didn't need her anymore. The show had attracted collectors, a new generation of well-off art lovers eager to acquire a piece by a fellow countryman, or people who were simply excited to spend their money on "something spectacularly useless."

"*Out of Africa* certainly made its mark, and I'm not just talking about Mozart's adagio for clarinet," Faith, the Kenyan, said in a solemn tone.

"She loves the sound of her own voice," Madam MinPublicWorks whispered in Katmé's ear.

That's when Gertrud spoke up. It had been her idea after all. She didn't even understand what the stakes were anymore. What were they on about? She had simply suggested taking orphaned children to see an art show. What was there to discuss? She suggested they vote and get it over with. Katmé's eyes met Djama's. She had gotten what she wanted. A vote. By show of hands. Only a few of the members had even been to Samuel's show. Djama felt certain she'd win.

Not long after being admitted to the Club, Katmé had looked beyond the smiles, embraces, and chitchat to map out the opposing camps and counterbalancing forces within the CFZ, which she labeled the Four Axes: Local, Western, Diplomatic, and Non-aligned. Within these blocs, there were smaller cliques: Christians, Muslims, White, Black, Arab, Asian, and the interracially wed. When opinions diverged irreconcilably concerning a destination or activity, they voted. Alliances formed and dissolved depending on the interests of each group. This was when the otherwise invisible demarcation lines became clear. The Friends belonging to the local axis had boycotted the exhibition. Not one of them had attended the preview or apologized for her absence. At lunch the following Friday, they had also refused to participate in the conversation started by enthusiastic expatriates in awe of Samuel Pankeu's talent.

Votes were rare at the FZC. The last vote had been to decide if the FZC should, as such, make a show of its presence at the celebrations in honor of the thirtieth anniversary of the president's party. The Mother of the Nation was the Club's honorary president, and the wife of the party's secretary-general was the vice-president, but was it necessary, relevant, or wise for the wives of ambassadors to sew outfits bearing the effigy of the president and wear local boubous to official rallies broadcast on national television?

As for whether the children would visit the show *Ante Mortem: Trance-Versal Therapies* by Samuel Pankoo—Gertrud deformed the final vowel, as always—and then enjoy an introduction to sculpting workshop, the diplomats from countries where freedom of speech is written in invisible ink, the local axis which parroted Djama's positions, and even Katmé, whose vote was only symbolic, voted no. Despite this strong opposition, and to everyone's surprise, the FZC voted to go ahead with the studio visit and sculpture workshop.

A week after Samuel led the introductory art workshop for the Vita House children, the following headline appeared in *Tropics Daily:*

ORPHANED CHILDREN LEFT IN THE HANDS OF HOMOSEXUAL ARTIST SAMUEL PANKEU, BROTHER-IN-LAW OF PREFECT TASHUN ABBIA

It would later become clear that the article had been commissioned by Tashun's opponent in the gubernatorial race in Haut-Fènn. A vengeful, obese woman and a member of the Central Committee, who'd earned an unshakeable nickname selling caramel candy in the Carrefour des Anges neighborhood: Mama Caramel Two-for-Ten.

7

A routine interrogation. The routine had been going on for three days now. The phone had rung while Katmé was packing her bag for a trip to Fènn. The final structural changes and the blueprints for the vault awaited her approval. The marble and fixtures ordered from Italy on Djama's advice hadn't been delivered on time, so the plumbing and floors in the bathrooms and new kitchen were behind schedule. More importantly, a distant cousin they'd hired to oversee the worksite (American, they called him—it would be too late by the time she discovered why) had been stealing materials in cahoots with the workers responsible for carting away the rubble. As soon as Katmé finished her conversation with Samuel's mother, she dialed Tashun's number. He was the first one to mention the *Tropics Daily* article. She started her car and raced to the police station in the Cité des Enseignants neighborhood. She hadn't set foot in a police station for years. The last time she'd come it was to apply for a national identity card, back before she got married. Officers slumped behind tiny desks, bookcases bowed under the weight of dusty forms, citizens with worry written all over their faces. A traffic cop recognized her, removed his beret, and led her to Samy following a brief exchange. He was sitting on a bench with five other people: two drunk teens, a drowsy old man, and two women in loud makeup. Samuel, whose head was resting on a thin particle board partition covered in Plexiglas, was wearing green polyester pants, a purple smock, and sneakers. He kept involuntarily gathering the two sides of his smock together. It, like his cheekbones and forehead, was dotted with white clay stains. The policeman took them to a light-filled office at the end of a dark hallway. No one had told Samuel why he'd been arrested, explained what he was doing there, or informed him what they thought he'd done. "You can't just arrest people with no explanation these days!"

He'd spent the night at his studio sculpting a panther with its head in the place of its belly. While waiting for the first quarter of an inch to dry so he could hollow it out, he'd been mixing the slip he used as glue, they'd banged on the door while he was making the slip, he'd finished sanding the dried clay and was mixing it with water, they'd pounded at the door as if it led to an arms dealer's lair, "Police, open up!" He doesn't even know what they think he did, he couldn't be gone long, the panther was drying, he had to hollow it out before, it had still been damp when he'd left the studio, ready to be hollowed out, if it was left to dry too long, it would harden, and if it hardened, it was ruined, the piece would be junk, he couldn't fire it with its belly full of bubbles, didn't Katmé remember the arm that had exploded in the kiln because he'd forgotten to hollow it out? That's what would happen, without a doubt, a panther three feet long and two feet tall, hollow it out, glue it back together, cut it, so it would fit in the kiln, the client, the one who had also bought the video installation on display at the gallery, would be unhappy if he didn't finish on time, he'd promised, he would have to start all over again if the panther hardened, he'd spent five days and five nights trying to tame the clay, and the struggle was far from over, the panther and its legs had been born, he would patinate it, the legs and paws would be blue, six legs, it would have six legs, the client had asked for a decapitated panther with blue legs, its head where its abdomen should be, like in *Ante Mortem,* a panther with six blue legs, the client would grow impatient, he couldn't let a client like that get angry with him, and the poor sculpture, the poor panther, it would grow weary of waiting if he didn't return, it would dry out, he had to go back to the studio, couldn't Katmé explain it to them? Tell them he couldn't stay here, stay here doing nothing, he could come back in the afternoon, he'd go back to the studio, finish his work, and come back, he'd come back so they could ask him all the questions they liked, what did they think he'd done? Since the show, he'd spent all his time between the gallery and the studio, what could he have done wrong there? The panther couldn't wait, he had to go, had to get back to the studio.

The door opened on the police chief. Samy paused his soliloquy. Having learned that "Madam Prefect" was at the station, he invited them to join him in his office, where he offered them coffee, tea, or beer. The phone rang and he picked up, vigorously nodding his head and repeating, "Of course, Your Excellency, my pleasure, Your Excellency, will do, Your Excellency." Then he handed the receiver to Katmé. Tashun asked her to leave the station *immediately,* he'd instructed the chief, there was no need to worry about Samuel. "Just your everyday, routine interrogation following the publication of the *Tropics Daily* article, typical procedure for this type of accusation," and, in any case, the presence of the Prefect's wife would only "complicate things." He spoke to Samuel next, who wanted to know if he'd be home in time to finish his panther sculpture, he'd finished the slip, he was about to begin hollowing it out when he'd been arrested, if he took too long, he'd have to start all over, Tashun couldn't imagine the amount of work it would be to start all over, and the client, the client would see red, the client, a collector who liked his work, he might lose his trust, he had to make his deadline, the client lived in Dubai, he wanted to go home with the finished sculpture. Tashun reiterated: There was nothing to worry about, he was doing everything in his power to get him home as soon as possible. As soon as possible, yes, but when? Within the hour? Possibly, why not, it was conceivable, he was doing his best. Katmé "forgot" an envelope on the chief's desk when he accompanied her back to her car, outside in the warm, dry air. In the yard, he waved off the paperclip-, envelope-, and official form-peddlers before they could swarm. Sita Félicie jumped out of a taxi wearing a wrapper tied over an orange, knit dress, her headscarf askew. Katmé got the chief to help her reassure Samy's mother. Her son would be leaving the station soon, no need to let Kizito know.

The next day, the press published more articles about "the Samuel Pankeu affair." Katmé learned from the papers that, before they banged on Samy's studio door like brutes, they'd paid a visit to Félix Éboué Middle School, where they'd called the students who had been in his art class to the teacher's lounge for questioning. They'd asked "a ton of questions," *Tropics Daily* reported, signing off with assurance that, "As we go to print and Samuel Pankeu begins his second night in holding at the Cité des Enseignants station, the police are still sifting through the answers." *Emancipation,* the paper where Ety worked and to which Samuel sometimes contributed articles for their arts and ideas section, published a short piece. The author, one of Ety's colleagues, reminded readers that the exhibition *Ante Mortem: Trance-Versal Therapies* would be closing at the end of the month and encouraged people to go see it. He also expressed his surprise at the zeal displayed by the police: "far from diligent when they should be, overeager when they shouldn't be."

Three days. Now Tashun was saying it would be counterproductive to get involved. It would do them all a disservice. He thought it would be easy to get Samuel out, but he was wrong, not at the moment, not in his position, not in a scandal like this one, in a country like this one, where it's better to be accused of embezzling public funds or murder, not when Samuel had made enemies of their friends with his accusatory exhibition. When you decide to rattle those in power, it's best to be beyond reproach. And Samuel wasn't even the target, it was Tashun himself, he was the one they wanted to drag through the mud, it was his rapid ascent through the party ranks they wanted to halt, that's what they wanted, for him to intervene so the press could attack him as the homosexual's protector and make him look like a homosexual himself, she knows what that would mean for his career, their family; so, they'd steer clear of it all, wait for things to fizzle out, the accusation was hollow, nothing but slander, no proof, sure Samuel was still in jail, but that didn't mean anything, he'd be released, without a doubt, he'd be released.

Samuel was two years older than Katmé and six inches taller, but in their final year of high school, whenever anyone bothered him, she was the one who bared her teeth. His sartorial preferences—suit jacket and tie, plenty of velvet—as well as his pompous vocabulary, affected mannerisms, and aloofness made him the target of teasing and the sort of humiliations that so quickly take shape in the minds of teens with too few outlets for expression. Samy was the brother life had granted her, the girls' godfather, part of the family. Tashun knew what Samy meant to his wife. If he himself hadn't been named in the *Tropics Daily* article, the inquiry wouldn't have lasted a day, and Samy wouldn't have been in this situation. But Samy *was* in this situation, which meant that Katmé was too. There was no way she could keep her distance. Stay. Wait. "You read the same articles I do in the opposition rags, you can see for yourself that *Tropics Daily* has it out for me, I'm doing what I can. They won't let it go as long as they can make him out to be my brother-in-law."

Katmé called Kizito. She learned that Samy was doing as well as a person locked in a twenty-by-twenty-foot cell with eighteen other people and an overflowing bucket of urine and feces could do. The envelope she had forgotten on the police chief's desk meant Samy escaped "the swing" and "hot coffee"—two forms of entertainment enjoyed by the sadistic officers at the Enseignants station.

At night Katmé could feel vicelike screws squeezing her temples, her eyelids spasmed, and the papaya leaf teas Bambili made her did nothing to slow her racing heart. Whenever the phone rang, she rushed over, certain it was good news. But the days passed and Samy remained in prison. She'd promised herself she would continue preparations for the funeral, go to her meetings with Djama, take Axelle and Alix to school, tend to the household with the steward, attend FZC lunches, and visit the house in Fènn, but she was unable to manage the ordinary things in her life when Samy's life was now anything but ordinary.

Tashun invited the newspaper publishers to a "discursive meeting" at the prefecture. The Editor-in-Chief at *Tropics Daily* presented his boss's apologies: A bad case of diarrhea. Too much hot pepper on his ground beef sandwich. He would be unable to attend.

"We know for sure now that that porker Mama Caramel Two-for-Ten and her lackeys are paying *Tropics Daily,*" said Tashun. He refused to tell her how much the discursive meeting with the publishers had cost him. "She'll do anything to take me out." After that, Prefect Abbia's name was kept out of articles about the Samuel Pankeu affair. Except in *Tropics Daily,* of course.

At the gallery, two clients demanded their deposits be refunded. "I don't want anything to do with a man who sleeps with other men," had said the would-be owner of the *Mastermind* sculpture, a banker with bulging eyes. The other was a car salesman who spent half the year in Guangzhou. He'd graced the labels of four photographs with red dots, then balked, "I'm okay with him criticizing the government in his work. We need people like him in this country, to speak up when things aren't right. But a man who does *that* with other men, when there are plenty of women around, ready and willing for us to shove our thing in any hole we like—for free even—I mean, they're fine with us doing whatever we like whenever we like wherever we like, and he's doing it with men! It's sorcery. You want me to hang something by someone like that in my home? I don't care if he's Ousmane Sow in the flesh, my sister, no vex but I want my money back." Keuna maintained that the *Tropics Daily* article was a load of nonsense, that the other papers had simply jumped on the story like rutting buffaloes on a hapless female, that Samuel had a girlfriend and that, regardless, the gallery would not refund deposits without a valid reason. But it was no use. Both buyers got so aggressive that she had to give their money back.

8

"Mr. Pankeu and my wife are not bound by blood and share no kin. He is not my brother-in-law. He cannot be my brother-in-law. *He's our girls' godfather?* I'm not saying we don't know him, I'm simply saying that he's not my brother-in-law as has been claimed in the press. He's an old classmate of my wife's, more of a superficial acquaintance who comes and goes than a true friend. Our daughters were born very preterm. Their lives were at risk. Mrs. Abbia and I were in a rush to have them baptized. Mr. Pankeu happened to be at the hospital that day, so we chose him. Pure chance. He became their godfather. But that was a long time ago, the girls are ten now. He plays no role in their upbringing, they never even see him. *My wife attended the preview for his show?* Mrs. Abbia likes art, I don't believe that's anything to be ashamed of. She was as surprised as I was by the nature of the works on display, but she'd made a commitment, so she kept her word. *The Minister of Culture pushed for the arrest to settle a score?* Nonsense. We live in a democracy. We don't have people arrested simply because they disagree with the government's positions. That's a thing of the past. Mr. Samuel Pankeu exercised his freedom of speech, his artistic freedom, both of which were established—it's important to remember to whom we owe our liberties—by the Father of the Nation. Why would we have him arrested for that? *What did I think of the exhibition?* Do you really want to know what I think? I've heard a few people use the terms 'audacity' and 'originality.' Personally, all I saw was an erratic, wandering, spasmodic expression of youthful creativity—though the artist's twentieth birthday is a distant memory. Too rash for my taste. *My take on this affair as a Christian?* First and foremost, let me remind you that we are a family of believers, a pious family, my wife's sister is a Redemptoristine nun. In the West these days, permissive, provocative literature on this topic is on the rise. Our adversaries are working hard to destigmatize and even normalize behaviors that are anything but normal. God's laws are clear on this subject. It's not about trends, it's about truth, and there can be no aggiornamento when it comes to the word of the Lord. As for Mr. Pankeu, an investigation is underway. If Mr. Pankeu gave in to any of these despicable temptations, he will have to answer for it in the courts of men and of God. He will have to repent because, as you know, God does not seek the sinner's death. Several party officials, including myself, are organizing a Mass to be led by the archbishop at the cathedral. This scandal is a wake-up call for all of us, we must pray tirelessly for our lost sheep. *Why haven't I pressed charges?* I am fully devoted to the task the Father of the Nation entrusted to me through the Ministry of the Interior. Managing a city like Akriba is exhilarating but demanding. I have no time to spare. I devote any spare time to my family, not to the spiteful maneuvers of easily manipulated, bribe-taking journalists. This may surprise you, but malicious insinuations leave me wholly indifferent. *Why am I speaking up now?* I'm a public figure, so attacks are to be expected. I thought that by keeping silent I could protect my honor and my family from being dragged through the mire. I see now that doing so only fanned the flames, encouraging the drivel of a rag unfit to be called a newspaper. I understand that people may seek to discredit me given my position, but when my daughters are viciously teased at school, told absurdities about their father's virility and lies about his morals, that's when I say stop, that's enough, you've gone too far, crossed a line. So, here's a warning for any scribblers who dare to write another word of drivel about me: I'll see you in court."

Katmé turned up at the prefecture holding a copy of *The Voice of Zambuena.*

"How many times do I have to tell you? I'm the one they're after with this scandal, not your precious Samuel! He's a small fry. Didn't you read the latest article published by that tabloid?" Tashun asked, alluding to one in which *Tropics Daily* insinuated that the prefect had bought the silence of their colleagues.

"The girls were teased at school? We don't know Samy?" Katmé protested.

"All right, all right, I may have gone a bit overboard, I admit."

"How could you drag our daughters into this? You went a *bit* overboard? I think that makes you the king of euphemisms."

It occurred to her then that her husband, battle-tested opportunist that he was, may have orchestrated the publication of the first article in *Tropics Daily* himself, betting that the "Samuel Pankeu ordeal" would, in the end, reflect positively on him and advance his career. "God's laws are clear on the subject" and "God does not seek the death of the sinner"—Mama Récia couldn't have said it better. Tashun never missed the very popular eleven o'clock Sunday Mass at the cathedral, where those who once mattered, those who still mattered, and those who hoped to matter one day always gathered. Afterward, on the esplanade outside, beneath the huge Mbigou soapstone crucifix, they greeted one other, embraced, and traded information of varying degrees of importance while the archbishop embraced, greeted, and chatted with the most generous collection donors. The president often boasted about his piety. Every Saturday evening at six o'clock, a dozen officials attended Mass in his private chapel. Uncle Ambroise was among them. Tashun was obsessed with someday earning an invitation. Her husband, defender of Christian virtues and outraged father. It was petty, underhanded, and cunning—it was smart.

"I might as well tell you now, since you'll find out soon enough: Samuel was transferred to the central prison yesterday."

Katmé felt her legs begin to wobble. "What did you just say, Tash?" she asked so quietly she could barely hear herself.

"I said what I said. Samuel was transferred to Central yesterday. That's why my interview came out today. Speaking of which, I don't see what your problem is with what I told them. Whether you like it or not, he's not your brother and he's not my brother-in-law, Kat. Plus, it's not like I told the reporter Samuel actually was . . . you know. Because he is, in fact, a fag, isn't he? He is and you know it, and you always assumed I didn't. You know what your problem is, you and your Samy? It's that you think I'm an idiot."

Tashun was seated. Katmé stood across from him. Suddenly unsteady on her feet, she pulled an armchair over and slumped down onto it. Two weeks. She hadn't seen Samy in two weeks. For two weeks she'd "kept her distance." For two weeks she'd had blinders on. Two weeks of naïve, absurd, irrational stupidity. Maybe Tashun *was* an idiot, but she was the one who'd been had. Yes, he'd known for a few days that

Samuel would be transferred to Central. No, he hadn't thought he should tell her, she was already making the whole thing such a big deal; he hadn't wanted to worry her "any more than necessary," being transferred to Central didn't mean anything per se, the holding cells at the neighborhood stations were too small; Samuel had been moved in the night, his family hadn't been informed yet.

"Now justice must run its course."

"Justice? What justice? Fourteen days in police custody and now prison based on the ravings of a paper you yourself call a rag, do you call that justice? The potential for life in prison if he's convicted, is that justice? We can't just leave Samy in there! Get Uncle Ambroise to have him let out on bail!" Katmé railed.

"There's zero risk Samuel will be convicted. Zero! All we can do is wait. I can't speed up the process. I won't take that kind of risk."

"But there's no evidence! None! I read the law, article sixteen, you have to be caught in the act. We aren't characters in a Kafka novel! This is an arbitrary arrest, unlawful imprisonment!"

"Woah, woah, woah! Don't get ahead of yourself. Apparently, you didn't read article sixteen all the way through. *Flagrante delicto,* allegation, or a series of indications. In this case, it's an allegation. Your directive remains the same: Keep your distance. Mama Caramel-Elephant-Belly has it out for me. She won't let up. She knows that Uncle Ambroise is throwing my name in the hat to be the next governor of Haut-Fènn."

"What are you talking about? Governor of Haut-Fènn? You? I don't understand," Katmé exclaimed.

Tashun crossed his arms over his chest, a look of defiance on his face.

Stunned, his wife sank deeper into the armchair.

They'd been married for nearly twelve years. She'd come to accept the unquenchable thirst for revenge that consumed her husband. Revenge for the hand he'd been dealt in life. "If my father had made the same political choices yours did, my career would never have lagged," he often said. Back when democratic ideals first began to gain traction, Tashun's father had been Minister of Finance and the Economy—until he resigned and founded his own party, certain that the time was finally right for a two-party system. The president, who was a boarding school classmate of his and had been in office for thirty years, ostracized him. Abbia, their name, became a synonym for betrayal. Though Tashun had graduated first in his class at the National School of Civil Service, his career stagnated until just before the last municipal elections, when the ruling party made him the candidate for deputy prefect of Maboma, an insignificant, arid, northern city that had been run by the opposition for over a decade. Tashun saw it as an opportunity; he worked hard on the campaign, did what needed to be done, and, to everyone's surprise, the APM won the election. The city of Maboma itself meant nothing, but as a symbol, it was everything. Tashun was rewarded with his first articles in the papers. Ambroise Béma, Uncle Ambroise, his godfather and former friend of his father, former Minister of Territorial Administration and current Secretary-General of the party, who had cut all ties to the Abbia family in the wake of the "betrayal," got back in touch with his godson and took him under his wing. Eighteen months later, at the age of thirty-three, Tashun was appointed prefect of Akriba—an extremely coveted position. It had only been a year, but that wasn't enough anymore. Now Uncle Ambroise was dangling the governorship of Haut-Fènn before his eyes. What would come next?

In Haut-Fènn, there was a common saying: "If you run into a Mének and a snake, kill the Mének and let the snake be." Tashun was a Mének. The opposition had held onto the governorship in the region since the first multi-party elections twenty years ago. He didn't stand a chance.

"The incumbent is unwell. He isn't running. This is my window. It's the province where there will be the fewest candidates for the party's primary. They're convinced we'll never win there. If I win the party's nomination, I swear on our daughters' lives that I'll win the election! Your mother's funeral will launch my campaign, and the health center will help me build ties with the local community."

"I don't see how inviting all those people to a private event that only holds meaning for my family is going to help get you elected," Katmé deadpanned.

"*A private event?* Did you really think your mother's funeral would be a private event? You're thinking like a white woman. Have the

Europeans at the FZC brainwashed you or something? Do we even live in the same country? I mean really, Christ, think ahead for once!"

"About what? A masquerade? Your political fantasies? Get Samy out of Central! He has nothing to do with any of this!"

"The Old Man has noticed me, Kat," Tashun continued. "They're about to invite me to join the Central Committee and make me the gubernatorial candidate in Haut-Fènn. Do you think that all just came together like that?" he asked, snapping his fingers. "I refuse to throw it all away for Samuel. He'll have to man up and get through this on his own. It won't kill him. As soon as I've taken office, we'll get him out."

Central Prison. She'd been there with the FZC. One of their "adventures in squalor." The rank courtyard, leprous walls, sickly prisoners begging, "We're hungry, help us, Madam, take my family's contact information, tell them I'm alive, I'm ill, Madam, buy me medicine, Madam, Madam, Madam . . ." Underage boys soliciting, "Give me your grits and you can fuck me in the ass—your beans and you can fuck me in the ass!" That's where Samy was now.

That day in their final year of high school when he sat down on the bench next to her and said, "I'm not like the other boys," the days when they left school together and took the shortcut past the dump on the way home, trading stories only they found funny, the days when they led the film club, the days when he shared with her his dreams and sorrows, the day when his father died in his sleep at the age of fifty-nine, the days when he lost himself in the haze of love then emerged from it scratched and bruised, those bitter days when he fled the harsh and horrid Loon, the days when he admitted, "I would have fallen in love with a girl like you if I had it in me," the days when he said, "you don't know what it's like to be in my shoes, Kat," the days when they told one another, "you're my better half," the days of solitude after Sennke left for the convent, the gristly days when the best had to be ahead of them, the days when each of them was the other's *airport,* the only viable landing strip, the days when he first started to see sculpting as his profession, reveling in the fact that he'd made it, days of joy, days of failure, days of absence, days of promise, days of loneliness, days of elation. Those days and so many others, they had always been there for one another. He would dizzy her with the breadth of his knowledge, his mastery of philosophical concepts, and his ardent love of sculpture and art, wrapping her in absolute, inalienable affection. As for her, she would turn into a doting little mother, a chosen sister, a protective older sister who loves, watches over, and defends.

She felt it was her responsibility to get him released.

So she begged her husband.

She begged him to call the Minister of Justice, Jean Tafeng, and get him to order Samy's immediate release. He was right, they were after him, Samy was just a distraction. A distraction locked up in Central because of him, because of them. They couldn't abandon Samy. Samy was facing a minimum of twenty-five years in prison and eight million CFA francs in fines, Samy could even be sentenced to life in prison. They couldn't put Samy's life in the hands of a judge. If he had Samy released, she'd never, ever forget it; she'd throw herself into the campaign, he'd see, he'd hardly be able to believe it. She'd scour every inch of earth and of the house in Haut-Fènn. He was right, he'd make an excellent governor, and she'd support him, she'd have kaba ngondos and boubous made for herself in the party's colors, bearing the Old Man's effigy; yes, he would win that election! "Nothing will be able to stand in your way, but please, I'm begging you, Tash, have Samy released from Central." She didn't notice when her husband's expression hardened, a thin veil fell over his eyes, and his fists clenched. He pushed his chair back and stood up. "Well, how about that," he said. "How about that . . ." His wife, his own wife, was willing to campaign by his side, scour every inch of earth, and knock on every door to get him elected. Not for him, not for their daughters, not for their future. For Samuel. She could read the disappointment on his face.

"I have to get back to work, Kat. Go home."

Now it was her turn to stand. He wouldn't do anything? He planned to leave Samy in prison? Fine. She marched to the door then spun back. "I won't sit around doing nothing while Samuel rots in prison. I'm going to see Jean Tafeng. I'll knock on the door of anyone who can help me get him out, whether you like it or not!"

He grabbed her before she made it out of the room, yanked her back, slammed the door behind her, and shoved her back to the armchair she'd just left. He forced her down, holding her with his full weight on her shoulders.

"Let me think about your request for a minute," he said as he returned to his chair, pushed up the sleeve of his wool suit jacket and stared at the face of his watch. "Tick, tock, tick, tock—a minute's up! Now let me explain things one last time: I will not take any risks for your friend. There are plenty of people waiting for me to do just that, so if I do, I'm done for. Do you even know the acrobatics Uncle Ambroise had to perform to get those reptiles to accept my candidacy? After the inauguration, that greaseball Mama Caramel and her friends will no longer have any hold over me. You want me to squander my future for some wimp, my so-called brother-in-law, whom I've been fed up with for years? Well, your little Latin champion will have to figure it out on his own." She'd saddled him with a pseudo-brother, whom he'd accepted out of love for her, because he wanted what was best for her, with no mother, no father, no sister, so he'd behaved toward Samuel as he would toward a real brother, because Samuel made her happy and her happiness was important to him. Of course he knew that she paid the rent on his studio, that she bought his materials; he knew and turned a blind eye. Her dear "brother," who floated so far above the constraints of this world but who didn't think twice about taking money from a corrupt and ambitious prefect. "You want to go see Tafeng? Go ahead, try it! Your 'better half' will cost you, Katmé. It will cost you big, just you wait and see. If I find out that you set foot at Central, you'll get what's coming to you. You know the scandal you caused when that worm was arrested could have destroyed me without Uncle Ambroise, don't you? I had nothing to do with what's happened to your friend. A person who prays for rain should have a leaf to cover himself up. So if he has to pay the piper for having some guy ream his asshole or for reaming someone else's when we all know that's illegal in this country, then too bad for him, he'll pay. He knew the law, right? You know what this *vulgum pecus* has to say? *Dura lex, sed lex,* there's a Latin phrase for you! Your beloved Samuel must know it."

With her husband, in their new world, she wasn't much. Without him, she was nothing at all. Defy Tashun and go see Samy in prison?

Ask the Minister of Justice for a meeting? They'd had dinner at one another's houses, and his wife, Mamiton Tafeng, was a member of the FZC. Contact a lawyer? A judge? The prison warden? What about the money? Kizito earned a modest salary as an adjunct professor at the university; his wife was a nurse and they had six children. Sita Félicie lived off an unpredictable pension, knitting to make ends meet. Samuel put into his sculpting every franc he earned as a substitute art teacher at Félix Éboué Middle School. As for herself, she was on indefinite leave from her job, no earnings, financially dependent.

Her father! Of course, her father! Innocent Patong would speak to Tashun. He and his son-in-law had grown close and enjoyed discussing politics, fine clothes, fine shoes, and cigars—her husband, who had never been a smoker, had taken up the habit. Innocent Patong had promised to introduce Tashun to prominent figures in Fènn. Her father knew how important Samy was to her. She'd explained it to him. He'd seen it for himself at the exhibition. He would plead her case to Tashun, he would urge him to help Samy, to get him released from prison. He would even persuade Tashun, yes, of course he would.

"*Soubanalai!* Your husband's future is on the line, your future, Katmé. You have to understand that."

"Samuel's *life* is on the line, Papa. Can't the two of you understand that?!"

"You and your husband are currently a trifecta, or maybe even a boxed first four. It's up to you to become a super high five. If you succeed, your life will change radically. You're not far from a super high five as it is. You're the wife of the prefect of Akriba, whereas that boy, Samuel, is a loser, a horse that won't even make it past the starting line. He's your past. As the drunks of Zambuena Pari-Mutuel always say, 'You can't dry today's laundry with yesterday's sun!' You have to keep moving forward, Katmé."

It had taken the news of Madeleine's exhumation, a stay in his coastal city of albatrosses and cormorants, weekends at the residence with Tashun and his granddaughters—when he pointed out the parts of her that she had gotten from him: her incorrigible resilience, her protruding chin and long, thin fingers; the way they both dropped their *R*s when they were tired; the quick, uneven pace of their speech; the way they stuttered when angry; a shared reluctance to stir up the past and bring dead memories back to life—it had taken his arms around her, his praise for her decision to defy Tashun's orders and attend Samy's show, his admiration for her sense of loyalty and friendship; it had taken him saying these words, words she no longer expected, words that cost a man like that, a man of his age, a man of his generation; it had taken all that to erase the years of terrible questions she'd asked herself, the bleak nights she'd spent trying to understand why he'd vanished from her life and Sennke's, to finally help the miserable feeling of being a leaf in the wind begin to fade. Her father was back in her life. He had a taste for fine clothes and shoes as well as luxury watches. Every day he selected his car to match the color of his suit and wore shoes that made Tashun say, "Any man who wears lizard-skin consul oxfords is a great man." He drank vintage champagne and black coffee sprinkled with lemon zest at breakfast with an egg-white omelet and always emptied his bread of its crumb. Cassava fufu with okra sauce was the only dish he considered a real meal. He cut his own hair while studying himself in the mirror, tapped his nose with his finger when he laughed, polished his own shoes, and grumbled at her valet, Motto, when he got too close. At mealtimes, he loved telling tales that were incredible but true, and the dinners he attended at their house always ran later than usual. Even sitting down, he was very tall. Her father forgot the twins' names, never mentioned Sennke, politely asked about the preparations for Madeleine's ceremony, turned up at their door empty-handed, and left laden with peaty Japanese whisky and Cohibas. He didn't call his daughter; she regularly checked in with him, but he only phoned Tashun.

How had she ever thought Innocent Patong would be any help?

She decided to flee. To flee the capital, her powerlessness, and her daughters, already unnerved by their mother's irritability. To flee and lose herself in the work on the house and the construction of the vault. Before booking the jacaranda room at the Zimanto Inn, before getting behind the wheel of her car, before she even realized what she was doing, Katmé called Aleksandre Fortès and told him she was coming.

9

One afternoon, Samy and Katmé had run into Fortès at the bottom of the hill, and he'd invited them over for a drink. His house—a modern take on the traditional conical, thatched-roof hut often occupied by the village chief—wasn't particularly comfortable. A sofa, two wrought-iron armchairs, an empty bamboo bookcase, a dining table, and two wooden chairs inlaid with cowrie shells and brass coins. The only hint of luxury was a woven raffia rug that hung on the wall—Kasai velvet. But Katmé and Samy were drawn to the spectacular quantity of DVDs that had colonized the bottom half of two of the living room walls. They eventually asked him if they could take a closer look, and in return he asked if they'd like to stay and watch a film. He'd heard them talk about their high-school film club at the dinner the mayor had hosted. As for him, his white grandfather, who'd raised him in Paris, had handed down his love of movies through screenings at the Pagoda, the Normandie, or the Sept Parnassiens theaters every Wednesday afternoon. As an adult, he'd begun exploring the few African films he could find in Paris. Now he attended every edition of the biennial Pan-African Film and Television Festival in Ouagadougou. It was around seven o'clock in the evening, it was dark, and no one was expecting them at the Zimanto Inn, so . . . Fortès took *The Camp at Thiaroye* out of its case.

When Samy joined Katmé on her trips to Fènn, Aleksandre Fortès would invite them over for dinner up on the hill, in the Tam-Tam neighborhood. Dinner and a movie. And those evenings were quite unlike the listless ones they spent sitting across from their corn on the cob and safous in the reddish half-light of the Zimanto Inn restaurant, eating to pass the time until they could return to Akriba. Over time, their movie nights quietly became opportunities to cautiously open up to one another. They talked about art and politics as well as progress made on the highway, the vault, and the health center. She and Tashun had given up on the idea of a center for unwed mothers, opting instead for this compromise. Fortès had been invited to dinner twice at their home in Akriba with Mival's CEO. On the rare occasions when Tashun was in Fènn, he invited Aleksandre to join them at the mayor's or deputy prefect's house. Most of the time Fortès claimed he had other plans. Katmé knew that he was avoiding the groveling competition which no one could escape at the politicians' tables. In his living room, after the film, the three of them would drink tea, and wine, lots of wine. Samy would talk freely about Ety, she might reluctantly mention Madeleine, and with a patented blend of fatalism and disconsolate self-deprecation, Aleksandre would evoke his Ivoirian mother who disappeared three days after he was born at Port-Royal Hospital in Paris. "Being abandoned by your mother is less common," he said one night as the credits rolled on *Sugar Cane Alley.*

Whenever he was away, on a trip to Akriba for work or in Paris to see his children, Fortès encouraged Katmé to get the keys from his cleaning lady, Inga, and enjoy his kitchen and video projector without him. Though she would have preferred to spend the evening in the company of tormented filmmakers and underground movies, she always chose to dine alone or with Samy at the Zimanto Inn. There was no sense in going to Aleksandre's house without him, she would have felt out of place amid the sterile decor, which would only underscore his absence. She still couldn't get used to his green eyes, his harelip scar, the way he would suddenly suck in his lower lip like a gecko slurping up an insect, his enigmatic sense of humor, the smell of ganja that clung to her clothes after dinner at his house, forcing her to have them washed at the inn before returning to Akriba, or the groundnut stew and rice he always served. And yet, when she hadn't driven herself to Fènn, when Tashun's driver, Célestin, was chauffeuring her and Samuel around, she would cancel their plans with Fortès, despite the feeling of loss it kindled in her.

Lampshades shaped like huge combs—a recent purchase—shrouded Aleksandre's living room in a bawdy glow. He'd served her a stoneware mug of lemongrass and ginger tea, which she clutched between her hands to warm them and keep herself grounded. She realized, as the uncomfortable, unpadded, wrought-iron chair dug into her posterior, that if Aleksandre weren't there, she wouldn't have had anyone to listen to her feverish, circular monologue, no one to tell that Samy was locked up in Central with rats, bedbugs, and fleas, locked up for an indefinite period, that she wasn't allowed to visit him, and that the last part was killing her. He listened to her as she expressed the powerlessness, fury, and dread she felt about the possibility of a trial. About the potential for humiliation and even conviction. He listened as she related the arrest, the police station, the remand order, and Tashun's rebuffs. Unlike the FZC members, Mama Récia, her former colleagues, and the principal of Félix Éboué Middle School, he listened without asking, "Is it true? Is *Tropics Daily* telling the truth?" As if the answer mattered, as if it could determine whether Samy deserved the public crucifixion he was being subjected to, as if the problem wasn't the despicable behavior of a newspaper or the intrusion of a failing, enfeebled, wholly objectionable state into the private life of a citizen, a state that claimed the moral high ground to protect certain people while devouring others as it saw fit.

Aleksandre pushed up the sleeves of his charcoal-gray abacost, crossed his legs, and broke the silence he'd observed since she began. "I saw that the public prosecutor is bringing charges. I thought you had to be caught in the act."

"The law in this country . . . In this sort of case, an anonymous call to the police is enough for the legal system to get involved, a simple allegation. So, as you might guess, since it was published in a newspaper . . ."

"But they don't actually have anything on Samuel, do they? I mean . . . He didn't," Aleksandre hesitated a second time. "He didn't flaunt it?"

Katmé shook her head. "But since the police and the prosecutor determined that Samy's mannerisms weren't 'sufficiently masculine,'" she said, using air quotes, "they had enough to get a judge to remand him. We don't know how long he'll be in prison before they even make a formal decision about moving ahead with a trial."

"A minimum sentence of twenty-five years, maximum of life . . . and an eight-million-franc fine . . . All for being gay. Your country is absurd."

"Accusing someone of this sort of offense is by far the easiest way to settle a score."

"You keep saying, 'offense' and 'case'. . ."

"I don't understand."

"Your best friend is in prison because he's been accused of homosexuality, but I haven't heard you say the word even once. That strikes me as strange, that's all."

"Well, I find your observation strange. To be honest, I think it's rather inappropriate," Katmé balked.

Aleksandre seemed to look right through her. "I'm sorry," he said. "It just jumped out at me, that's all. Let's forget it."

A heavy silence settled between them.

Was this a mistake? Had she been wrong to open up to him? Why was he trying to push her into the muddy waters of doubt and introspection? Did her unconscious refusal to say the word betray some unspeakable trait he'd already discerned in her? Or was it more like the primness that had led her to omit certain words from her vocabulary—words she heard and read but never said. Except for that time when she'd tried out one or two in bed and Tashun had swiftly called her to order. Of course she listened to Samy's stories and kept his secrets, but the religious education that had kept her legs firmly together until Tashun tepidly spread them, and the years she'd spent reading Barbara Cartland romance novels, had cultivated a prudishness in her that the realities of life, two children, and eleven years of marriage hadn't entirely vanquished. Samy loved men. She loved Samy. It was his life, his desire, his choice. She accepted it. But why should she shout it from the rooftops? Would saying the word, an abstraction really, an immaterial concept that her mind struggled to imagine or embody, help to anchor her feelings for Samy? It didn't matter what Samy had done or been accused of—she would have defended him, spurred by the same protective instincts, if she learned he'd committed murder. Her love for Samy was like the love from the hymn: *so high you can't get over it, so deep you can't get under it, so wide you can't get around it.* But Samy was no murderer. He was attracted to men; that was his crime in the eyes of Zambuena's laws; yet she couldn't bring herself to speak the word *homosexual.*

As if he could read her thoughts, Aleksandre apologized again. "Please forget what I said earlier. It wasn't my place. When do you plan to go see Samuel?"

"I told you, Tashun won't let me go."

"No one can keep you from visiting Samuel if you really want to. There's always a choice."

"That certainly sounds nice, there's always a choice. But did you have a choice when my husband made you fall in line with his calendar? And all the wheeling and dealing you've had to put up with to stay in the good graces of the Ministry of Public Works, did you have a choice about that?"

"Yes, Mival had the choice. The company could have said no, insisted that we'd signed a contract with an international funding organization, told the government that since a third party was paying for the project, any special requests would need to be directed to them, that we're not supposed to have direct contact with or take orders from a partner state. That was my position. But headquarters chose the more pragmatic, profitable, and cynical route. The company wants in on deals for other projects here, so it was an easy decision to make. You're not in the same position, Katmé. Far from it."

"I have to convince Tashun that it's in his best interest to have Samuel released. He needs a pretext of some kind—I don't know, something like, 'Justice Triumphs after Terrible Mistake!'"

"Do you really think your husband will ever lift a finger to get Samuel out? Come on, you're smarter than that."

"All that's happening to me, with Samuel, I—"

"I'm sorry to say so, Katmé, but nothing is happening to *you*. Something is happening to Samuel, something truly terrible. And if you won't take off your blinders, you won't be much help to him."

Aleksandre uncrossed his legs and jumped to his feet, as if suddenly spurred to action. He stood across from her, a wily look in his eyes. "If you really want to see Samuel, you'll need a disguise!"

"I'm sorry?"

"To get into the prison. It'll be easy to make you unrecognizable, and then, in this country where everything is for sale, easier still to have a fake ID made for your new persona! It won't change Samuel's circumstances, but at least you'll be able to see him and offer moral support. You'll be able to discuss things. It's better than nothing."

A disguise . . . Katmé's shoulders slumped. She finished her lemongrass and ginger tea, thanked Aleksandre for listening, and returned to the Zimanto Inn.

Still fully dressed in the espadrilles, black jeans, and pumpkin-hued blouse she'd put on before her visit, Katmé threw herself onto the bed, preparing for the night ahead, a night she knew she'd spend staring at the floral wallpaper until she could make out the early morning fog. Before dropping by Fortès's house, she had discussed cement and rebar with the construction workers at the house, counted the number of light switches installed by the electrician, and had a shouting match with her crook cousin, aka American, who refused to let her fire him because she "couldn't do that to her own blood." She'd yearned to escape the cold heat of the sun, to swallow the colors of the day and watch the evening take shape so she could see Aleksandre and lighten the load that weighed so heavy on her heart. A disguise. What next? Evidently, it wasn't enough to have watched *Muna Moto* together and shared their outrage at Teno's *Chef!* while eating overcooked rice swimming in groundnut stew; he didn't understand. Fortès was a foreigner. He worked for Mival, a foreign company. In twenty months at most, he'd pack his bags and disappear from her life and Samy's too. The pressure building up inside her had escaped through her lips; she'd confided aspects of her life in him as if they were real friends. She deserved a degree in the art of the faux pas. It seemed Samy's incarceration would also put an end to movie nights in Fènn.

10

The first time Katmé visited Central as cabaret singer Eulalie Nana, the guard at the first gate trained a hostile eye on her. Vaguely plump and wholly graceless, she wore a colorful cotton jersey broomstick skirt and scuffed boots with a faded khaki blouse, big, rectangular glasses, black lipstick, and purple blush, with her hair in dreads. The eye in question was certain it had recognized an easy woman, but the kind who wasn't monetizing her skills; he wouldn't get a thing out of her. She had to be some inmate's poor family member, the kind that didn't pay bribes, lengthened the line at the checkpoint, and whose useless presence took up space in the crowded yard where the prisoners and their visitors were already stepping on one another's feet. The families' poverty didn't kindle any pity among the Central guards; instead, it heightened their natural inclination to push people around. But at every step along the path toward Samuel, Katmé placed her closed fist in the guards' hands. Five- and ten-thousand-franc bills. The relatives of the inmates in the VIP block rarely gave more than three thousand, those in general population generally gave somewhere between five hundred francs and two thousand. "All that money, just to visit a cousin . . ." The next week, they welcomed her to Central like an old acquaintance.

Twice a week she got in her car and drove to Ety's. There she would trade her pants, blouse, and loafers for Eulalie Nana's worn, shapeless clothes. Camouflage, a farce, a ridiculous hoop she had to jump through to evade the watchful eye of her husband and everyone else who thought that it was best to let Samuel sort out his own problems. Tashun had repeated his warning: If she tried to see him, if she got mixed up in this mess, she'd get what was coming to her. To spend forty-five minutes with Samuel, Katmé scheduled a little over three hours from the moment she left home so she could drive to Ety's, get changed, and climb into the taxi which would wait for her during the visit in a makeshift parking lot across the road—a vacant lot with a view of the prison's tall walls. Afterward, she went back to Ety's, took off her makeup, changed back into her own clothes, and then drove home. Ety had come up with the disguise. A girdle to push up her butt and stomach, inordinately long dreads, and flashy makeup—it wasn't surprising that the guard inspected her like a fake bill. Ety had gone to "Customs," the part of the Joie neighborhood where forgeries of all sorts of official documents were bought and sold. A fellow named Belong, who had been Ety's source on an investigative reporting series he'd done on the neighborhood, got him a voter registration card featuring a picture of Katmé looking like a cabaret singer.

Samy trembled at the thought that her wig or glasses might fall off and someone would recognize her. "At least dressed like that, you're dodging a bullet with the warden," he would say. The warden, Tazi Djamen, had earned the nickname Uncle Lollipop by offering to improve the lives of those prisoners who were unfortunate enough to have female relatives both pretty and poor—for a special price. Two minutes with his penis in their mouths and the guards stopped searching and taking their cut of the meals they brought; for five minutes, the women could be alone with the prisoner in a closet; if he got to ejaculate, the inmate didn't have to do any chores for a week; and if the women swallowed, the inmate got to spend two nights in a private cell with freshly laundered sheets. Otherwise, it was strictly a cash business.

Since Katmé always paid a tidy sum, Samy migrated from gen pop to the VIP block and was allowed a visit from a doctor and medicine to help heal his torn anus, treat his scabies and ringworm, and extract the chiggers from between his toes. Dressed in an oversized shirt and pants, Samy was emaciated: his lips two thin, ragged lines; his irises cloudy, his skin covered in a whitish film. He looked like a bewildered scarecrow. He turned down the menthol for his lips, the palm oil for his skin, the cocoa butter for his cracked heels. After eating just two spoonfuls of kidney beans and a banana doughnut Bambili had made, he would whisper, "I'm full." Though they weren't in season, Sita Félicie had managed to get her hands on grasshoppers, termites, and palm weevil grubs; she'd seasoned them with garlic, salt, chili, white pepper, ginger, and basil, and let them marinate before roasting the grubs in a dry pan, and the termites and grasshoppers in a pan with a few drops of oil. In the past, Samy would have happily eaten poisoned grubs rather than pass them up. Now he skewered just two or three, chewed them slowly, then mumbled, "I'm full," after what felt like an eternity.

The day before he was transferred to Central, a gynecologist had examined him, shoving two fingers into his anus, inspecting the deformation of his rectum and strength of his sphincter. Equipped with a ring, he measured the circumference of his anus. In the prosecutor's office, a naked prostitute shimmied before him, touching herself while the other men in the room—the police chief and officers—poked Samy's penis with a ruler, saying, "Yoohoo, wakey wakey! Real men get hard watching a woman stroke her pussy, are you going to get a boner or what?" Since Samy's body didn't respond to their jeering, they played heads or tails. Heads, hot coffee, tails, the swing. The coin landed on the edge, so Samy got a mix of both. They bound his wrists and ankles, then hung him upside down with his knees over a bar while they whipped him with a machete.

"Have you ever sucked a man's penis? How many times? Did you like it? Answer! Is it part of your mystical practice? You were born that way? No one is born that way! Are you paid to do it? Answer! Do you take money? Why do you do it if you're not even paid? You want to make it as an artist, is that why you do it?"

An hour after he was admitted to Central—it was eight o'clock at night—the other inmates formed a circle around him and sodomized him until dawn.

With his hands clasped between his gaunt thighs and his head bobbing gently, he told Katmé about the recurring dream he'd been having since he'd been incarcerated. He's kneading clay, molding sculptures of children in a corner of the studio, and a panther with blue legs begins to sing:

You asked to see me, so here I am,
Look at me! Zimanto!
I'm the panther who falls on his right side,
I'm the panther who falls on his left side,
I'm the panther who raises his paws,
Here I am! Zimanto!

Then the panther comes over, walks in a circle around him, lies down, and raises its clay paws skyward, singing all the while.

"It sings while I sculpt children, I don't want to sculpt children, but all of my sculptures turn into children. Do you remember that interview Giacometti gave where he explained that his hands had a mind of their own, that they sculpted despite him? He would sculpt from real live models, but they shrank between his fingers, against his will, they became tiny, their bodies thin and spindly. No matter how hard he tried to render them as he saw them with his eyes, the result was always the one we know: anorexic bodies and shrunken heads. Do you remember? It's the same in my dream! At first, I'm working on a different sculpture, but in the end, I find myself with little statues of children, the neighborhood children, the children from the Joie neighborhood, Kizito's children. The other night it was Axelle and Alix, it's often my students from Félix Éboué. Every night I see these children again and again, it's driving me crazy. Crazy, Kat. I know it's just a dream but it's driving me crazy. The song is going to drive me crazy too. It's always in my head, sometimes I even hum it in the daytime:

You asked to see me, so here I am,
Look at me! Zimanto!
I'm the panther who falls on his right side,
I'm the panther who falls on his left side,
I'm the panther who raises his paws,
Here I am! Zimanto!

"At the Enseignants police station, I didn't have time to dream, I imagined myself in my studio, finishing my sculpture. When I was sent to gen pop at Central, I stayed awake, the racket, the smells, the terror of being raped again, thank God I wasn't hungry, I was never hungry, if I'd been hungry, I would have eaten the rats like the others. Rats and cockroaches. The guards wouldn't let my mother and Kizito bring me food, luckily I wasn't often hungry, I lived off half a bowl of corn or beans, or half a bowl of rice, they said if I'd arrived in September, there would have been grasshoppers, they collect them under the lamps in the yard, they said the prisoners fight over them, can you imagine me fighting other inmates for grasshoppers, with my physique? I would have ended up on their plates myself, so I'm actually lucky the article wasn't published in September, I'm afraid of cockroaches, I don't eat rats, but you know how much I love grasshoppers, so I could have been stabbed over them, the prisoners call it stabbing, they drive their fingers into your orbits and pull out your eyeballs, here you can lose an eye over grasshoppers.

"In the morning, I wake up and look at my hands, they're clean, not a trace of earth, but all night they danced with the clay, stroking it, bringing it to life, in the morning they're limp, useless, dead. What good are my hands if I can't bring anything into this world? If I can't sculpt, what good am I? If I can't be in the studio, why live at all? Wiping my butt, cleaning myself up after I poop, that's all my hands are good for, I scratch myself, masturbate, blow my nose, sometimes slap myself, I slap myself with these hands, look at them. I'd give a year of my life for a few minutes in the studio, just a few minutes, to regain my strength and energy, like Antaeus touching Mother Earth. My heart will explode, Kat, my soul is suffocating, it will die if it can't take flight through my hands. I'm going crazy, Katinétou. I'm going crazy, Mbindi."

Katmé thought she could see a light at the end of the tunnel when Mamiton Tafeng stopped by one day. Her husband disapproved of Samuel Pankeu's remand pending trial—an order slipped to the judges by certain members of the APM. He would secure Samy's release. She couldn't give Katmé an exact date. But soon. "Don't mention this to anyone, especially not Tashun, who's aligned with Ambroise and the rest of the backward faction. They won't stand for the slightest criticism of the Old Man." Times had changed, but those fools hadn't noticed. They hadn't cast off the yoke of colonization to live under the yoke of Ambroise Béma and his clique until the end of time. "My God, artists don't belong in prison! He and his creative impertinence are just what this country needs!"

Jean Tafeng, Minister of Justice, had ordered the arrest and deportation of street children, people with intellectual disabilities, and beggars from the capital two months before the pope's most recent visit to

Zambuena. The opposition newspapers claimed that the disabled had been executed and thrown into a common grave while the children and beggars had been transferred to a prison more than three hundred and fifty miles from the capital. At an FZC lunch, when Aline Dubois had questioned her about the topic, Mamiton had replied, "Even if it's true, I don't see what the big deal is, they're unproductive, we're better off without them." A few days later, at a dinner, Mamiton had brought the subject up again with Katmé. "Those white women are exhausting! Why don't they save their indignation for something worthwhile?" Katmé shooed the parasitic memories from her mind. No one is ever only one thing. Jean Tafeng was going to have Samy released!

11

As on every weekday morning, the accounts were the final order of business at Katmé's *daily briefing* with the steward. How much money did he still have on him, what had he done with the sum she'd given him the day before, how much more did he need? Adding, subtracting, and multiplying, five days a week. Katmé's eyes would zigzag across the ledger where the steward kept updated records in tidy schoolteacher's handwriting: revenue, expenditures, cash flow, purchases, and more. She would count, calculate, make mistakes, and get mixed up. Balancing these ridiculous books left an emptiness inside her. The prisoners at Central had only half a bowl of rice or beans to eat and here she was doing silly math problems. Samy kept his eyes open at night, dreading the panther's return to his dreams, while she tallied and tracked again and again until she felt sick to her stomach. Her FZC friends, who had more experience, had explained how to ensure the staff weren't stealing food or supplies. Conducting surprise inventories, weighing bags of rice, packages of meat, and boxes of laundry detergent, drawing a line on bottles of oil and cleaning products, having the guards check the staff's bags on their way out, having the steward check the guards' bags, checking the steward's bag herself, and always keeping the keys to the pantry on her person. A full-time job. Either you'd been trained to do it, or you hadn't. Katmé hadn't.

After her meeting with the steward, she received a dozen people who had come to request "a helping hand from the prefect and Mama." Again, as she did every morning, five days a week. No prefect's wife had ever turned into an ATM quite so quickly. The staff nicknamed her Caritas. In the tiny office she set up in a wing of the residence, a man sat across from her with a coarse, goat-turd, chinstrap beard covering his square jaw, home to teeth yellowed by kola nuts. He'd paid her a first visit a few months earlier. His wife had been nearing the term of a difficult pregnancy. Baby clothes, medical expenses—a cesarian. Katmé gave him an envelope. A little Katmé was born. A lifelong debt. Mama Prefect was their last hope the very last he swore Mama Prefect had to help him Mama Prefect has a good heart the heart of children of the good Lord Mama Prefect is a mama too she understands. Mama Prefect, Mama Prefect . . . New supplicants were always arriving, while those who had been successful in the past saw no reason to stop coming back. It was discouraging, endless. Katmé remembered watching her father flip off his own brother behind his back and call him a parasite. "Nobody forced him to spawn children left and right, why should I be the one to pay?" Madeleine had laughed. Because Madeleine laughed at everything Innocent Patong said. Katmé hoped she'd never reach that point herself, the point of seeing the needy people beaten down by life who besieged the residence gate from morning to evening as "parasites." What was it Samy had said again? "Instead of redistributing wealth among APM apparatchiks, they can give it to the people." She opened the desk drawer and was counting bills when Bambili cracked open the door. Without stopping, Katmé gestured for her to wait, slipped the money into an envelope, and gave it to the new father. The man left and Bambili handed Katmé a note. Keuna had tried to reach her.

Keuna was covered, from her scalp to the tip of her toes, in a fetid, dark-green paste. She was huddled in the fetal position, in a red dress with turquoise fringe, her teeth chattering. Katmé covered her nose and mouth with her hand. The stench of dried shit. Keuna had been visited by eight young men in their twenties. Jeans, T-shirts, backpacks, sneakers. Defenders of Morality who came to express their "inner artist." They slapped her hard, callously, and ordered her to lower the metal shutters and close the gallery. The two guards in their sixties whom she'd hired out of compassion had been trussed up with clothesline and locked in the garage. The Defenders of Morality had pissed on Samy's photographs, smashed the video installation and collages with a hammer, shit on the sculptures, and enveloped them in cling wrap to create a piece they dubbed "Caca Sarcophagus."

Then, Keuna explained, the one who seemed to be the leader started on the walls with the others dictating. He dipped a brush in the excrement and scrawled slogans on the wall in very fine handwriting: "There is no such thing as sexual determinism"; "No one is born a fag, it's a choice"; "We will triumph over homosexuality!"; "Long live the return [they hesitated about the word "return," some would have preferred "rise"] of a faggot-free society"; "Homosexuality is the opium of the decadent bourgeoisie"; "The white man's depravity will not win." Here too they discussed replacing "white man" with "Devil." One of them argued that the message had to be bold and straightforward; he convinced the rest and so they stuck with "white man" after all. Whenever their stock was running low, one of them would lower his pants, squat down, and provide new "paint." Shitting on demand was not something Keuna had previously thought possible. Upon completion of a given slogan, the calligrapher would step back from the wall, bite his lower lip as he admired his work, take a satisfied twirl, then return to add wings to the *E*s and *H*s, and clouds above the *I*s. "It was like being part of a scatological performance piece, like Piero Manzoni manufacturing his *merda d'artista* in front of the audience, you could almost take those madmen for a group of contemporary, transgressive, baroque artists."

Once they'd finished adorning the walls of the gallery with fecal matter, the calligrapher had shouted in Keuna's direction, "You're the star of the exhibition, the masterpiece. Strip, servant of Evil."

That's when her teeth had begun to chatter.

"Hey, why are you shaking like that? You afraid we'll rape you?"

The group guffawed.

"We're going to show you what real art is, not this nonsense you've been working on with Pankeu, *Ante Mortem* or whatever. Once you've seen real art, you'll thank us."

Each of them put on a pair of gloves and they made her stand on a folding chair. She closed her eyes, felt a hand fondling her butt.

"What is there to rape on her anyway?" she heard. "Tiny *mingili* butt, *mingili* breasts, no hips, no hair, just bones, nothing but bones, what are we supposed to do with this?"

"Mama!" said another voice, "Look at that! A shaved pussy!"

"Mtcheew, so ugly, oh! Who would want to touch a girl like this? Not a single hair on her pussy? Mtcheew!"

"I heard it's a white woman thing," someone shouted from off to the side. "But my God, who would want to marry this? White men are real sickos." Keuna recognized the leader's voice.

"Why are you crying? We're not going to touch you if that's what you're afraid of."

"Maybe that's what she wants," suggested another with a lewd chuckle.

They took turns slathering her in excrement, kneading her breasts, spreading her legs with their hands, prodding her clitoris. "You like that? You wet? You like it, don't you?"

For the grand finale, they unzipped their pants, pulled out their penises and showered her in urine. Since they couldn't decide on the piece's title—*Servant of Evil* or *Shitty Gallery Owner*—they drew straws.

"See, look," Keuna said pointing to the sheet of printer paper at her feet. "They settled on *Shitty Gallery Owner* in the end. A single look at me and you have to agree the shoe fits, right? They threatened to come back if I don't close the 'filthy fag's' show, which offends the moral and sexual ethics of the entire country. *Moral and sexual ethics,* those are the exact words they used."

When the jackasses were gone, Keuna put her clothes back on, untied the guards who now knew everything there was to know about their boss's anatomy and personal grooming habits, and called the residence. For the first time since Samy's arrest, Katmé was relieved that he was in prison. He wouldn't have to see his pieces destroyed, the gallery ransacked. Maybe the excremental version of Samy's work, the "Caca Sarcophagus," would interest some collector? As she looked at Keuna—a pagan Venus, a sacrificial totem, defeated, shriveled, and covered from head to toe in feces—Katmé did her best to convey only compassion. But how could she have been so stupid? Hiring two sickly old men as guards when Akriba was full of experienced private security agencies!

"How did this happen to me?" Keuna moaned. "Here. To me. In my country? I left everything to come back to this shitty country, this sewer, this cesspool! Thank goodness Xavier is at school. What would I have done if he'd been here? I guess there's no point going to the police! How could they do this to me? To me! Here!"

"People are attacked everywhere," Katmé whispered gently as she overcame her repulsion and took Keuna's hand.

In the wake of the Samuel Pankeu affair, another paper, *Insolence,* published a list of "homosexuals of the Republic" in its weekend edition. Ministers, governors, and CEOs were cited by name. The article's author was arrested, the newspaper seized, and its offices put under lock and key. The legal double standard that reigned in Zambuena outraged only the naïve, law students, young girls in flower, and Kizito Pankeu. The latter poured his soul into two articles: one—"Scapegoat Theory in Sunny Zambuena"—in *Counterpoint,* the journal he ran, the other—"The Crime of Celibacy: An Era of Suspicion"—in *Emancipation.* He did not mention his brother in either. His readers read between the lines. A few days later, he wrote a third article, "On Homosexuality in Politics: Janus Bifrons or the Two-Headed Beast," which had a bigger impact than the first two, leading to a summons from the university chancellor. As a man the university only tolerated because they lived in a democracy, a man who openly and frequently criticized the government without reprisal, Kizito needed to learn that there was a difference between open-minded generosity and laxity. If he could not demonstrate measure and restraint, he would have to resign. Kizito agreed to temper his fervor and his crusade against the justice system and the establishment, instead funneling all his energy into finding a lawyer to defend Samuel. Everyone he'd asked so far had refused. They didn't want to lose their existing clients.

The national radio station aired a press release from the principal of Félix Éboué Middle School inviting art teacher Samuel Pankeu to return to work within twenty-four hours. Failure to comply would amount to resignation. Seventy-two hours later, a second press release informed the public, all public and private schools, teachers, parents, partners, and friends of Félix Éboué Middle School that Mr. Samuel Pankeu, substitute art teacher, was no longer on staff.

Katmé first laid eyes on Samy's lawyer while watching the talk show *Clash* on Zam2. The weekly program aired at seven o'clock, in direct competition with Brazilian telenovelas. The host opened the episode by explaining that he'd begin by "grilling" his guest himself, after which he would be inviting his viewers to phone in. It seemed he liked his guests thoroughly grilled. Katmé never watched the shows on Zam2—"too low-brow for you, huh?" Tashun would tease. But tonight she had reserved her evening for Ms. Cécile Bessonguè and what turned out to be an interview conducted at cross-purposes. Samuel's lawyer was a plump woman in her forties with thin braids, round glasses, and a strong chin. In her black pantsuit and tobacco-brown blouse, she was there to talk about the law, abuses of power, and injustice. As for the fifty-something host and chief griller with his genial smile, pink floral tie, and black jacket, there was only one question worth the asking: Is Samuel Pankeu a homosexual or not? Cécile Bessonguè dodged the question and explained legal nuances the host couldn't have cared less about. The viewers who called in shouted, "Ms. Bessonguè, you know white people are the ones who imported this satanic practice to our country, don't you? Do you believe in God?" or "Ms. Bessonguè, are you doing it for the money? I feel sorry for the people who brought you into this world, I hope for your sake they're dead." "Ms. Bessonguè, does Samuel the Fag regret his actions?" "Ms. Bessonguè, why did you agree to defend an immoral man like Samuel the Fag?" With her hands clasped against her chest, the lawyer chose not to respond. The host seemed to find the situation rather amusing. The phone line crackled again, heralding the arrival of a new combatant: "Ms. Bessonguè, you are single yourself, you're a woman with no husband. Are you a lesbian, a homosexual like Samuel the Fag?" "Ms. Bessonguè, are you yourself keen on Samuel the Fag's practices?" "Ms. Bessonguè, by defending Samuel the Fag, you bring shame on all women, shame on our society." "Ms. Bessonguè, do you fear God? You know he destroyed Sodom and Gomorrah, don't you?" The show continued the way such shows always went on this channel. Cécile Bessonguè was like a Christian thrown to the Roman lions. What had she expected? Bessonguè didn't seem to understand, thought Katmé, that for the viewers whose voices shook with anger and hatred on the phone, *she* was the beast in the arena—the lawyer who had agreed to defend "Samuel the Fag."

Five minutes before the end, they aired a collection of street interviews. "Is it right to arrest homosexuals?" the reporter asked each participant.

"Just arrest them? They deserve to have their anuses ripped out and dissolved in lye," said a sweaty, bare-chested young man who was transporting bunches of plantains in a rickshaw.

"If my son were homosexual, I'd inform the police myself," affirmed a woman who had stopped to share her two cents before getting into a taxi.

"Those people, those people are like cancer, they must be eradicated, a full course of chemotherapy for their genitals," recommended a man in an orange bow tie.

"Homosexuals are sorcerers, they practice black magic, they need to be exorcised," exhorted another man.

"Of course, what kind of question is that!" a young woman balked, her lips burned by alcohol.

Only one person tried to introduce a hint of nuance; a woman in a boubou and headscarf. "Who are we to judge? The Lord on High alone may judge. We just have to keep them away from our children."

Back on set, the smiling host wrapped up the footage with a *"Vox populi, vox dei."*

"Vox populi, vox dei?" Cécile Bessonguè objected. "Those street interviews were conducted in poor neighborhoods where people are sociologically predisposed to say that sort of thing. That's hardly a reflection—"

The host cut her off. "Are you saying that the socio-economic status of the people we interviewed means their opinions on the topic are invalid? That some of your fellow citizens don't have enough formal education to know which behaviors they approve of and which they condemn? That the difference between good and evil depends on your milieu? The neighborhood you live in? That rich people know what's right, not poor people? That people who don't have a doctorate shouldn't be interviewed?"

Bessonguè shook her head in disgust. Katmé was dismayed. Kizito had gone with the first lawyer who agreed to take the case. He was hardly spoiled for choice. Before winding the episode to a close, the host thanked his "engaged viewers" for their interest in societal issues and willingness to speak their mind and ask hard-hitting questions, then dropped a few hints about the guest he'd be grilling the following week, leaving just the right amount of suspense in the air. Seconds before the credits rolled, he adjusted his tie clip and casually asked Bessonguè if Samuel Pankeu would plead not guilty at his trial. *In cauda venenum,* Samy would have said: the venom is in the tail.

"You'll find out when he has his day in court," she replied enigmatically.

Katmé leapt to her feet. Bessonguè had already chosen to mire herself in opaque turns of phrase couched in sentences a mile long instead of simply affirming, "No, he's not homosexual," and now this. With her ambiguous answers and poor performance, if she was in charge of Samy's defense at trial, she might get him convicted even if the judges were all paid off. Katmé had to meet this lawyer. But an open meeting was out of the question. How could she possibly explain why the wife of the prefect of Akriba had a bone to pick with Samuel Pankeu's lawyer?

12

It seemed Katmé had been blind to Samuel's latent penchant for heroism. She glanced toward the door, which had to remain open during their visits. Her scalp itched under the wig. She backed into the darkest part of the tiny cell, the part protected from prying eyes, and freed herself from the cascade of woven strands that imprisoned her own hair, then scratched the skin between her cornrows. Echoes from the soccer game in the yard below reached their ears. A few rays of sunshine filtered through the doorway into the windowless room, casting short shadows between Samuel's legs. Two teams of inmates were facing off with a new ball donated by a prisoners' rights charity. When Katmé arrived, she'd struggled to make her way through the only path left open by the crowd of spectators. A guard had walked ahead of her, clearing the way, pushing people aside to prevent them from jostling her or grabbing her purse. Samy was sitting tall on the straw twin mattress, his features staid and fingers knotted together. Apparently, accepting these miserable walls as the permanent confines of his existence was no longer out of the question for him. Asking Ety, Sita Félicie, Kizito, and Katmé to face the leprous building each week to bring him books, food, and clothes was no longer out of the question. Making them fret, pay off the guards and Uncle Lollipop, and put up with a slew of crude jokes and jealous prisoners. None of it was out of the question anymore. During one visit, a prisoner heading back to his cell after completing outdoor chores had slowed when he saw Katmé in the bleak hallway that led to the main yard.

"Sweetheart, haven't you found anyone better than that mingili fag to take care of you? You're fucking your cousin? You come see me if you want to taste a real plantain, good and hard—you got money, right? You want me to show you, you want to touch it? Why don't you share your money with all of us, you dirty whore?"

She generally turned a deaf ear to the comments guards and prisoners hurled her way.

"If she's his cousin, I'm the pope's boxers!"

"Ah, bro, maybe he humps her good. If he humps her real good, she'll follow him anywhere, even hell."

"What are you talking about? The VIP block is no hell, it's heaven on earth, brother. Heaven!"

Shouts of joy erupted outside. A goal. A commotion punctuated with insults followed.

Yet for Samy, putting all their lives in jail along with his own was no longer out of the question.

"We're working day and night to get you a court date, that's all we need to get you out. Kizito has a solid lead. Your mother and brother are convinced that your arrest was a pretext to make you suffer for your show. What will you tell them? Have you thought about what your sudden urge to plead guilty would mean for them? For our lives?"

"What do you think? Of course I've thought about it. I've been thinking about it since I was eleven years old, when I disgusted myself, loathed myself for being such a monster, since the day in catechism when I looked up at the sky and prayed, 'Dear Lord, please don't let me fall in love with a boy, don't let me fall in love with Antonin.' I won't let anyone blackmail me like that bastard Antonin ever again. Since the good Lord didn't listen, I'm considering making my own voice heard in court."

In the corner farthest from the door where Katmé stood with her back against the grainy roughcast, furiously scratching her scalp, she was going over events from the past few days, scanning Samy's face for clues that could explain why pleading guilty was "no longer out of the question." He seemed horrifyingly determined.

"Kizito didn't write those articles to defend his little brother's right to be homosexual if he likes, Samy," Katmé continued. "He wrote them because he's convinced his little brother *isn't* homosexual. You're going to be released. You'll go back to sculpting and photography, classes with your students and the neighborhood kids, you'll see Axelle and Alix again. You'll make pieces for a new show and move in with Ety if you want to. You'll do whatever you like. I'm just asking you to please be patient. As soon as we have a court date, we'll bribe the judge and other officials, and the very same day you'll be back at the studio. You'll get back to normal life soon, I guarantee it."

"Normal life?" Samuel fumed. "When have I *ever* led a normal life? Even *you,* Kat, you wanted to take me to see a priest at first."

"I thought you wanted help!"

"Do you even hear yourself? The trial doesn't matter, my fate is already sealed! Don't act like that's news to you."

"You're the one sealing your fate so you can play the hero!"

Samy left the bed to stand across from her. The bruises from the batons had faded and his face had regained its air of placid mystery, but his left index finger was still crooked. It should have been set and put in a cast after the beating at the station. "Socially, I'm already dead, Kat, and you know it. Don't lie."

"You have your studio, your talent, years ahead of you, no one can take that away from you, Samy, no one," Katmé countered, silently congratulating herself for convincing his visitors to keep the attack on the gallery and the destruction of his pieces from him.

"In this country, no matter what I do now, I'm dead. The panther comes every night, it won't leave me alone.

You asked to see me, so here I am,
Look at me! Zimanto!
I'm the panther who falls on his right side,
I'm the panther who falls on his left side,
I'm the panther who raises his paws,
Here I am! Zimanto!

If only you could hear its voice. At night it's in my dreams. During the day it's in my head. The panther's requiem. You know what, Katmé? The more I have this dream, the realer the nightmare ahead becomes."

"Oh, Samy, don't be so tragic! Your dream is easy to decipher: You were sculpting a panther when they arrested you and the article was about the orphans from Vita House. That's all there is to it. Plenty of people go to prison every day; it doesn't mean their lives are over."

"In our beautiful, beloved country, how many gay men have returned to their normal lives after being attacked in the papers and locked up?

I want names. Statistics. It's over for me, let's stop pretending. If this miserable life of mine can help save others from the same fate, I have to try. You don't know what it's like to be in my skin, Kat. You can't."

Samy walked toward the door. With his bare feet straddling the threshold and his hands on either side of the frame, he blocked the entrance with his body, giving her a view of his profile. Katmé returned the wig to her head. How did women like Djama manage to tolerate wigs all the time, she couldn't help but wonder. She pushed off the wall and sat down on the bed. Samy pivoted, still in the doorway, but with his back toward the hall this time. They heard the referee's whistle followed by boos. "I hope there won't be any fights after the game," said Samy. "The infirmary is closed for the day."

"Samy, doing this won't save anyone. You can start over somewhere else. Zambuena isn't the only country on earth. Many of the FZC members admire your work and were shocked by your arrest. They'll help you get a visa. You can start fresh, start over somewhere else."

"A visa so I can go live my never-ending quarantine under foreign skies? In gay heaven? Thank you, but no. I won't hide it anymore. There's no such place for people like me."

"And we're back to tragedy. Do you really think straight people have such a place? It won't be hard to get you a visa to move to a country where gay people aren't persecuted. You can start over. Hold on to that, don't throw your life out the window. You're an artist, you can live and work anywhere. Aren't I still your airport? I'm begging you—trust me."

"So you're offering me a life as a refugee? What the hell would I do somewhere else? My inspiration is here. I want to live here. Here. In this lousy country. If you're still my airport, it should be easy for you to understand. Thanks, but I'll pass on your visa for exile."

Katmé had gone out on a limb mentioning the visa. The women from FZC's Western axis "loved" the artist Samuel Pankeu. And their ambassador husbands knew and socialized with the Minister of Justice. But the universal nature of human rights stopped at Zambuena's borders. They'd told Katmé that, unfortunately, since the Samuel Pankeu case was a domestic affair, it would be out of line for them to get involved with things that didn't concern them. Diplomatic relations based on trust were difficult to establish, and getting mixed up in this affair came with the risk of angering the highest authorities in the country and elsewhere. And, of course, in other words, with that said, and in all honesty, the people of Zambuena are largely in favor of the law, in favor of conviction and punishment, of course legal and cultural relativism is to be avoided, but nevertheless, however, regardless, when you stare the situation in the face coolly and dispassionately, without wasting any emotional energy, if a country's laws express the will of its people, it's not a good idea to upend them, to import an outside view or impose a "turnkey" approach too far removed from local realities, after all, laws are made for the people, not against them. Juliana, the wife of the European Union ambassador, had promised that her husband would nevertheless bring it up with the Minister of Justice. Katmé was still waiting. When Mamiton Tafeng crossed paths with Katmé at government or FZC events, she was careful never to be alone with her. The Minister's wife met Katmé's questioning gaze with such an enigmatic expression that she began to wonder if she hadn't dreamt up the promises made by the Minister of Justice and his wife.

"*Alea iacta est,* Kat. The die is cast," Samuel said as he emerged from his thoughts.

She stood up. "Are you saying you've made up your mind?" she asked frantically. "Answer me!"

Samy refused to meet her eyes.

"I introduce you as my brother to everyone I know, you're the girls' godfather. Do you know what it will do to me, to Tashun, my husband and Axelle and Alix's father, if you get on the stand and advocate for this cause? I suppose your thirst for the truth will lead you to say we all knew—failure to report a crime—and that I know your friends and Ety, that I invited him into my home—accessory to a crime. Not so long ago all you wanted to do was sculpt, walk through the door to your studio, breathe in the smell of clay, and shape it with your hands. You can have that again. For goodness' sake, Samy, don't be so self-centered. Get a grip!"

"*I* need to get a grip?" he replied with an icy laugh. "It scares you, doesn't it? Your social status in jeopardy, your privileges slipping through your fingers, and all because of your friend the fairy."

"Oh, Samy, you've grown so bitter. It sounds like you want to punish me for something. It's not just about me though, Samy, it's about your family too, Sita Félicie and Kizito, you're risking your life. It might feel worthless to you now, but it still means a great deal to me. Getting convicted won't change a thing, except that we'll be crucified along with you. Is that really what you want?"

"I can't be a sellout anymore, Katmé. A series of compromises doesn't add up to a life. Look at you, at me. In the beginning, Mama Caramel Two-for-Ten was looking to settle a score with Tashun, right? So why am I here? Why doesn't he get me released?"

"He will, after he takes office!"

"Do you really believe that? I don't. I'm tired of being a burden on myself, on others, on you, living off your good graces at my age. All the money you're wasting, you and Kizito and my mother who'll eventually go blind from knitting so many awful wool outfits for newborns when it's a stifling hundred degrees outside. Why should I accept that? Without you I would be in gen pop. I can't keep living life as a sellout, Katmé."

"I never said you should. I'm just asking," Katmé said as she placed her hands on his shoulders and looked him in the eyes, their faces almost touching. Samy met her gaze but she couldn't tell what he was thinking. "I'm just asking you to be patient. Don't sell your skin, our skins, to the highest bidder."

A long whistle followed by a round of applause signaled the end of the soccer game. Shouts followed. Katmé still had her hands on Samy's shoulders when the VIP inmates who'd been playing in or else watching the game returned to their cells. One of them stopped in the hall. With his back to the door, Samy couldn't see him. Katmé recognized the former Minister of Sports in a goalkeeper's uniform. He'd been arrested for stashing the bags of money set aside as bonuses for the players who'd participated in the last World Cup at his mistress's house. The mistress had the good sense to use it to buy traveler's checks, hop on a flight to the United States, and vanish into thin air.

Samy and Katmé were so close to one another that their position seemed to corroborate the lovers hypothesis. Samuel read her face and turned around. The former minister shook their hands, then gestured to Samuel to come with him. Apologizing for the interruption, he stepped aside with him.

Katmé sat down on the side of the bed. So Samy wanted to start a crusade. In Zambuena. In a country where a judge could openly say, "I can render a fair ruling when both parties pay me the same amount." If she couldn't make him see reason, who could? Ety? She doubted it. Did he even know? Kizito, Sita Félicie? Telling them would mean betraying Samy in more ways than one. He was going to plead guilty because, "Do you even know what it's like to be in my shoes, Kat?" One day when he'd seemed troubled, as he often did, she had offered to take him to see Father Evariste, her spiritual guide. Father Evariste was as unyielding as the Stone Tablets and shouted from the pulpit every Sunday that, "A child is like a river, which needs two opposite banks to keep it on course." She only learned later that he had not come up with this adage on his own—nor the Bible verses he presented as his own words.

"So you think only prayer can heal me, like I've got an incurable disease?" Samy had asked, furious. He had read in a brochure that it was about whether Yin, the feminine energy, or Yang, the masculine energy, was more dominant in a person. "I have more Yin, so I like boys. You have more Yin too, that's why you like boys, but since you're a girl, that makes you heterosexual. If you had more Yang, you'd be attracted to girls and would be homosexual."

"If I've understood correctly, you mean your sexual identity is feminine and that's why you like boys. Which means that even though you look like a boy, you're actually a girl? So, if we continue to follow this logic, you're actually heterosexual and appearances are just deceiving?"

"Sure, if that works for you. Let's say I'm a straight woman in a male body who is attracted to people of the same sex."

They were in Samy's room, sitting on the mat near the fan that was always on high to combat the heat. His parents were in the living room. Despite his castrato voice, which hadn't dropped during puberty, despite his narrow hips, and his suspicious love of flowers, cooking, and knitting, Samy was seeing a girl, taking her to his room, spending the afternoon with her behind locked doors; everyone was pleased, everyone saw it as a win. Except for Mama Récia, who at first wasn't keen on this stick-thin, tar-skinned boy, whom she suspected had impure intentions, spending time with her niece.

Samuel returned, his face impenetrable. He lay down on the bed clutching the small, beige, rabbit-shaped pillow she'd given him as a joke for his twenty-fifth birthday. He used it to prop up his head.

"What does Bessonguè think about your decision? I find it hard to believe she'd encourage this madness."

He pushed himself up onto his elbows. "She's prepared to follow my lead. People can't keep shrugging it off and saying that's just the way things are. The 'those people don't have to be homosexual' argument has to stop. She wants to fight to change the law."

"She thinks *she's* going to change the law? That's laughable. She had her head handed to her on a silly television show and she thinks she has the power to reform the whole country? This is Zambuena. If you decide to do your little song and dance on the stand, you're done. D-O-N-E done! Us too, sure, but you especially. So please, Samy, wake up!"

Katmé saw a flash of hesitation in his eyes. It rekindled her hope.

Samy clapped his hands together a single time. "I didn't think I'd ever have to ask you this question, Katmé. Will you be on my side come what may?"

That was all it took! Monsoon winds put out the flicker. "I didn't think I'd ever have to tell you this, Samuel, but I don't give a shit about the homosexuals of Zambuena or anywhere else, I couldn't care less. Do you hear me?" she asked, her voice trembling with anger. "I'm not fighting for gay rights or the legalization of homosexuality in this country. People can do what they want with their bodies, I don't care. But pleading guilty is madness, it's suicide! I'm fighting to get you out of this rank, vile place where I can't stand seeing you waste away, more unrecognizable each week! I'm not fighting for a cause, Samy. I'm fighting for you."

"'The nations slumbered, but Fate made sure that they not fall asleep.' Hölderlin. This cause is me too, Kat."

"Samuel Pankeu, you can shove your goddamn quotes and fuck off!"

He was losing his mind, the lights were on but no one seemed to be home anymore, a vessel must have burst or maybe a synapse or something had short-circuited, a month in prison and he'd lost it. She would stop paying Cécile Bessonguè's fees, they'd see how far she could coast on altruism alone. Samy had to attend the trial as a free man, that was the only solution, the only way to knock some sense back into him. Out on bail a week or two before the trial date so he could breathe the air of the Cité des Enseignants neighborhood, return to the studio, put his hands in the clay, pour his mind and body into a new piece; start over with the blue-pawed panther, complete it, perfect it—that was the only way she could think of to stamp out Samy's crusade against Zambuena's legislators. "This cause is me too, Kat." Really? She'd find the money, all the money they needed, she'd take it from the health center fund if she had to. Syringes, medicine, examination tables, and white coats could wait. The emergency was Samuel. The health center wouldn't be built for months, there'd be time to explain everything to Tashun, now the time had come to get Samuel released. Yes, she was a coward, yes, she was a sellout. At the age of thirteen, on her mother's grave, she'd learned that life promised much and delivered little. You have to cling to whatever you can carry. And that's what she would do.

13

Katmé siphoned money from the residence's monthly budget and from the amount set aside for the funeral, the work on the house, and the vault; she siphoned off the money and, via Kizito, filled the pockets of every scoundrel who swore he had a solution, had hatched a scheme, or knew someone who could get Samy back on the streets. Kizito had some reservations about this heightened zeal to get Samy out of prison before the trial, whatever the cost.

"Once we have a date, we'll have to pay the judges, and they'll be greedy, believe me," he argued. "Let's not spread ourselves too thin, we don't have an endless supply of money."

Katmé had tried to borrow money from her father. He acted surprised. "My property belongs to your brothers, darling. I don't own a thing anymore. Your brothers pay me an allowance each month to buy cigars and champagne. Your husband is the prefect of Akriba and you're short on funds? I'll talk to him! A man who doesn't take good care of his wife is no man at all." Katmé chose not to remind him what sort of man he had been with Madeleine.

Then Aleksandre offered to loan her some money, but she refused. He was a kind ear and a potentially friendly shoulder—she hadn't ventured that far yet—and that was enough. She wouldn't add the heinous question of money to a relationship whose contours she sometimes struggled to see clearly. Mama Récia was a member of several tontines. Katmé took a chance and told her that Samuel, whom she called "my son", needed her help. The fact that her purveyor of funds had attempted, before God, to relieve her of her savings shocked Mama Récia less than what Katmé intended to use them for.

"Those people will not enter the Kingdom of Heaven. If Samuel is a sodomite, pray for him and keep your distance. Don't mix the wheat with the chaff, think of your soul, of your children's souls."

The line of alms-seekers outside the residence gates was as long as ever, but many of them left empty-handed. Keuna had waived her commission and given Sita Félicie all of the money from the sale of the few sculptures that had escaped the would-be artists' vengeful expedition and their determination to uphold morality. Katmé only visited Central once a week now, bringing Samy books, food, and clothes. After fifteen minutes, she'd leave. Something between them had broken. Ety admired Samuel's nerve. Since he'd been in prison, they'd shared an intimacy and proximity unhindered by the studio. Ety would bring Samy potted African violets. As the scent of the flowers filled the room, Samy would close his eyes and imagine himself at the foot of the studio stairs. On the stand, Ety explained to Katmé, Samy wouldn't provide a single name, he wouldn't out anyone, he'd simply plead his cause, their cause. No one has ever pleaded guilty in a trial like this, Samy will be the first, others will follow, the law has to change, we aren't criminals, the government has made us outlaws, someone has to have the courage to stand up to the law.

April 30, Samy's birthday and Zambuena's National Day, put a stop to Katmé's prison visits. "It's a holiday today, no work in honor of my birthday," he'd always told Axelle and Alix when they were little. On National Day, beneath relentlessly sunny skies, the twins—yellow blouses, brown skirts, green ties—proudly marched up Boulevard du Trente-Avril with their classmates, directly behind the military, civil servants, and representatives from political parties as well as society at large. Thanks to Uncle Ambroise, Katmé and Tashun had escaped the torture of the bleachers with their merciless corrugated metal roofs; instead, they watched the parade from seats in the last row of the presidential platform. Afterward, Djama and her husband hosted their traditional National Day Lunch, which was followed by the six o'clock cocktail party the Old Man always organized in the gardens of the presidential palace.

When Katmé and Tashun returned home after lunch, they found their daughters in the kitchen with aprons tied over their frilly cotton dresses—one sky blue, the other off-white. With help from Bambili, they had baked a heart-shaped mango cake for their godfather.

"When will Uncle Samy be here, Mama?" asked Axelle.

The day after Mamiton Tafeng had stopped by, Katmé had promised the girls that Samuel would be back from his trip "by his birthday at the latest," and she'd believed it herself, at the time.

Katmé's eyes met Tashun's. "It would be better to tell them the truth," he'd been warning her for some time.

"Mama, you said that he'd be back for his birthday," Alix chimed in. "Why doesn't he ever come to see us anymore, Mama? Is he mad at us?"

"Of course not! His work has taken him far away, like I told you, and it's taking longer than expected. The people there have commissioned huge sculptures. As soon as he's finished, he'll come home and we'll make him an enormous cake."

"Well, since your godfather isn't here, why don't *I* taste the cake, here and now!" said Tashun. "I might get jealous, the first cake you make and it's not for your papa, huh? Oh, come on, don't look so sad . . . Let's find a knife."

The twins exchanged a glance. "Mama, can we freeze the cake? That way when he comes back, he can have his real cake that we made on his real birthday," said Axelle.

Tashun helped his daughters wrap the cake in aluminum foil and find a place for it in the freezer compartment of the refrigerator; then Axelle and Alix left the kitchen holding hands, heads hung low, followed by Bambili.

"Why did you tell them he'd be home by his birthday?" Tashun asked as soon as they were alone.

Katmé shrugged. "I had to tell them something."

"Your story about a trip doesn't make sense. Why doesn't he ever call if he's on a trip, huh? What will you do if someone at school or one of the household employees braves your wrath and lets the cat out of the bag? They're nine years old, you can't keep the truth from them forever."

"I don't plan to. Samy will get out of prison once you're done scheming. To the girls, he's magical. We can't ruin that for them."

"Will you please get your head out of the clouds for once? You can tell them that their magical uncle is the poor, innocent victim of an unjust system if you like. But for goodness' sake tell them that he's in jail! You're wrong to lie to them, it's not healthy."

If Axelle and Alix had persisted, savvily exasperating their mother the way children do to get what they want, she would have gotten cross and cut them off, would have told them to stop acting like such willful babies since it wasn't anyone's fault that their godfather was working far away, so that was quite enough whining for one day . . . but the fact that her daughters hadn't even blamed her for kindling their false hope, that they were doing their best to put on a brave face and hide their sadness behind weak smiles when she looked into their eyes which held back tears—that unsettled Katmé. It pushed her to shed the cautiousness that had been with her every second since she'd begun stepping into Eulalie Nana's shoes. Tashun had gone upstairs for a nap. She looked at her watch. She had about two hours. Even if her husband woke up, he wouldn't come down before it was time to leave for the cocktail party at the presidential palace. Central was twenty minutes away, forty minutes round trip, sixty with traffic; if she spent twenty or thirty minutes there to do what needed to be done, she'd still be back in an hour and a half at most. On holidays, the number of visitors at the prison tripled; the guards would be so busy inspecting all the gifts, food, and lengthy lines of people, that they would be less attentive, they wouldn't notice her. Now that she knew all of them, from the greediest to the kindest, she wouldn't waste any time. She'd give the envelope to Janvier right away. It was Wednesday, so he'd be on duty outside. She'd add an extra bill or two to get him to ensure she got her access badge quickly. She didn't have time to go change at Ety's; she'd put her hair up in a turban and wear her reading glasses, that would have to do. She'd say she'd forgotten her ID at home, she'd be convincing, she'd pay, it would have to do.

No one recognized Katmé or assailed her ears with their usual, irritating "Madam Prefect." Before Samuel could ask, she opened the basket she held in her hand. "Eulalie Nana couldn't make it, so I'm filling in. Your birthday cake, baked by your goddaughters. Find us a quiet place where we can take a picture and then I have to go."

Katmé didn't have the same privileges as Eulalie Nana. Access to Samy's cell required a special pass from Uncle Lollipop. To get a picture of him eating a piece of his cake as she had planned, they'd need a bit of privacy. Next to her, a woman dressed in a gray pant suit and freshly shined black leather shoes and whose scalp bore the stigmata of advanced alopecia was lecturing a prisoner whose legs were covered in blisters—her son, no doubt. The yard full of wicker baskets like hers gave off the same excitement as Christmas or New Year's Day. The smell of food and sweat saturated the air. Katmé didn't regret coming; she'd been right, in the dense crowd surrounding them, no one paid her any attention.

"This is crazy," Samuel scolded. "It isn't worth—"

"Can we go to your cell?" Katmé asked, warily scanning the yard.

Samuel shook his head.

"That's what I thought. Can you find us somewhere else? I don't have much time."

Samuel made his way toward a guard whom Katmé recognized as Auguste. Every time she visited, he tried ever harder than the others to get as much cash out of her as he could. He and six others were keeping an eye on the crowd, guns in hand. Samy whispered in his ear and slipped a bill into his pocket. Five minutes later, they were sitting atop empty beer crates in the laundry room amid yellowed, roughly mended sheets that reeked of bleach.

"I suppose you came up with this idea?" Samy asked.

"Wrong. Not this time. I didn't even know about it. Tashun and I were at the parade this morning, the girls too. Afterward, we went to lunch at Djama and Uncle Ambroise's house but the twins went home with Bambili. They showed us the cake when we got back."

"They came up with the idea all on their own? To make a cake for a sad sack like me?"

Samuel's eyes welled with tears. Katmé took the cake and a Polaroid camera from the basket, found a sheet in better shape than most, and put the cake in Samy's hands. Find a neutral, unidentifiable background, come up with a plausible lie, develop a credible story, show the girls—only the girls—the photo and ask them to keep it a secret. She pressed the shutter button on the instant-print camera. Samy smiled a smile she hadn't seen in a long time.

"Tashun says it's unhealthy to let them believe you're away for work. Maybe he's right? You vanished so quickly from their lives, they're starting to think they don't matter to you."

"We've talked about this before. The answer is no. Don't tell them anything," he begged. "If you do, I won't be able to look them in the eyes anymore when I get out. Please don't."

Katmé pushed the shutter button again. "And on the stand, when you officially come out of the closet so you don't have to live your life as a sellout anymore, do you think I'll keep telling them you're on Jupiter?"

"Please, Kat . . . Not today . . ."

"I'm just asking you to pick a line and stick to it, that's all."

A knock on the door made them jump. "Auguste gave us ten minutes," Samy explained.

Exactly fifty-six seconds after they'd returned to the courtyard, Katmé was furious at Bambili for making the heart-shaped mango cake, enraged at Tashun for letting Samy rot in prison, livid with that scheming heap of crow droppings otherwise known as Mama Caramel, incensed with *Tropics Daily* for its shitty articles, and again furious with herself for being so irrational. And she'd only just said goodbye to Samuel when two former ministers, accused of misappropriating State funds to found their own party, rushed toward her. She and Tashun enjoyed dinner at their homes several times before their arrests. Katmé Abbia, the wife of Prefect Abbia! Who could she be visiting? News of her presence flitted around the yard, crept down the hallways, wriggled through fences, and climbed over walls until, panting, it finally found its way to the warden's ear. He was, of course, on duty for a day as juicy as National Day. Uncle Lollipop came running to present his "respects," asking after "His Excellency." A group of inmates from the VIP block were gathering around her as well: the former Minister of Communication, the CEO of the national refinery, and the CEO of the national pension fund, who had vacationed in the French Riviera with the pensions of retirees like Sita Félicie, but whose gravest crime was criticizing the Old Man. Off to the side, hands clasped behind his head, Samuel watched in horror.

"Mama, Papa is looking for you," Axelle and Alix announced as soon as she'd parked her car in front of the stone steps to the residence. "He's waiting for you upstairs, in your room."

Katmé ran up the stairs with the girls on her heels. With a good idea of what awaited, she shut and locked the door in their faces as soon as she stepped inside to make sure they couldn't follow her.

Tashun spun around to face her when he heard the door slam. "Where have you been?"

Before she could open her mouth or utter any sort of explanation, his right palm barreled into one cheek, the back of his hand into the other.

"What's gotten into you, Tashun! Are you crazy?" Katmé raised her arms to protect her face.

"Me? You think *I'm* crazy? You're the crazy one! Completely crazy! You went to Central?" he shouted as his blows continued to fall. "Answer me! Did you go to Central?"

He used his left hand to grab her wrists and prevent her from escaping the wrath of his right.

"What do I have to do to make you understand? I am your husband! Your husband, do you hear me? I'll get that green dog Samuel Pankeu out of your head! You dare risk my reputation for that maggot? That nobody? Is it witchcraft? Have you lost your mind? Are you looking to ruin me? Your behavior is beneath the wife of the prefect of Akriba, it's a disgrace! If you ever go against me again, I swear you'll see stars, do you hear me? I swear on the souls of my parents, if you go against me again, you'll see a whole new side of me."

Katmé's head whipped from side to side. Tashun hit her again and again, alternating slaps and punches. She held back her screams and cries, bottled them up in her throat. The girls could be right on the other side of the door, in the hallway. Her cheeks burned, she'd slather them with cream later, Bambili had a recipe for everything, or better yet there was the cream she'd bought for Alix that time when oil from a frying pan of plantains had burned her thumb, it must be in the medicine cabinet, hopefully it hadn't expired, she'd put cream on her cheeks instead of the salt Mama Récia usually suggested, because salt caused swelling down the line—salt packed its own punch, so to speak!—she'd laugh later, she'd definitely laugh, her cheeks would stop burning, and she'd laugh, she'd think about the quicklime searing her cheeks and she'd laugh, she'd find it all funny.

She passed out.

The following afternoon in the blue sitting room, Djama fanned herself with a copy of *Insolence* featuring a caricature of Katmé as the life of the party in the prison yard. Josephine Baker in a banana belt, her breasts bare, performing a lively dance. Samuel was cast as a balafon player, his penis erect, as the warden and prisoners including the disgraced ministers watched with glee and applauded vigorously.

"You're a *B*, Katmé. A *B* cannot regress to become a *C* or a *D*. With the cards you drew, you could even be an *A* someday. I think I've already told you, but my father always used to say that the millipede only gets lost if it walks alone, without any company. You're losing your way, my dear. You're not allowed to forget who you are and where you want to go . . . How could you have put us in such a position? You know that people are whispering behind your back? They're saying that young man is your lover, you know. I spoke to Tashun, he was so angry he lost it, he could have killed you. He'd forbidden you to go, hadn't he?"

Katmé looked up at the thirty-by-fifty-inch frame on the wall. Her lips began to curl into a smile. Djama's voice became background noise. The photo had been taken at an FZC lunch. The Mother of the Nation—what they called the president's wife in all seriousness—stood surrounded by a group of women in elegant dresses, except for one. Katmé was wearing white jeans and a short-sleeved, navy-blue blouse. The Mother of the Nation did not generally attend FZC meetings, but on occasion she would surprise them by "appearing" as Juliana, the wife of the EU ambassador and the host that day, had put it in a tone thick with gratitude. She would *appear* like a supernatural being. Katmé had noticed that these apparitions were reserved exclusively for Western ambassadors' wives. Tashun, who had had the picture framed and hung it next to the portrait of the Old Man, the Father of the Nation, always felt obliged to explain, whenever a guest studied the photograph closely, that Katmé hadn't been informed about the dress code or that the Mother of the Nation would be there—otherwise she would have dressed up. She might as well have been naked in his book. Classic Tashun. She completely forgot about Djama, left her armchair, and moved closer to the wall.

"What are you doing? I'm talking to you!" Djama shouted.

Startled, Katmé returned to her chair like the poorly behaved little girl she became around Uncle Ambroise's wife.

"Do you really want to compromise your family's honor, your husband's career, and your children's future for someone who is not even a *D*? For someone who's not even eligible for ranking? A zero, Katmé! He's a zero! Zeroes are beneath us. Thank God we have them, because we need them—to serve us, to be around only when required, but that's it. God himself established a hierarchy in Heaven, He must have had his reasons, no? God the Father, Jesus Christ, the Virgin Mary, the angels, the archangels, the saints, messengers of light, and so on, they are not equals, and believe me, that's not a coincidence. You're young, your daughters are little, focus on them, their education, their well-being . . . Later, if the time comes—I'm speaking as your own mother would if she were still alive—if you need what women my age call 'something to calm your nerves,' when that day comes, and it will, dear, choose an *A*, nothing less. Choose an *A* and opt for silence and discretion. Why must you proclaim your friendship from the rooftops like that and end up in the papers? It's beyond me, truly beyond me. With all your responsibilities, where do you find the time to go on day trips to prison? We have many enemies, even within the party, you know. You can't be a pebble in your husband's shoe or in ours. Your husband has a reputation to keep up, a campaign to run, which means you do too. Tashun isn't perfect, but you can count on him, he's a husband, a real husband. Men who are true husbands don't grow on trees."

In the late afternoon, Mama Récia helped Bambili prepare the concoction to soothe the fire burning on Katmé's cheeks. "Every married woman goes through this at least once in her life," she mumbled. "No need to make a big deal out of it."

Five days later, Eulalie Nana visited Samuel in prison with a scarf wrapped around her swollen face.

"Tell Eulalie Nana to never, ever, set foot in prison again, I mean it. You tell that cabaret singer it's over. Done. I was too careless," Tashun barked, his features twisted with fury, when he turned up in the middle of the dinner she was sharing with the girls in the kitchen. He looked up at the ceiling fixture. "That orange light is from Christmas! Don't you have anything better to do than to make a spectacle of yourself at Central? Like take care of the house! From now on, the prefecture will receive a list of every person—every single one—who visits inmate Samuel Pankeu."

"Papa, do you mean Uncle Samy? Why did you call him an inmate?" asked Alix.

Katmé tried to get Tashun to meet her gaze. *"Moïndjamoto,* what Papa means is that . . . Uncle Samy—"

"What Papa means is that your godfather is in prison," Tashun said, cutting her off.

"Uncle Samy is in prison?"

"He's not on a trip, Mama?"

Two pairs of anxious eyes stared at Katmé. Since she'd gone mute, they turned to their father.

"My sweet, sweet girls, your godfather is in prison," he repeated.

Katmé placed her elbows on the table and tried to slow her racing heart.

"Is that true, Mama?" The girls' voices comingled and Katmé could hear the kind of wavering that generally preceded sobs. "You always say only bad people go to jail. Does that mean Uncle Samy is bad? Uncle Samy is good, so why is he in prison, Mama?"

Katmé untied the scarf beneath her chin, she couldn't breathe. Oh well, the girls would see the marks their father had left on her cheeks. She was forgetting that the orangish glow in the kitchen faded the bruises on her skin.

"Why did you lie to us, Mama? You always tell us not to lie, you say God is watching, but you lied, Mama."

Katmé took a deep breath. *"Moïndjamoto* . . . I . . . I . . . Uncle Samy is good, he'll always be good . . . He . . . He's . . ."

Her eyes begged Tashun. For their daughters, she begged him. Against her better judgment. Choosing to ignore her request for a truce, Tashun sat back in his chair with his arms across his chest, joining the girls, it seemed, in their quest for answers. Far worse than his slaps, this time, without laying a hand on her, he was hitting her where he knew it would hurt most.

"Mama, is it true what Papa says? Are you mad at Uncle Samy, Papa?"

Axelle and Alix were crying.

Tashun stood up, walked around the table, and bent down between their chairs to wrap his arms around their shoulders. "You know," he began in a confident tone, "your uncle, your real uncle, is Uncle Henri, my brother, and your real aunt is Mama's sister, Auntie Sennke who lives in a convent. You'll see her at the ceremony we're organizing for your grandmother. Uncle Samy did some bad things. Papa will find you a new godfather, someone even nicer than Samuel. Now, do big girls cry? Don't you trust your papa? Go on, no more crying. Are you big girls, or aren't you?"

He stood up and, before leaving the room, cast a hateful glance at Katmé.

14

Samedi—or maybe someone else, but no matter—was telling a story that began to stretch Katmé's lips into a smile. Samedi, a carpenter who also held a university degree in French literature but could never find a teaching job, had a firmer grasp of the art of storytelling than the masons, painters, or locksmiths. He used a varied repertoire of voices, always included a twist, and knew how to captivate his audience. They were in the courtyard, some of them seated on empty drink cases they'd forgotten to return. It was early afternoon, the sun was in full revolt, and Katmé's eyelids spasmed in a continuous vibrato. Dr. Abba at the Hommes Capables Clinic had diagnosed the phenomenon as a benign twitch and prescribed magnesium supplements. Despite the pair of small white diamonds she slipped under her tongue morning, noon, and night, her spirited eyelids continued to dance to an unruly bend-skin beat. Samedi was done with the shelves in the bedroom upstairs where she would be sleeping the following week. He'd finished for the day—the last of the work he had to do on the house. It was his final day, and before he left, he was telling the story of his uncle the customs officer who, upon returning from a six-month internship in Switzerland, had begun holding the girls and young women in the family a bit too close, kissing them on the lips, and trying to put his tongue in their mouths because, "That's how white people, civilized people, say hello." Kneeling in the dirt, Katmé was using cardboard and burlap to protect the roots of the dwarf spruces she'd just planted. "Who goes to church in Europe today?" Samedi grumbled, imitating the voice of his uncle who had banished religious objects from his home and threatened to behead his wife and children if they ever set foot in a church again. "Us! Dimwitted Negroes! Those of us who live in places where everything's a mess, us and everyone else relegated to third-world status, we're the ones who fill their churches! How can people who have vanquished tsetse flies and witchcraft still believe in God? As they say, 'if God existed, he would show himself rather than prove himself.' So I'm done with all your Saint Peter medals—they bring nothing but bad luck into a home." Just six months in Switzerland and his uncle had come home lewd and faithless. Katmé laughed heartily and each of the workers took a turn sharing a story about the strange behavior of a relative who'd returned from Europe or North America.

Since Katmé came to Fènn three times a week now and was the first to arrive at the worksite in the morning—in rubber boots, baggy pants, and a T-shirt with yellow stains under her arms—and the last to leave, the workers had stopped calling her Mama Prefect and opted for Mama Katmé instead. She had also learned each of their names and details about their families, and begun occasionally enjoying a nice cold *mimbo* with them at lunch. She would fetch water from the well or pond for them, had expressed an interest in the process of manufacturing cinderblocks, even making one herself, and had planted an entire colony of pines around the house all on her own. Working alongside them soothed the metallic buzzing that had filled her body since she'd been banned from prison, since Tashun had beaten her. The mayor stopped by from time to time to make sure she had everything she needed, and the prefect regularly invited her to dinner with his family. Every time they'd find her dressed like a *buyam-sellam* market woman, deep in conversation with the contractor, workers, and craftsmen. She would mix the concrete—gravel, sand, and cement—dampen the molds, oversee the framing, and help finish the slabs. Once, the mayor dared to ask if she'd visited her mother's grave. Katmé looked up at him with a calculated delay, then plastered false remorse over her face.

When she returned to Fènn the following week, she would no longer be staying at the Zimanto Inn. She'd move into the upstairs bedroom with the veiny, gray tile, the one next to the sitting room and the secondary kitchen. From the terrace she'd watch the sun set over the pond, the stand of eucalyptus trees, the pine saplings, Aleksandre's house with its vernacular architecture: the conical thatch roof and location of the yard behind the building. Aleksandre was on vacation with his children in Portugal. His absence suited her. She couldn't imagine telling him—or anyone else—what had happened on Samuel's birthday and the days that followed. She still couldn't quite put it all together herself. She'd been banished from Central; Ety had been forbidden to go anywhere near her; Belong had been arrested for forgery and the whole network of ID forgers had been dismantled; Djama, like a bird on stilt-legs with a cactus tongue and steel heart, had admonished her directly; Axelle and Alix had begun sculpting skinny, mangled figures from self-drying clay and hiding them under their beds; she had constant headaches whenever she returned to Akriba, the eyelid twitch was unrelenting; and to top it all off, in their bed at night, Tashun would have his way with her, whispering in her ear, "If I look dead after, I'm just sleeping," as if everything were normal.

Katmé was piling earth onto the pieces of cardboard to weigh them down and fixing the burlap to the base of the trunks. Samedi was saying his goodbyes; he wouldn't be back. She stood up, took off her glove, and shook his hand firmly, her grip filled with the sort of regret you feel for an old colleague on the eve of retirement, someone you promise you'll see soon, though you know you never will. Of course, she'd contact him if there was ever any more work to be done. Then she returned to her knees and continued her work at the foot of the spruces. According to *The Clever Pine,* the book Samy had gifted her after their first trip to Fènn, covering the roots locked in moisture, prevented weeds from taking hold, and encouraged rapid growth, resulting in trees that looked three years old after just two years. In Akriba, when the legions of shadows threatened to overtake her, she would pick up the book and reread the whole thing, making sure she'd done everything just right so the trees would "quickly grow into beautiful, healthy specimens." If the book wasn't enough to fight off the hordes, she would sit down Axelle and Alix and undo their cornrows, however recent. Despite the girls' protests—they would cry from exasperation—she'd then zealously comb their hair and rebraid it. The twins also protested—this time in disgust—when their mother would lay sloppy kisses on their chests as she mumbled blessings and protections, then hold them so tight it hurt, as if she feared that upon her return from Fènn a law might have been passed to prevent parents from hugging their children. The girls had written a letter for Uncle

Samy—they didn't want a new godfather. They'd wait for him to get out of prison. "When will he be free, Mama?" Tashun observed all this with indifference, content simply to ensure, via his many informants, that Katmé was no longer defying his orders, that she was staying away from Central as well as Sita Félicie, Kizito, and Ety.

One day, when the legions were more aggressive than usual, Katmé got behind the wheel of her car. Find Keuna, talk. Since the attack of the so-called Defenders of Morality, the bath Katmé had given Keuna in her apartment on the top floor of the same building as the gallery, the lemongrass, honey, and lemon tea she'd prepared, and the way she'd brought Keuna's son Xavier home from middle school to give Keuna enough time to stop shivering and pull herself together, the two women had grown closer. True. But what would she say to Keuna? That Tashun had tried out his talents as a drummer on her cheeks? Katmé didn't open up easily. Her exclusive, all-encompassing, slash-and-burn friendship with Samy had quashed all other attempts at fellowship around her. Before Samuel was incarcerated, she'd never even considered confiding in someone else. She'd gone beyond her comfort zone by divulging even the smallest bits of information about her life to Aleksandre—a situation which continued to astound her. But now adding Keuna to the list? She wasn't inclined to multiply her confidants. Keuna would listen, of course, and she wouldn't harp like Mama Récia that "every married woman goes through this at least once in her life; no need to make a big deal." Keuna was a far cry from the type of woman who listens to you and feels sorry for you but tells you that since the dawn of time men have been men, that's just the way it is; she wasn't the type to put things in perspective by arguing that marriage is a *burdenation,* not the type who knows all too well that you have no intention of changing anything, that you're simply after a sympathetic female ear—perhaps the ear of a woman whose lot in life is less enviable than your own.

After her run-in with the Defenders, Keuna had closed the gallery, declaring that she would be "officially depressed for at least a month." Her depression lasted forty-eight hours. She had everything cleaned up, reinforced the doors and windows, signed a contract with the best security agency in Akriba, and called her attackers "bicycle chicken dicks" in a feature article published by *Emancipation.* A lot of good it would do her if Keuna, who feared nothing, smoked cigarettes, and drank whisky neat, took it upon herself to convince her to file charges against her husband, or even to leave him. Keuna couldn't stand the idea of an educated woman like Katmé, a woman with a degree, a teacher who could make her own living and was still young, clinging to the comfort of her marriage—especially since when it came to love, she hadn't felt that for her husband in quite some time. There was no need to prevaricate—she and Keuna were not cut from the same cloth. Behind the wheel of her car on Boulevard du Trente-Avril as she made her way to Bubinga Project, it had occurred to Katmé that without the patient, savvy, constantly renewed weaving of compromises and perpetual adjustments, her life and the lives of so many other women would be utterly impossible. Who can claim to be fully whole and intact? We're all just limping through life, as Samy liked to say. That was before, "a series of compromises doesn't add up to a life." You can't upend your existence and the lives of those around you over a few slaps. You put up with it—like painful periods or premature ejaculation. So she shifted the car into reverse and turned around.

Despite the sunless sky, Katmé's face was dripping with sweat—or at least she firmly believed it was. She began rifling through the pockets of her alpaca pants, which were two sizes too big, to find a tissue. It wasn't until the locksmith, Dieunedort, expressed his concern—"Mama Katmé, are you all right?"—that she realized sweat rarely pools in your eyes before streaming down your cheeks.

15

When he returned from Portugal, Fortès didn't ask any questions. Katmé was still wearing the silk scarf to hide her cheeks; her eyelids continued their seemingly intoxicated dance. As usual, he suggested watching a film. And though the magnesium had failed to tame her eyelids, *Dancing in the Dust,* Demi-Dieu, and his six wives were able to make them see reason in eighty-eight minutes. The last time Katmé had laughed her relaxed, carefree laugh, which always made Aleksandre laugh in turn—he had found the film middling at best and had been surprised to hear her laugh so much—was the day she and Samy had been heartily insulted by the dishonest man trying to sell them a plot of land. Katmé wished Samy were there now, wished he could watch the film with them. With his incredible memory, he would have learned the funniest dialogues by heart and performed them afterward to make her laugh. Back in high school, the film club put on a *Name That Line* contest twice a month, and Samy won six times in a row. Katmé noticed that the twitching had suddenly stopped. When the laughter stopped, she untied her scarf and let it slide down onto her shoulders, revealing her bare, raw, haggard face and the pattern left behind by Tashun's fingers.

Aleksandre's home became a drop box. Katmé would leave the money there, and when Kizito came to pick it up, he delivered letters from Samy passed to him by Ety.

Not once did she hear Aleksandre say, "Sorry, I don't have time to have dinner with you tonight, or watch a movie, or accept delivery from Kizito." He made himself available, never expressed any boredom when she grumbled repeatedly about how angry and frustrated she was with Samuel's situation. Together they would remember evenings spent with him, the arguments he'd presented for or against a particular film, his ramblings after four glasses of wine, the exhibition preview—details of little interest which Katmé cherished and regularly revisited to keep Samy there with them. Even when she dropped in unannounced, Katmé never ran into anyone else—a woman?—at Aleksandre's house. "My sexual therapy phase is behind me," he said when she finally pressed him. He'd been married twice. Two times too many, according to him. He kept his distance from the expat social scene in Fènn, but when the villagers invited him over to sample a local dish or attend a baptism or wedding, he would go, wearing his usual abacost—in fact, she'd never seen him dressed any other way.

One evening, he didn't hear her come in. She found him sitting at his desk. Legs crossed, glasses perched at the end of his nose, focused, typing feverishly at his computer. An ephemeral scene. Inescapably ephemeral. An evening would come when Aleksandre wouldn't be seated with his legs crossed staring at his computer, she thought. An evening would come when Aleksandre would be dead. Like Madeleine. Buried, rotting, skeleton.

Aleksandre was mortal.

This was Katmé's barometer. The indicator that revealed her degree of attachment.

Her hairdresser, for example—a man on the outskirts of her existence who often said, "God denied us everything, honey. Even easy hair," as he struggled to detangle her tight coils. When she began to worry about his death, she knew that, though she had always hopped from salon to salon before, now she'd stick with him until the end. Dead people walking—that's what the living were to her. Corpses endowed for a few years with the ability to breathe, laugh, gesture, love, make love, fight, and hate. She would look at a person and wonder: How much longer?

How do you begin a life of adultery? By choosing the right location and weapons for the job, like gangsters? How much deception and manipulation of the truth should one expect? Aleksandre's harelip scar, the bulge of flesh, exploring its thickness, its hardness, his thin lips on her hers, touching—fragile visions, heavy as the wings of a steel butterfly. How do you move from the first man to the second? From your husband to your lover? How do you juggle the two? Assigned days or weeks? Or both in one day, to ensure absolute fairness? How many hours between them? What about gaffes? And getting caught? And morality? And sin: Was it venial or mortal? She'd stopped believing in all that poppycock long ago, but you never knew. Thank God that good, kind Jesus took a stand against stoning adulterous women two thousand years ago. What about Axelle and Alix? Oh, for Heaven's sake! Tashun surely hadn't worried about all this. Aleksandre continued to welcome her with the same courteousness, the same ineffable patience, only now it disgusted her, leaving her wondering if he saw in her nothing more than a fellow movie lover. That said, he did sometimes remark on her different hairstyles, and he would take her by the shoulders and reduce the space between them when he kissed her cheeks in greeting and again when she left. It wasn't much. Could the skin beneath his abacost have been permanently sated by "two marriages too many" and his "sexual therapy period"? Ridiculous. Who could she talk to about it? This was where a friendship with an older, more experienced woman—like Djama without the Ginger Jones aspect of her personality—would have been beneficial. With Keuna, she couldn't get over the feeling that she was a counterfeit, fake leather.

"Why did you leave your husband?" Katmé had finally dared to ask her one day. In her circle, a divorced woman with no husband who had chosen to raise her son alone, smoked openly, and drank whisky and dry gin just as openly, was far from banal.

"Because Aurélien wasn't as smart as he wanted everyone to believe, and because you can't go on indefinitely sucking the dick of a man who's sponging off you," Keuna replied before taking a drag on her cigarillo. "Screwing a guy who didn't do jack shit—other than jerking off, of course—with his days just got to be too much for me. One day I picked up my son and got the hell out. I had to be ready and willing morning and night. Before work, after work. At first, well, you know what it's like."

Katmé thought to herself that she didn't.

"We fucked like rabbits. It was fantastic! Only a life-threatening emergency could get us out of bed. He wanted to go at it all the time and so did I! But by the time I realized that beyond 'take me in your mouth again, please' and 'get on all fours, please' there was no one home, we were already married and I was pregnant. He always had a good reason to quit whatever work he had going: All his jobs were too this or not enough that. Imagine a guy who pulls out his dick every morning to shove it in your mouth when you have to rush to drop the baby at daycare and catch the 7:55 commuter train to get to work on time. I worked in an art gallery in the Marais—you know where that is?"

Katmé said she did. It was the neighborhood where Tashun's brother lived in Paris. They'd stayed there once on their way to Rome.

"I was the curator for exhibitions on sub-Saharan Africa, so Aurélien knew that I'd pay the bills, or worst-case scenario, there was always *mommy and daddy.* He's an only child and his parents' mission in life is to prevent their son from cutting the cord. Even now, when he's broke, mommy and daddy are waiting for him. They almost thank him for sponging off them! Aurélien wasn't done being his parents' child, so how could he be a husband and father? When I told him I was done, you know what he asked me in his whiny voice? 'Keuna, are you saying you don't love me anymore?' 'Actually, I don't love myself anymore!' I answered. Ten months later I came back to Zambuena, and after eight horrible months slaving away at the French Embassy, I quit—well, I was basically fired—and a year after that I opened Bubinga Project."

Katmé had been unable to keep from asking Keuna if she'd found someone new, and then if she wasn't afraid of being alone for the rest of her life.

"I'm not scared at all! I'm free, free from the servitude that comes with believing relationships are mandatory."

A series of compromises doesn't add up to a life, as Samy said. Life as a sellout wasn't worth the living. Keuna was living life on her own terms, that much was clear.

Standing naked across from her mirror, Katmé conducted a merciless inventory of her body's rugged geography. The rolling hills her breasts had once formed were now topographical depressions. Stretchmark paths covered her stomach and behind; her butt was a plateau; her hips a river, her arms two brooks; the tuft of hair atop her pubic bone a graying forest; her thighs and legs choked by clumps of cellulite.

What did the "other women" look like, the ones Tashun visited before coming home? Were they mothers as well? Were their stomachs flat? Their breasts mountainous? And their butts—plains or hills? At the age of thirty-three, with two children, she was already thinking like a woman who had retired from the game of physical attraction.

Under Mama Récia's roof and incandescent faith, every child had been required to hand over the reins to his or her soul to a spiritual guide. Father Evariste preached abstinence, of course, discouraging sexuality before marriage. "You can have feelings without acting on them," he would say. Years later, during the Pre-Cana course she and Tashun completed before the wedding, he reiterated again and again: "Don't forget, my children, even after marriage, your bodies must come together in a way that honors God." Tashun was cheating on her and there was nothing she could do about it. Even if she'd wanted some kind of revenge, it wasn't an option. Not with the kind of ammunition she had at hand—some innocuous glance directed her way, from Aleksandre for example. So she was doomed to be faithful to her husband—her first and only lover, whom she'd married before God and man, a husband she no longer loved—all because of a body she didn't love. She'd rushed into marriage because she lost her virginity; she refused to rush into adultery because she'd lost her breasts. Her motivation was far from noble, but God would have to make do. Trapped—now she was a real woman. A real woman discovering the blinding radiance of faithfulness motivated by resignation and obligation. Because her desire for Aleksandre came from deep within. A crude, primitive desire that had little to do with her messy feelings. She felt feverish. She was unable to explain it. All she knew was that the same questions kept whirling around in her head. Katmé fancied herself a pioneer, the first to experience the hesitation that precedes the first expedition beyond the confines of the conjugal bed, but she was meticulously ticking off every trope on the list.

When exactly did they begin saying ridiculous things to one another, like "We both have a K in our names"?

And, "Do you know how old I am?"

"Well, I know how old you make me feel."

Or, "I can tell you're going to be an important part of my life."

"Would that be good or bad?"

And even though they still addressed one another with the formal *vous,* "Do you ever dream about me?"

"You've been a relentless presence in my dreams for a while now."

Whenever he challenged her opinion of a film, she would grumble, "I hate you," and he'd reply, "I hate you too." Together they'd reminisce about their "first fight" at his office. Aleksandre would tease her about saying, ". . . and I'm out," claiming it was the only interesting thing she'd said that day, adding that the phrase was what had first led him to believe she might be a suitable neighbor. Katmé would leave notes listing all of the reasons she was grateful to him, and he would write in reply, "You are an apparition which was not supposed to appear—a stream of moonlight in the middle of the desert." She confessed to him that she didn't like colored eyes, which were a cause of suspicion in Zambuena.

"Colored eyes?" he asked.

"I mean, not black, brown, or—if push comes to shove—hazel."

Aleksandre laughed. He'd been showered in compliments about his beautiful eyes since birth, so he shared the story of a middle school classmate he had bullied who one day finally exploded, shouting, "Your eyes are the only nice thing about you. Every other part of you is ugly and mean!"

And now Katmé realized she'd finally done it. Finally made the move she'd imagined making so many times. And he snatched her finger between his lips. They were in the kitchen, at the table, sitting across from one another. She hadn't escaped the usual groundnut stew and rice. Outside the animals were vocal. Aleksandre had laughed at his story about the color of his eyes, she'd reached out her hand and run her index finger along the scar on his upper lip, and now his tongue was circling her finger, making her nipples hard beneath her black satin blouse.

16

Amédée, one of Mama Récia's seven sons, had once declared, "Once I'm married, I'll only touch my wife to have children. I want three children, so I'll touch her three times."

With Aleksandre, Katmé was pretty far off Cousin Amédée's quota. Sometimes he was inside her two or even three times the same night. Regardless of where he placed them on her body, his lips felt like magic. Keuna had used the phrase "fuck like rabbits." Now, at thirty-three, Katmé finally understood what that meant. Aleksandre took her peremptorily, making love to her like a general in the middle of a campaign, a commander in chief who believed every battle decisive. Besiege the adversary, dominate her, then beg her to ask for mercy to end the torture of the wait. Her husband had clumsily introduced her to lovemaking; now Fortès was teaching her about pleasure. The kind that mounts slowly, inescapably, and leaves you spent.

"I'm glad you're not a Greenland shark," he said one day, still addressing her using the formal you.

"What do you mean?" she replied, following suit.

"Greenland sharks live for two hundred to four hundred years and reach sexual maturity at 186."

"I'm not sure how to take that . . ."

"As a compliment; you've made swift progress."

Katmé got used to the contortions of adultery just as swiftly. Sometimes she was so carried away by her heady desire that she minimized the extent of the risks she was taking.

While her husband thrust in and out of her, she would imagine Aleksandre and stifle the moans rising in her throat. With Tashun she bridled all expressions of her own pleasure; she never "squawked" or indulged in any risky logorrhea. Like a real wife. Less than a year after their wedding, he had put a lid on her verbal outpourings during sex. The night she'd moaned louder than usual and said things, all rather incoherent, all inescapably crude. She had thought it was her fault that he was stepping out, that it was because she lacked experience, so she'd decided to learn; after all, she was a teacher, she knew that a bit of serious studying could pay off. In the absence of hands-on experience, a theoretical foundation could rectify many shortcomings. She had wanted to surprise him, to get him to stop sheathing his penis between other women's legs. *How to Keep Your Man,* a manual she procured for herself from a second-hand bookseller, became her tutor. According to the jargony incipit of the book, which was published in the late sixties, sex was all about vocabulary, gestures, sighs, oral ravings, whispers, cries, and positions; no man could resist. Tashun resisted. He pulled out of her in a state of shock. Such vulgarity . . . sounds worthy of a working girl from the Joie neighborhood . . . He said "sounds" and Katmé heard a heifer low, a sow squeal, and a camel cow grunt. Huddled into a ball, so ashamed that she seemed to actually shrink, becoming smaller and smaller on the bed, she was served a sermon on the values of discretion, respect, dignity, and self-worth a married woman must embody. Tashun was applying—at least with her—the precepts Father Evariste had taught them by *coming together* with her "in a way that honors God." Singing is twice as good as praying, they always said at the Eucharistic Youth Movement group she had attended. So was having holy relations with your wife. It goes without saying that Katmé never read beyond the first chapter of *How to Keep Your Man;* she tore it to pieces and threw it out.

As for Aleksandre, he was in a constant dialogue with her body, encouraging her to whisper or shout whatever was going through her mind, to moan loudly, and scream her pleasure in unison with his. With him, her vagina aspired to be permanently occupied. When the distance between them grew, she felt starved for dopamine, serotonin, choline, and endorphins. So lost that she would throw caution to the wind and insist that they spend the night together, spooning naked, him inside of her. Was she becoming unhinged? Turning into a nymphomaniac? At the hair salon one day, she happened upon a magazine article about a woman in her forties who became a sex addict while her mother was in the hospital dying of cancer. "I felt guilty about have sex while my mother was at the hospital. I was constantly horny, every minute, it was like an animal instinct in me had suddenly awakened. My partner at the time wasn't enough for me, so I found others.

In hindsight, pleasures of the flesh kept me going while I took care of my mother. It helped me to let her go, and it helped my partner at the time, whom I put to work in the evenings, grow closer to his own mother, with whom things had been conflictual." Madeleine had been dead for twenty years. Samy wasn't dying in prison. Her situation was hardly comparable.

She behaved rather brazenly with Tashun one night. She'd gotten her period before leaving for Fènn, and her husband—unlike Aleksandre, who used his tongue to explore the hollow between her thighs even when she was bleeding—tended to let her be while "nature was running its course." After dinner, the day she returned, once Axelle and Alix were in bed, he closed their bedroom door and pounced on her. In the early days of their marriage, she liked it when he was hungry for her. It was a sign, she thought, that he hadn't been carrying on with other women. His desire reassured her. She responded gratefully; if he wanted her, then she was his favorite. So that night, without thinking, she fell to her knees and unzipped his pants.

"Who else has been touching you?" he asked, backing away.

She mumbled weak excuses, feigned tears and bewilderment, and managed to assuage his suspicions. Later, once they'd finished, he flipped onto his side and asked the usual question: "Good, right?" She nodded and smiled. He smiled back, then turned over and went to sleep. Tashun was content with a nod rather than any audible, uncontrollable expression of his wife's pleasure.

"I don't have any expectations for this relationship," Aleksandre would often say.

"If only we could really have no expectations," Katmé would reply.

Beyond the red-walled bedroom, the wrought-iron sofa, the kitchen counter, the bathtub, the tile floor in the shower, and the soft bed of foliage next to the pond where they would get lost in one another surrounded by eucalyptus trees and the croaking of toads with only a kerosene lamp and moonlight to see by, it occurred to Katmé that Aleksandre would never be as committed to her as she wanted. Besides, did she even know what she wanted? For the moment, his lips, hands, skin, and member had made her body burn hotter than she ever could have imagined, and that meant something.

PART THREE

17

It was hardly a relaxing stroll through the countryside, but they were making headway. The scent of clay rising from the damp ground, the morning dew, the song of robins perched on tree branches, and the wild beauty of the flowers all tempered the cruelty of the journey. It was a miracle no one had fallen flat on their face yet. The wet grass tickled their bare ankles and the tree leaves scratched their exposed arms. Stumbling and staggering, they all kept moving as best they could. The machete slashed left, the machete slashed right—blades of tall grass fluttered through the air like green sequins until the glamour wore off and they fell to the ground. With his feet firmly rooted to the earth and his hand steady in the air, the young guide cut through the dew-drenched vegetation. Their path amid wild shrubs, cacao trees, banana plantations, hordes of striped ground squirrels, snakes, and creeping plants, had all the hallmarks of an expedition through hostile bush. No one complained, everyone was doing their best. From time to time a groan rang out, that was all. They clung to branches, steadied themselves on the shoulder in front of them or their own hips or knees. Machete in hand, the stocky, muscular guide hacked through dense thickets to create a path through the underbrush. With every swing of the machete, Katmé measured just how little foresight she'd demonstrated. Mama Récia's kaba ngondo and her own, Sennke's blue choir dress—the dresses, boubous, and pants of all those pressing toward Madeleine's grave—bore constellations of thorns from the brambles, with tears here and there. Standing tall and proud, unaided, his breath steady despite his seventy-six years of age, Katmé's father exuded the austere, majestic air of a lord surveying his lands, preceded by his faithful doungourou. His immaculate white bazin gandoura embroidered with gold thread was perfectly tailored to his six-foot-six frame, which made all the others look small. Only someone with his confidence and self-assured bearing would wear such a fervent outfit to the heart of the backcountry where he hadn't set foot for over twenty years. By way of comparison, Tashun's black suit and black shirt made him look like one of the gravediggers from the Last Smile funeral home who were bringing up the rear. It was nine o'clock in the morning, there was a cool breeze, and the sky was the color of soot. The guide reassured the many pairs of eyes raised toward the heavens that it wouldn't rain. Not today or tomorrow. That's all they needed—two days of gray, threatening skies would do as long as there was no precipitation. To ward off showers, Mama Récia had buried the blade of a knife, right up to the handle, in the ground near a woodfire.

Only the family had been invited to the exhumation. "Thank goodness," Tashun had griped after tripping on a vine. Innocent Patong was family. The others—mayor Edouard Limu, who had joined the APM as expected and was now Tashun's running mate for the gubernatorial campaign, the prefect, and the Last Smile gravediggers (inmates on labor duty with their guard)—didn't count. The guests, the many guests, would arrive in the late afternoon or tomorrow morning before the funeral Mass. Katmé's husband would never have forgiven her for sharing this ordeal with their new friends. Busy mounting his campaign and worn out by his duties as prefect, he had only loosely followed her preparations. His visits to Fènn had focused on expanding his team, polishing his platform, and meeting various local dignitaries through Katmé's father. She tried to remember Samy's proverb about caution. *Cautela non* something or other . . . Who would believe that she had planned to have the brush cut back, the path to the grave cleared? She thought she would have time. She thought she would have time, but then it had slipped her mind. She and Kizito had explored so many different options for getting Samy out of Central that it was hardly surprising she had forgotten to tend to the path to Madeleine's resting place. The day the metal bars had slammed shut behind Samy, her priorities were upended, and the bombastic ceremony Tashun wanted went back to being what it had been from the start, what it had always been: a burden she didn't know how to escape.

Though he'd been the picture of composure and stateliness to this point, Katmé's father was now berating the guide. "Are you taking us to the ends of the earth or what? It's been at least thirty minutes since you told us we were almost there. We're not in the same shape you are, son!"

Katmé saw Mama Récia bite her lower lip hard—the sign she had reached maximum irritation. Her aunt must be terribly upset with her for issuing no warning about Innocent Patong's presence.

"We'll be there soon, Papa," said the guide. To prove he wasn't lying, he raised his right hand, his thumb and index finger joined at the tips and the other three fingers spread and pointing skyward.

"When is soon?"

"Not even ten minutes, Papa."

Mama Récia's murderous glances at Innocent Patong intensified. Katmé could easily guess what her aunt was thinking upon seeing her father for the first time after all these years. She must have found that time had left less of a mark on him than she expected. She'd have reminded herself of his age and thought about her sister Madeleine, dead and buried for two decades now, while he, with his arrogant features showcased by the blinding white of his bazin gandoura, went on living, smiling his haughty smile like an aging Don Juan. A charisma that camouflaged a fair dose of depravity. Mama Récia only read the Bible and biographies of saints. She hadn't read *The Picture of Dorian Gray.* Nevertheless, Katmé was convinced that the troubled soul her aunt imagined in her father was reminiscent of Wilde's character.

Katmé's paternal and maternal families hated one another with passion and precision. In Madeleine's room at the mortuary—a hideous room where piss-yellow neon light shone on cracked walls with chipped paint—the two families hurled insults at one another as the undertakers looked on in consternation. Madeleine lay naked on the stainless-steel table, her lips smeared with bright red lipstick, her breasts erect, frozen in place by the ice, her pubic hair so glossy it could have been gelled, her wig askew, waiting for them to decide her fate. Each clan wanted to ensure she'd wear the accessories they'd chosen for her. Katmé could still see her left hand in a white glove slipped between her mother's frozen fingers; the pale pink first communion dress she was wearing; her new shoes, purchased by the principal at the high school where Madeleine had taught, which hurt her feet; her right hand holding Sennke's; she and Sennke standing before their mother's dead body, her skin the color of ripe papaya, their minds exiled to an imaginary haven to escape the negotiations underway. Mama Récia and her daughters won the battle for the dress. They put Madeleine in a white lace wedding dress dotted with sparkling little stars. No one would have been surprised see the outfit light up like a Christmas decoration. Speaking of which, it was December. Innocent Patong secured the right to use an ugly particleboard coffin which provided a fairly clear picture of the hard line he must have taken in negotiations with the funeral home's carpenter. Tacky gilt handles, fake satin cushions, a ridiculously thin zinc liner, and quick-dry varnish. Her father disqualified himself from the competition—not because he'd applied what he felt were the financial and aesthetic standards worthy of her mother's family, but simply because the coffin turned out to be too narrow for the body. He hadn't realized that Madeleine had gained quite a bit of weight over the past few years. Her father adopted the moderately disgruntled attitude of a person seeking a minor role in a play, out of politeness; once exiled from the stage, sent to mingle with the anonymous crowd, he bowed out gracefully.

The guide stopped short. He pointed—at what exactly? A rise? A knoll? A vague pile of debris, really. Remnants of concrete and steel rebar which would have gone undetected without the young man's keen eye. Her mother's grave. Open. To the vegetation. The wind. The sun. The rain. No name, no cross, no epitaph. Katmé felt twenty pairs of accusatory eyes on her. What kind of daughter of Fènn—an abomination of nature?—could abandon the grave of the woman who brought her into the world? A ground squirrel emerged from the hole and the assembly recoiled in panic. Tashun only just managed to catch Katmé's waist, wrapping his arm around her firmly; Sennke staggered and clung to Edouard Limu's arm; Mama Récia let out the screech of a bird of prey—nothing hysterical, just what was required to kick off the concert of weeping. Four of her sons yelped as the luxurious gray ebony casket inlaid by Djama's carpenter slipped from their grasp. The coffin made of rare wood ("gray ebony comes from a tree felled before it reaches maturity," Djama had explained) was now badly dented. Mama Récia was pounding her chest and pulling her hair. Why hadn't Katmé's aunt, who never missed an opportunity to cry floods of tears over the premature death of her younger sister, visited the grave either?

Thorns grew inside of Katmé. Innocent Patong wiped at a tear that was not welling at the corner of his eye, then placed an awkward hand on Sennke's veil as she cried candidly; she pulled away. Wearing his solemnity like a badge, Tashun gravely handed her a handkerchief embroidered, like his shirt and socks, with his initials; she declined it. He used the handkerchief to stem the flow streaming from Katmé's nose and staining his expensive bespoke suit. Mama Récia was doubled over, massaging her calves and humming a chant in which her twelve children and their husbands, wives, and adult children all joined. The mayor, the prefect, and even the undertakers from the Last Smile funeral home adopted expressions suited to the circumstances. Reuniting with Madeleine twenty years later was, on the whole, trying for everyone—at least to all appearances—except the five inmate gravediggers and their guard, who eagerly awaited the order to begin. Mama Récia, whose pragmatism never failed her, took the situation in hand and instructed them to open the grave. Open, so to speak. With pieces of the slab here and there, nothing substantial, it was hard to say it was truly closed. Mama Récia explained that she would only be fully convinced that it was, in fact, her sister's grave, once they'd found the dagger—all skeletons look the same, don't they. The mayor and prefect suggested a moment of silence. They tried to read the official decrees authorizing the disinterment of Madeleine Lapteu in a single voice. Their uneven tempo, overlapping and interrupted sentences, and repetitions were laughable. No one laughed.

When the first pick hit the ground, Mama Récia struck her chest hard once more. Katmé stared at her aunt and her spectacular grief. The reason her aunt had never visited the grave of her sister Mado was hidden away in a dark corner of her hardened Christian soul. "Keep your distance from sin, my children." You don't visit the grave of a sinner. Katmé remembered what Mama Récia said at the hospital right after her mother shut her eyes for the last time. "Bless our Lord Jesus Christ, your mother suffered greatly before she died. The Lord purified her. Through her suffering, she earned a place in heaven, praise God, she won't go to hell!" Madeleine had been living in mortal sin because she was in a relationship with Innocent Patong outside the sacred bonds of marriage. That's why—to "purify" her—Mama Récia's Good Lord arranged for Madeleine's vehicle to collide with that drunken driver's truck, arranged for her to survive long enough to be thrown from the car while a piece of her dress kept her tethered to the vehicle, arranged for her to be dragged on her back at full speed, at the diabolical speed of a runaway car, for the skin and flesh of her back to be ripped off from the bottom of her neck to her tailbone, for her car to end up in a village without electricity where the residents stole her jewelry and money, and arranged for the hospital—which she finally reached thanks to a bus driver feeling more than usually charitable when he passed the wreck—to refuse to treat her until her family came out to pay them upfront for saving her life. Next, the Good Lord arranged for the doctors to take two days to detect her internal hemorrhaging, arranged the unbearable, drug-resistant pain that made Madeleine's whole body writhe, arranged for her to howl like something from beyond the grave until at last her voice gave out, arranged for the doctors to realize on the third day that her lower limbs were numb and that she would be paralyzed for life, arranged for her to begin peeing blood soon thereafter, and even arranged for her to be discharged on that same third day, mute from so much screaming, mute from so much suffering, from so much crying. Mama Récia's Good Lord—choreographer of torture, architect of redemption.

When the gravediggers' picks hit the ground the second time, a partial cave-in pulled concrete and steel into the hole. Katmé freed herself from Tashun's embrace and shouted for them to be more careful. "They're bones, darling. We'll clean them. If they don't hurry, we'll fall behind schedule," her father whispered in her ear. She hadn't felt his approach. He put his arm around her shoulders. "*Soubanalai!* Hurry up!" he said to the diggers, who had paused. "This can't take all day." Her father knew that time was money. To amass a fortune like his, you had to know the exact worth of each passing second. *Bones.* Over the past few months, Katmé had thought back to the woman who suffered so much before her death, the woman who was a mother for just over ten years and would never be a grandmother; the woman who wasn't there when she got her first period, when she had her first doubts, her many sorrows, her rare joys; the intrepid woman who stood up on her Vespa and had traveled the world but was unable to come to her wedding; the woman with brown eyes and skin the color of ripe papaya, who exuded health, strength, and authority, but had had been unable to protect Sennke and her from the violence, the beatings and physical torture that Mama Récia's oldest daughter, Rosine, had inflicted upon them when her mother wasn't looking. Dead opportunities, missed dreams, inaudible questions, and unswallowed anger paraded through Katmé's memory. After two hundred and forty months of banishment, her mother was no longer completely exiled from her thoughts. Madeleine full of life, then dead, stiff, naked in the room at the funeral home, exposed to the shameless gaze of everyone present, she had pictured that many times. But she had never, not once, imagined her mother as *bones.* That was her father. Innocent Patong was a man of action, there was no room for the superfluous in his vocabulary.

Once the entrance to the grave had been cleared, Katmé leaned forward to glimpse the famous bones amid the dirt. Three gravediggers jumped into the hole, landing on both feet—there was no ladder. The other two threw them shovels, which they caught before they hit the ground. In return, they tossed up what looked like a femur. Sennke and Mama Récia screamed. "A curse! A curse upon you!" shouted her aunt. "You fiends!" The inmates didn't understand what they'd done wrong, so they looked to the guard, who turned to Tashun and asked for the family members to "lend a hand as well." Mama Récia's sons—the ones thanks to whom the brand-new coffin looked like it had come from a junkyard—made their way to the edge of the grave, lay down on the ground, and stretched their arms down into the hole. Their bare hands gathered the dislocated pieces of Madeleine's skeleton, then handed them to the two gravediggers, who passed them to the undertakers, who reassembled them in the coffin. Wearing gloves and armed with rags, the Last Smile employees cleaned the bones before placing them inside the casket. Katmé sniffled. Tashun's handkerchief was now so full of snot and saliva that it could absorb no more. They extracted the tattered remains of the once sparkling white dress, a quarter of the wig, and half a glove. Katmé stopped swallowing the viscous liquid that dripped from her nostrils down to her lips, then continued its path along her chin and neck. Her father tightened his arm around her shoulders. Tashun slipped her a clean handkerchief, which, like the matching ascot he was wearing, bore the party insignia and an effigy of the president—the gubernatorial campaign was set to begin in just two days' time, on Monday. They brought up a sculpted handle made of tarnished silver and a rusty, partially disintegrated blade. "The dagger! They found the dagger!" Mama Récia rejoiced. "It's Mado's grave, praise be to Jesus Christ, it's Mado's grave!"

The dagger. Katmé hadn't forgotten. Her aunt had pressed it into her mother's rigid hand before they closed the coffin at the funeral home, so she could defend herself if someone—like Innocent Patong, as a not-very-random example—tried to steal her corpse, resurrect her, and smuggle her to some kind of parallel universe where she would be forced to toil away to build up a great fortune *he* would nonetheless be able to enjoy in this world. Yes, indeed—do keep up! A rosary had already been placed in her left hand. With his strong forehead, ox-like neck, and nails and cuticles ragged from biting, the marabout spread a thick brown paste on the face of the deceased and sprinkled the contents of a black vial beneath her body. Chanting incantations, he called for the irremediable death of Madeleine's "mystical murderer" nine days after her burial. To conclude, he licked the dagger from end to end and placed it flat on Mama Récia's joined palms. Rosary on the left, dagger on the right—Madeleine would have her choice of weapons if someone picked a quarrel with her during her eternal rest. The dagger would slay Innocent Patong, whose fortune—as everyone knew—came from the money he made delivering naïve souls to the dark powers he served. Indeed. Did the man perched on a chair at the back of the room with a camcorder on his shoulder (filming the scene from above, unbeknownst to all) stagger as a result of his attempt to zoom in on the deceased's hands? Whatever the cause, the creak of the precarious step he'd climbed onto to film the ceremony betrayed his presence. Katmé still remembered the devastated faces of Mado's packaging committee for her odyssey through the great beyond. "We asked everyone to leave, EVERYONE! Except the children and immediate family of the deceased. What are you doing here?" The marabout was livid. His voice trembled with fury. Dressed in a tight white polo and black jeans with pagne insert bellbottoms, the owner of the VHS video camera was not afforded the time to reply. Amédée vigorously kicked the foot of the chair, and the man and his material went flying. The family confiscated the camcorder, and Amédée used his teeth to scratch the film. "Shame on you! Christians practicing witchcraft like this," the intruder bellowed as they directed him to the exit with repeated kicks to his backside. "You call yourselves children of God? *Minalmi!* Hell is what awaits you, you pack of devils!" As soon as he was outside, he began sharing the story of the séance he'd just witnessed urbi et orbi.

For Mama Récia and her daughters, "rabid zealots" as Katmé's father called them, nothing about the situation was incongruous. Not even the idea that, after burial, a body might be dug up by evil, rapacious forces, brought back to life, and forced into slavery in a parallel universe to produce riches that would benefit someone in the tangible world. Indeed. So, officially, at her mother's first funeral, there was the priest, a man of God representing the Church, a worshiper of the Host and the wafer box; more discreetly, there was also a marabout, his chest weighed down by cowry shells beneath his red boubou—the unofficial supplier of the dagger and mystical philter. Nine days after the funeral, Innocent Patong was not only alive; he had turned up at Mama Récia's house to give her "a bit of money for the children" looking the picture of health in a meteor-blue safari jacket that matched the color of his Lexus. Katmé's aunt hadn't had the heart to spit on the "satanic" money, so she simply asked him to place the bills on the table in the kitchen so she wouldn't have to touch his skin. Once he had gone, she spritzed the bills in holy water from Lourdes mixed with holy oil from Jerusalem while uttering a dozen Hail Marys, then explained to her household that Innocent Patong had escaped the marabout's plans for him by pilfering a handful of dirt from Mado's grave. "That's how he wasted the work of our marabout: He gave him the dirt from Mado's grave and together he and his own marabout blocked everything. Poor Mado, only God knows where she is now." If Katmé followed her aunt's logic carefully, Madeleine had been the victim of both divine wrath and human sorcery. Poor Madeleine, surrounded on all sides. Mama Récia would have been surprised to learn she practiced a particularly flexible brand of syncretism.

Katmé blew her nose on the Father of the Nation's face and decided she'd cried enough. She glanced at Sennke. Her little sister was crying freely in Mama Récia's arms, wholly indifferent to the acceptable volume of tears that can be shed in the presence of others, not caring at all that she might appear weak and breakable, like the low-quality grave slab which had crumbled over time and yielded without much resistance. Five months after Madeleine's death, Sennke and Katmé's aunt had taken them to a new, "terribly powerful" marabout—more powerful than the one from the funeral home. Papa Vérité scarified their skin above the solar plexus, beneath their breasts, on their lower abdomens and at the top of their buttocks: *bullet-proofing,* a shield against sorcery created using the corner of a razor blade dipped in a bloody, foul-smelling, molasses-thick paste. He had a bucket of water brought over and told the girls to focus intently on the bottom of the container. Since they saw nothing but water and the plastic the bucket was made of, he got angry, uttered sacred words, and declared when he was done that they had wasted their opportunity to see their mother "die her real death this time." Their mother had been working as a cook "in the mystical world that belongs to the country's wealthy men, including your father." He, Papa Vérité, had just killed her for real, no one would be able to take advantage of her unrivaled culinary talents anymore. Now Mado was finally setting out on her real path to God the Father's purgatory; she would soon reach heaven. Papa Vérité was going to destroy the fortune amassed by Innocent Patong in the shadow kingdom, they should expect to see their father ruined, a beggar, in under three months. Three months later, the only notable event in the girls' lives was the severe pneumonia they struggled to get over—a reminder of the two hours spent in their underwear, their chests bare in the moonlight during the rainy season, while the "terribly powerful" Papa Vérité mutilated their skin.

Katmé broke free of her father's embrace, walked over to her sister and took her hand. Their fingers recognized one another and instinctively united. Like when they were little, to resist punishment or ask for a miracle; like in the hospital the day their mother died, when they were so certain they could bring her back to life; like later, when they tried to bring back their father who'd walked out of their lives in a pair of Weston Oxfords. This morning, at the edge of their mother's dilapidated grave, the knots they tied their fingers into would keep them both from breaking, from crumbling.

The tears had stopped. Katmé's eyes burned. She would fight and win the battle of the tears. She had lost so many others of late. She needed to start somewhere. And Monday, Monday afternoon, a day after her mother's second burial, she would win another, provided everything went to plan. After four months and seventeen days, Samy would finally be leaving Central.

Shy rays of sunshine filtered between the tree leaves. Noon was edging ever closer. The guide warned them "at exactly noon, at twelve o'clock on the dot," they would have to stop and finish the disinterment the next day. No one knew why, but in Haut-Fènn, you had to bury or exhume a body before noon. Like the ban on women eating chicken gizzards and sitting on the same bed as their mothers once married, it was one of those rules everyone followed without asking where it came from or whether it made any sense; they'd always seemed ridiculous to Katmé. People said that once, when a family braved the rule and buried their loved one at twelve thirty, lightning had zigzagged across the sky and struck the deceased's youngest child, forcing the family to bury not one body but two. Everyone in Fènn knew the story, so no one dared step out of line. If the pre-burial formalities (Mass, speeches, eulogies, thank-yous, drum-playing, crying, and singing) weren't finished before the fateful hour, families would push the burial to the next day. To escape the long wake that awaited them later that night, Katmé had tried to schedule the exhumation and the burial on the same day. Despite her best efforts and the arguments she put forward, including a few that made sense (the event would cost less if they didn't have to feed the village for two whole days, for example), Tashun, Innocent Patong, Mama Récia, the village chief, and Djama had opposed the idea. The invitation read:

Wake for the deceased Saturday night.
Mass on Sunday morning at ten o'clock.
Burial. Light meal.
Eleven o'clock on Monday, official opening ceremony for the
Madeleine Lapteu Health Center
and a segment of the new highway from Fènn to Akriba
alongside the province's administrative and traditional authorities
and constitutional bodies.

"Defy tradition and rush such an important ceremony? Why on earth? To save on chicken thighs and groundnuts?" Tashun balked. She had to be joking.

Two green mambas made the poor decision to slither sneakily through the small crowd, so the guide's machete made quick work of them, chopping them in half. No one had time to be afraid. Four strips of neon-green vines now lay near the coffin. As for the ground squirrels, they enjoyed special treatment. Resting upright on their tiny back legs, they carefully studied the scene. Whenever one of the gravediggers victoriously announced they'd found a new bone, the shyest among them would scurry off. The others remained, bobbing their heads up and down to the beat of the shovels combing through the dirt to find Madeleine's remains. Like the ground squirrels, Mama Récia, Sennke, and Katmé followed the dancing shovels with their eyes and heads, their feet firmly planted at the edge of the grave. The gravediggers had asked them to step back a number of times since the unstable ground could collapse beneath them at any moment, and their closeness hampered their work. With their bare chests dotted with beads of sweat and their belts pulled tight through the loops around the tops of their pants, the men didn't appreciate the three women's supervisory looks. The sisters monitored each of their movements, scolded the men if a shovel inadvertently struck a knuckle, identified the parts of the skeleton, named them aloud, and counted them. Other members of the family had made themselves comfortable on patches of cool grass, boulders, and tree trunks. The red earth had exacted revenge from Innocent Patong's gorgeous gandoura; the circle of bazin around him looked like a bride's dress stained by the sudden arrival of her period. Sitting on a log with Tashun, the mayor and the prefect, he looked, despite his sullied clothes, like a village chief preparing for an audience, surrounded by his advisors. Like Tashun, Katmé's father was the relentless type, determined to make life cough up everything it had to offer so he could savor every last drop of its digestive juices. The opposite of Madeleine. Katmé's mother hailed from the tribe for whom life is a bitch. Unbearable suffering, only thirty-nine years old. A pitiful end, only thirty-nine years old. A discount funeral, only thirty-nine years old.

The prison guard informed them that the task had been completed; they were moving out. Katmé and Sennke knelt down next to their mother's coffin to meticulously inspect the skeleton. "The tally's off." Knuckles, fibulas, ulnas, ribs, and vertebrae were missing.

"We won't close the casket until there's a complete skeleton inside," said Katmé.

"Keep looking," the sisters said in unison.

The guard turned to Innocent Patong and Tashun, silently imploring them. It was quite clear that any support he could hope for would come from them. The inmate gravediggers were covered in sweat, their chins resting on the tops of their shovels as they waited. They'd combed through the dirt every which way, putting aside their picks and shovels to hunt for trapped bones with their bare hands. They were done.

"What if we don't find all the bones?" Tashun asked, nudged by the guard's silent supplication.

"They're here," said Katmé. "I won't leave without every last one."

Sennke nodded and tightened her hand around her sister's. Innocent Patong hadn't said a word since he'd urged the gravediggers to pick up the pace. He left his throne and took Katmé aside.

Surmising his intent, Mama Récia spoke up. "I'm warning you, leaving Madeleine's remains here will call down a curse on us and our children. The road will be coming through here, we can't let cars drive over her."

"Darling," began Innocent Patong as he ripped his irritated gaze from Mama Récia, "we have to be reasonable. It would take a miracle to find every single bone."

"We'll just have to wait for a miracle then, Papa," replied Katmé, turning to the gravediggers. "Keep digging, please. We can't leave anything behind."

Something that looked like a femur emerged. In his black suit and gloves, the undertaker from the Last Smile funeral home, who had been retrieving the bones and slowly but surely reassembling the skeleton in the coffin like a human puzzle master, cleared his throat. Unless Madam Prefect's mother had three femurs, there was one too many. Katmé looked at her mother's skeleton: two femurs. One of the three bones belonged to an animal.

"A sieve, we need a sieve, to sift through the dirt," she said as she stared at Tashun, who was now standing alongside her father and other family members around the grave. "We need a mason's sieve. You know, like the one they used for the construction work on the house."

"All right, Katmé. We need a sieve. A mason's sieve. Where do you suggest we find one? If you'd properly prepared for your mother's exhumation rather than messing around at Central, we wouldn't be in this position. You should have thought of this earlier. Weeks ago, damn it!"

"Come, come, children. Let's not get worked up," said Innocent Patong in a soothing voice.

"Be reasonable, Katmé," said Tanga, one of Mama Récia's sons.

She glared at him.

The pale pink whistle—a broken toy—meowed timidly at first, then louder and louder. Noon. The ground squirrels scampered off. The gravediggers drove their shovels into the ground and trained their eyes, full of early relief and established resentment, on Katmé. The tiny object clenched between the guide's teeth was screeching now. Innocent Patong, Tashun, the prison guard, the inmates, the mayor, the prefect, her cousins, the coffin, the heaps of earth, the eviscerated grave, the trees, the driver ants, and the dried dew were waiting for

Katmé to raise her right arm and then lower it again, signaling her consent to end the excavations. So she did. Immediately afterward, her hand groped for Sennke's and imprisoned it in her own. Their mother would be laid to rest incomplete in her new marble and slate abode, that was just the way it was. To save her, they would have had to go back in time twenty years, to the hospital room where Mama Récia claimed Madeleine was washing away her sins through excruciating pain. "The whole skeleton," as if that could change anything, as if that could bring her back. You saved the living, not the dead, that was just the way it was. Samy could be saved, not Madeleine. Since Jesus and Lazarus and Mary Shelley and Frankenstein, no one had found a way to bring the dead back to life. The dead remained dead, became *bones.* Bits of bones that got lost in the earth, pieces of femurs, ulnas, radiuses, and other Latin mouthfuls, that could only be found with a sieve. A life after this life, malarkey. *Hic et nunc,* as Samy said, here and now. Those were the last rites. Now they had something new in common: they'd both looked up at the heavens and thought, there's nothing up there. Katmé felt like crying, but a snigger rose to her lips. A wail of distress cut through the air—Mama Récia! Katmé let go of her sister's hand and wrapped her arms around her sobbing aunt, who was so tall she had to stand on her tiptoes to reach.

"You always say we should fear what corrupts the soul, not our earthly bodies, right, Mama? Her soul isn't here. We found almost all the pieces of her skeleton, Mama. The rest is with God, Mama. The rest is with God."

Katmé heard the quavering in her aunt's voice subside.

18

They had received four steers (Mama Récia was keeping track in a little notebook), ten pigs, five sows, a hundred and fifty village chickens, forty-seven guinea pigs, twenty-five goats, dozens of crates of champagne and wine, a hundred demijohns of raffia wine, ten barrels of palm oil, three tanks of draught beer, kola nuts, bitter kola, and twenty-five bags of groundnuts as well as money: envelopes full of bills. What goes around comes around, you reap what you sow, etc.—an endless cycle the people of Zambuena call solidarity. Tashun and Katmé had done as much at more than a few funerals, weddings, and baptisms. An elderly man in a chechia stood in the doorway to the kitchen asking Katmé to "come over for a minute." She left the plate of tomatoes she was cutting on the sideboard and stepped over Axelle and Alix, who were on their knees on the floor, leaning over their tools to learn how to mill spices with a grinding stone. Outside, moonlight diluted the darkness. Katmé filled her lungs with air, emptying them of the stuffiness that clung to the traditional mudbrick kitchen, where that morning Mama Récia had driven a knife into the ground near the woodfire to keep the rain at bay. It hadn't rained all day. Now the cold had them under siege. The surface of the black pond rippled, enveloped in a chorus of frogs and crickets. Three hundred yards up the hill, the terrace in the yard amplified the indistinct murmur of human voices, the echo of balafons, and the rhapsodies of the choir. "From the Tam-Tam neighborhood diaspora tontine," said the man. Corn in burlap sacks, boxes of peanut oil, and two rams tied to a eucalyptus. She thanked him, rummaged through the pockets of her kaba ngondo, and slipped a five-thousand-franc bill into his hand. He removed his chechia, bowed, and left. She walked over to the rams, then backed off when they started bleating; now was no time to get gored. Her steps led her to the edge of the pond, where her eyes were drawn to the far side of the water. Aleksandre's house. A light was on in the screened porch; the rest of the house was dark. It had been a month since she'd walked along the edge of the pond—the most salient border between the two houses—guided by the flickering flame of a kerosene lamp or the coruscant beam of a flashlight. After three months together, twelve weeks, he'd bitterly declared, "The only things you like about me are my dick and my DVDs. There's no point seeing one another again if you insist on being so full of yourself."

Katmé found Axelle and Alix in the position they'd been in when she'd left. Each of them held the small, round, baby stone in her hands and was grinding tomato and garlic on the larger, flat, oval stone beneath. The process required practice and technique, both of which they were lacking. The girls' clumsiness provoked nostalgic banter among the women gathered in the mudbrick kitchen. They'd had the kitchen built due to Mama Récia's insistence that traditional dishes wouldn't taste right if prepared on a modern stove. Katmé had to agree; ekoki cooked on an electric burner had neither the enticing smell nor the delicious flavor of ekoki simmered over a wood fire. A caterer would be handling the meal served after the funeral tomorrow, but her aunt and cousins were against letting "outsiders mess with our traditional dishes," so they'd called in a few village women as reinforcements. Katmé picked up the plate of tomatoes and went back to her place on the stool next to Sennke—shapeless dress, turtleneck blouse, and crucifix on her chest—who was peeling garlic with exemplary patience.

After the exhumation, once the casket had been placed on the altar, Katmé's father had quickly left, taking Tashun with him to the Montagne neighborhood, where they would welcome friends from the capital. Before they took off, her aunt had asked them to join in "a quick prayer with Madeleine"; a quick prayer in Mama Récia's book was never less than half an hour long. Innocent Patong had rebuffed her. Praying and the all-night vigil, those were women's tasks; the men had hired the choir, balafon players, and criers so they wouldn't have to sit through endless prayers. Mama Récia had bit her lower lip. The yard was growing increasingly crowded. Guests were drinking coffee and tea, eating groundnuts and puff-puff and beans as they prayed, sang, listened to the kinds of stories told at wakes, and led those who wanted to "pay their respects to the departed" to the living room. In an amber frame with an ochre mat, Madeleine welcomed them wearing a wrap dress, her hair pulled up into a bun on the top of her head, and her clever eyes trained on the lens, full of life. A curtain of real white flowers—lilies, gardenias, four-o'clocks, roses, and daisies—designed by Djama's florist cascaded down the sides of the coffin, and the walls were adorned with mauve lace. The latex, polyurethane, and plastic bouquets and funeral wreaths sent by friends, strangers, various organizations, and party members were piling up in a corner of the room. Nine five-arm candelabras framed the altar. Nine, in case of a blackout, and because nine is the number of mourning according to Djama, who had overseen the decorations. Katmé had simply placed the orders with the suppliers and paid the bills.

The twins were doing their best to follow Mama Récia's instructions. "Not so hard, not so hard, you have to hold the stone with your hand, not your fingers, hold it in your palm. Now you push, yes, like that, keep pressing, that's right, just like that, push, no, no, not like that!" No matter how hard they tried, the poorly crushed tomatoes ended up on the earthen floor or splattered all around the girls rather than in the bowls placed next to the grinding stones. Katmé and Sennke traded looks that contained the memory of their grandmother and her grinding stone lessons. Turning vegetables and spices into powder or purée on the rudimentary rock. Tomatoes and garlic for beginners; ginger, groundnuts, njangsa, and pepper for more experienced hands. It took regular practice to develop the right technique. The twins, who lived in Akriba with modern appliances, had no reason to learn to use a grinding stone. Except that they refused to go back out to play with the village children and their many cousins. Since they'd spent thirty minutes of prayer getting up close and personal with the long, gray ebony box containing their grandmother's skeleton, Axelle and Alix, who were generally rather independent, had clung to their mother, refusing to leave her side.

The women—a dozen or so—were cooking, emptying beer crates, and sharing the latest salacious gossip from the village, despite the presence of Sennke the nun and the two young girls. The women roared with laughter. Axelle and Alix didn't understand what was so funny; Sister Marie of Divine Providence fondled her crucifix. Katmé figured she had a little less than an hour—the time it would take for blood alcohol levels to peak in the armada of women who had come to help her aunt showcase the many qualities of Fènn's gastronomic tradition—to sneak off with Sennke and the twins without upsetting them. She knew she could count on her ferocious aunt and equally ferocious cousins Rosine and Sokjou to make sure none of the evening's cooks made off with half the dishes when it was time to go home.

A new squirt of tomato landed on Sennke.

"I'm about ready to go in the pan with all the tomato on me," she said.

"Here, wipe it with this," said Mama Récia, taking off the cardigan she was wearing over her kaba ngondo. Then she turned to the girls. "That's enough for tonight. Now that we have the house here, we'll come back regularly. Soon you'll know how to use a grinding stone better than me."

When the girls stood up, their shoes were covered in dust. With their hands sticky from grinding tomato and garlic, they brushed the dust off their velvet pants and mohair sweaters. Sennke had nearly finished cleaning her dress when Alix, who had wanted to show off the amount of tomato she had successfully crushed, tripped and spilled the contents of the bowl onto the dress. To avoid falling, she grabbed onto Sennke's sleeve with her grubby hand too. A laugh erupted from Katmé. Sennke smiled shyly at first, then began laughing as well. Everyone around Katmé was used to her brusque, cold mannerisms, half-hearted smiles, big, dry, impenetrable eyes, laconic answers, and long silences, so when she let loose, her laugh could be unnerving. The stark contrast between the distant, undemonstrative—introverted, some thought—Katmé they were used to and this sudden fit of mirth made those around her so uncomfortable that they felt obliged to join in, regardless of how overblown the reaction seemed, given the cause. With the back of her hand, Katmé wiped away the crystal beads of glee that had formed at the corners of her eyes. Then she noticed the girls watching her. Their mother was laughing. The woman whose laugh had been replaced by the tight braids she laced flat against their scalps with syncopated movements, the woman whose laugh hadn't been heard at home since the day their father had said Eulalie Nana was never, ever to go see Uncle Samy at Central again. She was laughing.

"Sweet Jesus! I'm fully seasoned now!" exclaimed Sennke.

"Sorry, Auntie Sennke."

Sennke leaned down toward Alix, lifted the girl's chin with her index finger, and kissed her forehead. Mama Récia was mixing fresh corn with macabo leaves in a steel basin. Her daughters, Sokjou and Rosine, were peeling green bananas. The embers were red-hot. Sennke adjusted her coif, looked around as if searching for something while fiddling with her cross, then said, "Excuse me, I'm going to go change. I missed compline . . ."

"Can we come with you?" asked Axelle.

Sennke looked to Katmé for approval.

"Go ahead, I'll be there in a minute," said Katmé. She watched her little sister leave the kitchen holding her daughters' hands. Sennke arrived at midday the day before, after a fifteen-hour train journey. Solemn, enigmatic, and covered in dust. She'd slept all afternoon, then remained silent at dinner. Impressed by their aunt's cumbersome habit, Axelle and Alix studied her from their chairs, noticing how tired she looked. Long red tunic, scapular over her torso, coif—a sort of long, white cowl that covered her shoulders, neck, and chest, revealing only her face—and a black veil layered over a white one attached to the coif. Shrouded in these many layers of fabric, Sennke spoke little and softly. Conserving her words and her breath, she answered the questions Tashun asked without taking any initiative. The nun seemed to have fully replaced the impetuous young woman who could be biting in conversation and relentless in debate—the queen of quibbling and ridiculous sophisms. As she'd watched her sister pick at her plate, Katmé had thought back on just how dissimilar and close they'd been. Ten years earlier, she was the one who'd been afraid to say the wrong thing, the one who repeated a sentence ten times in her head before speaking it, or became talkative and stuttered, tripping over words in an attempt to line them up as fast as her thoughts; she was the one who wavered, going back and forth on her decisions, full of doubt. Back then Sennke was determined; she took up space, always knew what she wanted, and saw things through—that is until she quit her second year of medical school to take her vows. Last night, after the required small talk—the uncomfortable train, the long journey, the heat, the dust, and so on—Katmé had followed her little sister's lead and repudiated speech. How do you pick up a conversation you left off eleven years earlier? Tashun had spoken for everyone. Sennke said a prayer before the meal then asked to retire to her room as soon as the table was cleared. In the dead of night, Katmé, unable to sleep, nudged open her sister's door, hoping to find her awake. She was sleeping. But this morning, on the edge of the grave that contained their mother's disassembled skeleton, their interwoven fingers had, like an unconscious shrug, spontaneously conveyed the legacy of their childhood, of a time when they shared a room and a bed, a time when their mother's epidermis was still intact, before it had been peeled off by miles of asphalt. Had Sister Marie of Divine Providence truly vaporized Sennke with her big mouth and short skirts?

Katmé hugged and thanked the women who had come to help, shaking both their hands as she promised to have "a little something" brought to them the next day. Then she spoke to Mama Récia separately and left. As she walked down the side path Sennke and the girls had taken, she greeted and embraced. In the yard, she crossed paths with distant cousins, aunts, and uncles, conversed with nosey neighbors, choir members, and altar boys who had come to prepare morning Mass, and led several people who wanted to pay their respects to her mother's casket. She took the guide's father—a former classmate of her mother's, who had sold them the land where she'd been buried in the bush—to her side. The jilted lover who had "asked for her hand in marriage even after you were born, and again after your sister was born," he explained, his voice rich with emotion as they entered the living room. Thirty years later, it seemed he still hadn't gotten over his misfortune. "Patong was a good dancer, Patong was a good speaker, Patong's wallet jangled, he bin turn her head, what could I do?" Standing beside the casket, he mumbled prayers in the Fènn language and crossed himself multiple times. He took both Katmé's hands, kissed her palms, covering them in spittle and words of blessing, then left.

Instead of returning to the yard, she left the living room through an inside door that led to a series of bedrooms. To get to the second floor, where Sennke and the girls were surely waiting for her, she had to walk down the hallway (the former Turkish bath, through the beige granite kitchen, and around the first staircase, then climb the steps of a second to reach a narrow hallway that led to the terrace. The girls' bedroom was next to theirs (hers and Tashun's) at the far end of the same hallway. Télésphore Zambo, their architect, could only perform so many miracles.

She was about to turn the doorknob to the girl's room when the voices coming through the varnished wood barrier gave her pause.

"Do you pray a lot where you live?" asked Alix.

"You can never pray too much, my sweet girls. The world needs prayers, so whenever I can, I pray."

"Do you pray for us too?"

"Now I do. Before meeting you yesterday, I didn't even know your pretty little faces existed. I prayed for your mother."

"Mama didn't tell you when we were born?"

"The place where I live is very far away, you know. It's hard for news to reach us."

"We're sorry about the tomatoes." Now it was Axelle.

"Look, I cleaned it up and it's all gone, not a spot left. Your mother and I did the same thing when our grandmother taught us how to use the grinding stone. It's normal. In a few months, you'll be experts."

"Did your grandmother massage your breasts with the little stone like she did Mama's?"

Katmé didn't hear an answer. Sennke must have nodded.

"You have big, big breasts. Mama's are *mingili.*"

"What's it like living in a convent?" asked Alix.

"It's like . . . living with your family, your brothers and sisters, but we devote our lives to loving God, with Jesus as our constant companion."

"Will we ever visit you where you live?" Alix ventured.

"I hope so, my sweet girls. I'll talk to your mother about it. Good night, girls."

"Good night, Auntie Sennke."

Katmé had kept her ear glued to the door and barely had time to stand up straight before Sennke opened it. Katmé resisted the urge to go in and kiss the girls, instead following her sister into the confined passageway. Sennke suggested they go pray with their mother in the living room.

"Again? We've prayed so many times today I lost count!"

"One little prayer, Kat. Just the two of us."

"What about your compline? I thought it was urgent?"

They trotted down the hall, one after the other, until they reached the terrace. There hadn't been enough time to finish putting in electrical sockets and light switches in this part of the house, but light from the round, full moon splashed onto the tile floor. Katmé couldn't help but notice the thatched roof on Aleksandre's house on the other side of the pond made tame by the diaphanous light of the celestial body.

"I'll say my compline before I go to sleep."

"An umpteenth prayer won't bring her back, you know."

Sennke let out a short laugh, then turned around to face her sister. "Are you still mad at her, Kat?" she asked in a voice aiming for indulgence, though her gaze was full of reproach. "You know you're fighting with a skeleton, right?" She smiled softly and added, "Not even a complete skeleton . . ."

"A truly *little* prayer, okay? Not one of Mama Récia's traps. I've had my fill of *Ave*s for the week."

"We'll pray for Samy too. We'll ask the Virgin to intercede on his behalf in heaven, if she can."

"Hmm . . ."

As they made their way downstairs to the wake room, they heard a muffled bang followed by a clamor outside. Power outage. Was it the grid? Or the breaker? While waiting for the generator to come online, they carefully climbed back up the stairs and returned to the terrace, where they got comfortable on the wicker armchairs that should have been taken back into the sitting room at nightfall. Through the Plexiglas balustrade, they could make out dozens of lit candles in the yard below; the villagers had come prepared. The flames leaned this way and that according to the whims of the mountain breeze. A memorial candlelight procession. Katmé listened in vain for the distinctive roar of the generator coming to life. She'd recently hired a new caretaker to watch over the compound; he lived with his family in one of the outbuildings. It seemed he'd have to turn it on manually. Hidden away in the shadows above the crowd, Sennke and Katmé had a clear view of the figures coming and going below, gathered at the counters to secure ground-beef sandwiches, fried fish, draught beer, plastic-bag whisky, and raffia wine. Like at an ordinary party that drags on, they'd close the bar at two or three o'clock in the morning so the merrymakers, impressed by this "real wake," by this "real time of mourning," "not at all like the so-called time of mourning they'd participated in at So-and-So's house," would finally leave. So they could go home and rest up, to come back a few hours later without missing a morsel of the feast that would conclude the funeral.

19

They sat with their backs to the chalky moon. Katmé could hear her little sister breathing. It was slow, deep, regular, almost a purr; as if she'd been lulled to sleep by the ballad sung by the frogs, crickets, and bats perched in the eucalyptus trees. Her clothes smelled of woodfire, ash, and smoke. Her shapeless dress, oversized blouse, and the cardigan Mama Récia had lent her hadn't hindered Axelle's inspection, which had spotted her aunt's "big, big breasts." In middle school they'd called her "Chesty." Her upturned eyes gave her a wild, feline allure; her full, welcoming lips made her look kind, even when she was angry and saying the cruelest things, which was often when they were teens; her fingers were slender, her feet gracefully arched, and her round, shapely backside was the ember that set all the boys aflame when she wore tight clothes. "God was full of energy the day he created you!" a classmate had told her one day.

"Senn," Katmé began.

"Huh?"

"Do you remember when I was the wailing wall for all of your rejected suitors?"

Her little sister didn't answer right away. "That's all in the past," she finally whispered.

"Are your feet still freezing all the time? Who warms them up for you now?"

"Call me big sister and I'll let you go!" said Sennke, bursting into laughter. Katmé joined her. "No one warms them up for me anymore. No one at all, Katinétou . . ."

Even after Sennke had spent a year as a postulant and two as a novice, Katmé still hoped her little sister might change her mind and realize her place wasn't in the convent, that she wasn't meant to live dressed up like Mrs. Claus in her blood-red tunic and white button-up shirt with her thick hair hidden away beneath an austere veil, sleeping in a cold cell, spending her days with other Mother Christmases who were nothing to her; far from the only true sister Providence had given her. The last time she'd seen Sennke was at the end of her novitiate period, when she professed her temporary vows. When she'd received the invitation to Sister Marie of Divine Providence's perpetual vows, visions of her sister being buried alive to Gregorian chants danced before her eyes, so she'd tucked the invitation away in a closet. Seeing her little sister's sweet, determined face again now was too much. Sennke could have become a diocesan sister and lived in Akriba, the same city as her, if she felt so strongly about devoting her life to God; they could have continued to see one another. But no, she wanted the works: the convent! Loosening the ties that bound them was, for Katmé, a way to lessen her suffering, a way to stop ruminating about what she should and shouldn't have done to annihilate Sennke's distressing interest in monastic life. She must have done something to make her sister want to get away, to make her prefer the cloister and Jesus's love to her own. But what? It had been eleven years now and she still didn't know.

"Married to Jesus . . . A guy who can't even make you come . . ."

"Katmé!"

"Sorry, sorry, I take it back."

Sennke—a bundle of admonishments in a shapeless tunic—left her chair and made her way to the far end of the terrace. Sister Marie of Divine Providence did not have Sennke's sense of humor or her ability to put Katmé in her place with biting witticisms. Katmé stood up and joined her sister, who kept her eyes trained on the lines of inebriated guests below, which had grown even longer.

"I really am sorry, Senn. I didn't mean to upset you."

"I'm not upset, Katmé," she replied as she turned around to face her sister, leaning on the balustrade.

"You're doing a good job of pretending, then."

"Don't let the devil worm his way into your mockery. He's sly. Clever. He often uses humor to destroy, to do his work by tricking God's children. Don't let him use you . . ."

Katmé stifled an exasperated sigh. "I said I was sorry!"

The zigzagging halo of a flashlight on the stairs announced a visitor. Instinctively, the sisters moved closer to one another. The power was still out, the girls were sleeping in the room next door, the women were in the traditional kitchen, and the revelers in the yard came from all sorts of backgrounds. Who on earth could it be? The beam came closer. The caretaker, Kossam, appeared. He needed money to buy some diesel at the gas station downtown, the generator tank was empty, the outage was from the grid, not the breaker. In other words, there was no point hoping the national electrical company would get the power back on before the wee hours, or worse, the next day, or even two or three days later.

Kossam left and Sennke adjusted her coif. "Goodnight, Kat. I have my compline to say. I'll pray for Samy, for the Virgin to wrap him in her protective mantle until he's released." Since she and Kizito had failed so many times, Katmé had preferred not to tell Sennke that he was scheduled to be released on bail on Monday. Conventional wisdom in Haut-Fènn says that you don't announce a pregnancy, you welcome a child.

"I have my doubts about your Virgin's ability to free Samy. My life would be as simple as yours if I still believed in that sort of thing. I've become a practicing nonbeliever, Senn."

"A practicing nonbeliever . . . You're only saying that because it sounds so clever, aren't you? You and Samy were always so good at that. Expressions so catchy that people didn't even notice just how empty they were. A practicing nonbeliever . . . You don't lose your faith like your keys, Katmé. You're a daughter of the Virgin. You can't deny it, even if you wanted to. Samy didn't choose the easiest path—"

"Because you think Samy chose this? You think he woke up one morning wondering how to fill his day and decided to ruin the rest of his existence by loving men?"

"So he *is* homosexual . . . You've never come out and said it before. Then they haven't wrongfully accused him . . ."

Katmé bit her lip; she'd spoken without thinking.

"To be honest, I'm not surprised. Do you remember the day he came over with a bouquet of daisies for Mama Récia? I knew then that there was something off about him."

"That there was something *off* about him?" objected Katmé, her voice climbing. "What do you mean?"

"Easy, Katmé. No need to take such a prosecutorial tone," Sennke replied as she left the balustrade, returned to the wicker chair, and pressed her palms and fingers together over her chest. "What I mean is that he seemed a little too drawn to girly things. Flowers, helping his mother in the kitchen, knitting, and even the way he walked and spoke. He looked like a person on his way to masculinity but who hadn't made it to the end of the journey, as if he'd gotten off at the wrong station, two stops too early, unfinished, really, you know what I mean."

Katmé came to stand across from her sister, hands on her hips, forcing Sennke to look up at her. "I suppose this is the sort of simplistic conclusion cloistered people reach? To think that you finished two years of medical school before cutting yourself off from the real world! I can hardly believe you just said that!"

"Don't get angry," said Sennke, holding out her hand. "Come sit down, Katinétou."

Refusing her sister's outstretched hand, Katmé returned to her seat.

"Kat, you love Samy so much that you're willing to accept that he has inverted the order of things. God loves Samy, but He doesn't love the sin he's committing."

"But who are you and your lot to decide what's a sin and what isn't? You should have heard the homily Monsignor Umtu gave at the cathedral in Akriba when Tashun asked for that so-called Mass of repentance for sinners. When he speaks, nuance is on leave."

"The clergy aren't an example of perfection either. What I said about Samy is true for all of us. God loves us. He doesn't love sin."

Katmé shook her head and turned toward her little sister. "Sister Marie of Divine Providence, huh? You want to know the truth, Senn? Heaven, purgatory, angels, hell, and all that—I don't believe in any of it anymore. Don't ask me how I got here, all I know is that it started when you left to join the Redemptoristines. Something in me started to shrivel. Our mother, you, Samy. The way Mama Récia told us not to have friends who weren't Catholic because we wouldn't see them again in heaven. The sheer quantity of nonsense we had to choke down! If the God you believe in doesn't like Samy's choices, when in reality he didn't choose any of it, then he can fuck off!"

Katmé immediately regretted her brutal sincerity. She could see her sister was stunned. Sennke cracked her knuckles in the wan gleam of the moon. "Don't be angry with me, Senn . . . Come on, I don't want to ruin what little time we have together . . ."

Katmé stifled the urge to take her sister's hand. Sennke was there with her. Until Monday. On Monday morning, she'd vanish. Again. Unless there was a third funeral for their mother, it would be some time before they had a new opportunity to see one another. So why try?

Sennke broke the silence, her voice heavy. "It's not easy for me to hear what I've just heard. All I can say is that no matter what happens, no matter what has happened, remember that the Lord alone has the last word. You must be humble enough to accept God's will."

Katmé lost her temper. "Was it God's will that Samy should rot in prison for four months? God's will for him to risk the death penalty? Why? Can you even tell me?"

"Katmé . . . Nothing happens without the will of the Father. You'll find the answer to your question in prayer."

"I'll find the answer to my question in prayer? Stop talking like a Sunday school teacher, for pity's sake! I'm still waiting for Him to tell me why you took off."

"There's so much resentment in you, Katmé. Is that why you didn't come to my perpetual profession or answer my letters?"

"You chose to leave, to leave me. What was left to say after that?"

"Did you even wonder whether it might be a true vocation for me? If I'd felt a calling so strong, stronger than anything this world had to offer, a voice that pulled me in, that transcended me? The only thing that matters to you is you, you and your feelings, you and your love for me, you and your desire to take charge of my life, you who knew better what choices were right for me. You wanted me to come live with you after you were married, you wanted me to be yours, but I couldn't be your doll and let you braid my hair until the end of time. You're only two years older than me but you acted like you were my mother. You probably don't remember the first time I tried to talk to you about the call I was hearing and how it troubled me, but do you know what you told me? 'Don't insult my intelligence, I know you better than you know yourself.' 'Don't insult my intelligence,' as if it had anything to do with intelligence. As for knowing me better than I know myself, it turned out you were wrong. I'm happy with my community, I've found my place. It was my vocation, and you didn't understand, couldn't accept it. My community is—"

"Your so-called vocation came from somewhere," Katmé said, cutting off her sister. "You became a nun because everyone harped on and on about how our parents weren't married, how we were the children of adultery and that we had to wash ourselves of original sin, and so on. Instead of staying to face the world, you chose to split. A refugee among the Redemptoristines, what an enviable fate. The community, the community—it sounds more like a cult!"

Sennke leapt to her feet, furious. Katmé followed suit. They loomed across from one another.

"I'm living the life I chose! You just can't accept that anyone would choose this life, a life of humility, without title, without recognition, without glory, and without money. You think you chose better because you stayed to face the world? It's not my place to judge your life, but are you really facing it? Your husband takes care of you, you don't work even though you have a degree, you live in comfort and safety, in a bubble funded by our country's corrupt government. I'm not saying this because I'm angry, but because it's true. I get up every morning at four o'clock, and after my prayers I work all day: the beehives, the apple trees, the cassava crop, cooking, laundry, the orphans at the school. Despite all your husband's money, you didn't even tend Mama's grave. We could have twisted our ankles out in the bush; thank goodness the guide knew the way. You let Mama's grave rot, and apparently half the Zambuenan government will be at the funeral. Why is that? All the money you've spent on this house and the vault, I would have used it to pay the school fees of every child in the eastern provinces who spends their days in the streets because their parents can't even afford to feed them every other day. Unlike you, I cried for my mother, I understood that she was dead and that Mama Récia could never replace her. A phony mother, an escape into marriage, a phony brother in Samy, are you sure you're living your true life now, Katmé?"

Katmé could tell that it was Sennke's heart beating now beneath her red tunic. Sister Marie of Divine Providence wouldn't have spoken like that. A feeling of great loneliness washed over Katmé. She had missed her sister much more than Sennke had missed her all these years apart.

"Each of us fled in our own way. You won't change my mind about that," said Katmé, her voice quavering.

Sennke shook her head, disappointment written clearly on her face. "So obsessed with being right. You haven't changed. I became a nun because that was my path, my mission in life. It was *your* dream for me to become a doctor, not mine. I became what I wanted to be. When will you accept that? It's been nearly twenty-one years since Mama passed away, and you still can't accept her death; I've been gone for eleven years, and you still can't accept that I took a path that didn't suit you. Samy is in prison, and you talk about it as though you're willing to fight God himself for putting him there. Get down on your knees, Kat, and beg the Lord to free Samy. That's what I'd do in your shoes in any case."

"Do you honestly expect me to stand back and leave Samy's freedom in your God's hands? Never! Never, do you hear me? There's nothing at all up there, Sennke, nothing! Just a lot of hot air! And seeing you wear that horrible uniform, watching you sacrifice your gifts, your talents, for hot air, for a thief, for God the kleptomaniac, it makes me sick."

Sennke's face hardened into stone. She stood tall, almost threateningly across from Katmé.

"The Virgin has given you so much, you say! What she *should* give you is her pity!" shouted Katmé.

Sennke took a step back. "I . . . I'm going to say my compline prayers now."

"Oh, Senn, wait, I'm sorry. I'll come with you, we can't—"

Sennke raised her open palm toward Katmé.

Alone on the terrace, the feeling of extreme loneliness that Katmé had felt moments before crushed her again. She looked up at the sky. Was there really no one up there? The pallid moon was at its zenith. The vague, dark shape you could see in its middle was Lot's wife, their grandmother had always said. The woman carrying a baby on her back who had been turned into a pillar of salt for disobeying her husband. She appeared when the moon was full to remind women of the punishment reserved for any who would dare flout the word of the Lord, any who were not "women of virtue." It was under a full moon like this one that she had for the first time fallen to her knees before Aleksandre and unbuttoned his pants. She would have liked to be able to confide in her little sister about that, instead of having a futile, hurtful exchange about Sennke's vocation and what was left of her own faith. But Sister Marie of Divine Providence was not her little sister. Samy would be released from prison on Monday. On Monday, he'd be back, and on Tuesday she'd see her brother again. The one person she could share everything with. Katmé's eyes were drawn to the column of smoke rising from the mudbrick kitchen, which she could only partially make out through the branches of the eucalyptus trees. She thought back to the women and the dirty jokes they told as they cooked earlier. How many of them had become Lot's wife?

20

She opened her eyes. Tashun was staring down at her. "Samuel was released at eleven o'clock last night." Katmé's mouth watered as she propped herself up on her elbows. Her saliva tasted like the untamable fibers and sweet, juicy flesh of ripe cassimango. "I wanted to tell you last night when I came home from your father's, but you were asleep." The alarm clock on the nightstand read six o'clock. In the enclosure behind the woodfire kitchen, the roosters hailed the dawn with their cock-a-doodle-doos, the goats bleated, and the crickets chirped. Through the shutters she glimpsed a small piece of sky, the tops of the eucalyptus trees, and the cheerful birds perched on their branches. The sun was rising, finally swallowing the months-long night.

Katmé cleared her throat. "I thought he . . ."

She had almost said, "I thought he was being released on Monday." Instead she said, "I thought . . . that it was impossible to have him released until the elections were over."

"It wasn't easy. What's that saying again? An incorruptible man simply costs more than most? Look, this is coming out tomorrow," he said, brandishing *Counterpoint.* His photograph featured on the cover above the caption:

TASHUN ABBIA: THE FUTURE OF HAUT-FÈNN

"Samuel was scheduled to be released on Monday, the first day of the campaign, a terrible idea. The Pankeus got him back a day early, they're pleased. I didn't say anything because I wanted to surprise you."

Katmé feigned astonishment. Thanked him. Leaning against the headboard and a stack of pillows, she flipped through the journal, which focused on the gubernatorial race in Haut-Fènn. A dithyrambic editorial on would-be Governor Abbia by Kizito Pankeu, articles praising his extraordinary accomplishments as prefect of the capital, photos of him on nearly every page, an endless interview (his vision for the future and goals for the province), obsequious text boxes devoted to the Old Man and the APM. The final pages contained a hasty presentation of the other candidates.

"Here, look at this too. It'll be published daily for a month."

Katmé took the four-page leaflet from his outstretched hand: *Campaign Tam-Tam.*

"Kizito and his team will publish an issue every morning for thirty days. Articles on my campaign. With the health center, the gifts I'm handing out to the villagers, your father's backing, and support from *Counterpoint,* if I lose it'll be because the devil himself made a fool of me."

Katmé reassured him half-heartedly. There was nothing to worry about, God was campaigning for him. While he sketched a glorious picture of their glorious lives in the governor's mansion, she was thinking about Kizito's side of the story. He and Sita Félicie had been ushered into the prefecture after nightfall to plead their case for Samuel's release; he was depressed, too skinny, catatonic, "withered from the inside out." Tashun suggested a "family agreement." *Counterpoint,* which had always been the voice of the opposition, a social and intellectual alternative to the Old Man's regime, would become the APM's *Pravda,* relaying every detail of the campaign in Haut-Fènn. Kizito Pankeu cost more than most. His price was named Samuel. Tashun Abbia, a scumbag hustler through and through.

Samy was free. Free! At last! Today was the funeral. Monday the campaign launch and unveiling ceremonies. And on Tuesday she'd finally see Samy again.

Katmé burst into Sennke's room. Dressed in a long-sleeved, pink-and-blue, polka-dot nightgown with a Peter Pan collar, her little sister was sitting up in bed with the covers tucked around her waist. When Sennke saw Katmé, she placed her left index finger over her mouth, raised the prayer beads in her right hand, gestured for her to come in, and whispered "rosary." The rosary. Three times around the strand of beads. Three repetitions of the five decades on the little beads, prayers and mysteries on the big ones, she would be champing at the bit for over an hour and a half if Sennke had just begun. Katmé took off her shoes, lifted the blanket off the bed, and lay down underneath it. A few minutes later, eyes closed and beads still in hand as she mumbled a few *Aves,* Sennke trapped Katmé's legs between her own. Her little sister's ice-cold feet! Katmé tried in vain to escape her vicelike grip, fighting for a moment before giving up. Sennke had had plenty of practice. As a little girl, a teenager, and almost up until she left for the convent, she had often rubbed her frozen lower limbs against Katmé's to warm them up. They would fight beneath the sheets on days when Katmé didn't feel like playing the hot water bottle, when she wasn't in the mood for Sennke's little game. Without letting go, Sister Marie of Divine Providence crossed herself, kissed the rosary cross, wrapped the strand around her wrist like a bracelet, and leaned closer to her sister with a playful wink. "Call me big sister and I'll let you go." Sennke flipped over, loosened her hold for a moment, and collapsed on top of her sister. With her legs placed firmly on either side of Katmé, she put all her weight on her sister and tried to keep a straight face as she repeated, "Come on, say it and I'll let you go. Just accept it, I'm the big sister here." Katmé shook her head and laughed so uproariously it brought tears to her eyes and prevented her from gathering the strength to push Sennke off. They'd traveled twenty years back in time, they'd never left the Enseignants neighborhood, their room, or their bed, their mother wasn't dead, her little sister hadn't run off to join the Redemptoristines. After a while, Katmé complied, feigning reluctance. "Big sister, big sister, you're the big sister! All right? Will you let me go now?" Sennke slid onto her side and raised her fingers in a victory symbol. Katmé shook her head and got out of bed to catch her breath.

Then, unable to wait any longer, she announced, "Samy has been released, Senn! He's free." Sennke's eyes widened as she threw off the covers, tossed her rosary onto the nightstand, and threw herself into Katmé's arms.

"Our good Lord took pity on him, he heard our prayers. Last night, after I left you, I prayed the rosary for him before going to sleep. God is great, God is truly great."

They began spinning around the room, their nightgowns fluttering through the air. The euphoria that seized them made quick work of their eleven years of separation.

Monsignor Umtu invited the family to say a word or two about Madeleine. Unlike Katmé, Sennke, and Mama Récia, who were succinct, and Innocent Patong, who opted for silence, Tashun invoked God, the ancestors, the weather, the party, the president, and Uncle Ambroise. His godfather took the stage next, launching straight into a panegyric about his godson, a man of honor, responsibility, and commitment, with shoulders broad enough to carry the demands of the governorship. A son who was the pride of his parents, his family, his friends, and the party, and who was ready to put his talent and his many personal qualities to work for the magnificent Haut-Fènn region if its residents put their trust in him in thirty days' time. Tashun hadn't chosen the Haut-Fènn province at random, since his heart had been rooted here for some time—"Isn't that right, my dear Katmé?" Katmé's eyes met those of Aleksandre Fortès, who was sitting with the other Mival executives in a row perpendicular to hers. She watched as Tashun's party friends raised their hands to applaud and then quickly lowered them again. The campaign officially began on Monday, the APM had gotten a head start. Uncle Ambroise returned to his seat. Djama whispered something in his ear and he stood back up, embarrassed. He had forgotten to say a word about the deceased. He floundered through a few trite observations about his exceptional godson's mother-in-law, then sat down again. Katmé's saliva became as bitter as the flesh of green cassimango.

While she was sharing her joy over Samy's release with Sennke, a team of young party volunteers had been outside decorating the yard with campaign materials. In addition to the covered porch, every spruce, eucalyptus, tent, wall, and chair was adorned—the APM was everywhere. Banners six feet long had been nailed to eucalyptus trees, huge signs staked into the ground at the entrance to the compound. Even Mama Récia, who let everything slide with her son-in-law-sent-by-God-himself-in-his-immeasurable-bounty, had been unable to stifle a "this is all a bit much, isn't it?" as she passed the television crew setting up a camera near the altar. Her son Tanga, "future Director of Statistics for the governor if Tashun is elected," had raised both eyebrows but refrained from commenting. Not long after, Sennke had calmly and methodically torn down every poster on the walls of the pavilion where their mother's casket awaited, sheltered from the heavy clouds. When he'd greeted Katmé before the ceremony, Aleksandre had noticed she was staring at a torn poster of Tashun's sales-rep smile. "Here we are." They hadn't seen one another for a month, and now here they were. But where exactly?

Six hundred, eight hundred, it was hard to determine exactly how many people attended her mother's funeral. Ministers, CEOs, prefects, members of the Central Committee, editors-in-chief, journalists, the local branch of the FZC, villagers, and busybodies. The crowd made it difficult to believe that Madeleine Lapteu hadn't been a major public figure in Zambuena, that her death wasn't recent, and that most of these people had never even met her. A dozen tents had been set up on either side of the pavilion. There weren't enough chairs for everyone, so latecomers stood. Twenty years ago, only thirty people or so had turned up for her funeral. The yard overflowed with plastic funeral wreaths. The inordinately tall bouquet of real flowers sent by the FZC's honorary president, the Mother of the Nation and wife of the Old Man, had been placed at the entrance to the vault. With their party scarves draped ostentatiously around their necks, Tashun's APM colleagues sang the couplets to the Gregorian chants and recited the credo and the Pater Noster in Latin without so much as a glance at the booklet they'd been given. Their intimate familiarity with the rituals of Mass and the visible ease of their genuflections reminded Katmé that they had all attended religious boarding schools. Like Samy.

During the sign of peace, when the faithful shake hands or hug their neighbors, Katmé watched Aleksandre leave his row and make his way toward her unequivocally. Her stomach tied itself in knots. He shook her hand, then Sennke's, Mama Récia's, and Tashun's. Silky-smooth palm and friendly smile. Whose skin, whose body, were those soft hands that had caressed her own skin and body so many times caressing now? Katmé scanned the crowd. Such honorable women, they looked so pious. As she had on the terrace the night before, she wondered how many of them had become Lot's wife, how many of them had found and then given up "something to calm their nerves" as Djama prudishly put it.

His dick and his DVDs, sure. But not only. Their affair—he hated it when she used that word and preferred "relationship," which she hated—helped her to triumph over Samy's incarceration, the preparations for her mother's funeral, and Tashun's excesses; in short, it had kept her mentally afloat. "We're at a point in our relationship where we need to talk about what it means." Nothing made sense anymore! She was so caught off guard that, "You aren't suggesting we get married, are you Aleksandre?" was all she could think to reply, still addressing him formally. "Who said anything about marriage? Grow up!" he'd replied, annoyed. She could go back to teaching, dissolve her meaningless marriage, take back her independence, and they could live their story out in the open, like adults, she didn't love her husband anymore, hated her role as the wife of the prefect, so what was holding her back? She objected that it would be a scandal and cause chaos in their girls' lives. "Unhappy couples often hide behind children when they aren't brave enough to live bigger lives," he had countered. Despite three children, he had been brave. Aleksandre. A divorcé who followed his impulses. Letting the children's mothers raise them alone. Selfish with his time. With his life. And he dared bring up bravery. If being brave enough to live a bigger life meant neglecting her responsibilities as a mother, sacrificing the future of her children, and upending her world just because he'd taken her body to the peak of female desire, just because she turned into a fountain when he touched her, because she found herself in another universe when his tongue explored her; well, then maybe he was right, she wasn't done being full of herself.

Two divorces, three children, and yet a disconcerting sentimentalism she'd failed to see at first had survived in Aleksandre. He wanted to be with her in a place where they could walk hand in hand and lock eyes over their meals with no need to hide; to drip mango and pomegranate juice onto her lips before feeling his tongue on her, in her; to taste the sweetness of her skin at any time of day or night. He wanted unbridled lovemaking, impassioned debate, incontrollable laughter, groundnut stew and rice, and legs interwoven beneath the covers while it rained outside. Was this the same man who had said he didn't expect anything from their relationship?

"We're at a point in our relationship where we need to talk about what it means."

She had thought they were on the same page! Apparently her book was right-side up, his upside down. Soon after their first night together, he had started writing her letters wreathed in hearts, notes that had the flavor and consistency of soursop: sweet, suave, and fibrous. He would read them to her when they got together and demand that she reply. Which she did while he cooked. He had bought flowerpots and filled them with nothing but white lilies since he'd found out they were her favorite flower. He would give her gifts which she left at his house, and some evenings, after telling her about the hard day he'd had at the construction site, he would light cinnamon- and cardamom-scented candles, lay her naked on the bed, and massage her body at length with coconut oil. Every time she knocked on his door, she knew she would laugh, bicker, and, once he was inside her, cry. Afterward they'd have lighthearted philosophic discussions and share stories from thoughtfully chosen parts of their lives, treading carefully to avoid hurting one another. Aleksandre's house was the only place she could talk about Samy, Zambuena, and humankind without holding back; she could discover new filmmakers, leave money and letters for Samy, and meet with Kizito in secret.

Like all lovers, she and Aleksandre had broken up and gotten back together more than once. He wanted more, he wanted better, he wanted everything, her, the girls, a new life, he wanted to . . . try. Where did Tashun fit in all his plans? He would brush the question aside with a wave of his hand. Risk her marriage, her family, and her reputation to "try"? Katmé started to dread evenings with Aleksandre, until he came out with it: "Let's get married then! Since you love being married so much, let's get married!" He'd started sleeping with other women, a return to sexual therapy—or so he'd said, though how could she know for sure? That night, in his bedroom with its red walls, for a brief moment, a fleeting moment, because she'd seen an unusual glimmer in his eyes, she'd thought to herself, "He's in love with me! I'm breaking his heart!" She'd immediately scolded herself: breaking his heart! As if you could break the heart of a fifty-one-year-old man with three children who had been divorced twice, abandoned by his Black mother at birth, neglected by his father, raised by his white grandfather, become a ruthless corporate lawyer turned corporate social responsibility executive, a former alcoholic and cocaine addict who had wandered with his ghosts through five African countries before Mival hired him and he dropped anchor in Fènn's Tam-Tam neighborhood. Maybe you can scratch a heart like that, maybe even crumple it if you try hard enough, but break it? A heart like that doesn't break.

She hadn't seen Aleksandre since. One morning she woke up to find a letter slipped through the crack under her door. She'd read it, ripped it up, taped it back together, read it again, wrapped it in a black plastic bag, and buried it behind the mudbrick kitchen.

I stretched out my arms and cautiously embraced
The shadow of our memories.
I close my eyes so as not to see
That you are gone.
I drift through the sea of possibilities that I imagine
And reimagine again and again.
Wherever I go, I crash into your absence.
I've tamed the silence, which people say
Is great.
And yet I feel weak.

I dreaded the power of distance,
Which people say erases
Even the most stubborn passion.
But my memory retains every image.

I walked the path of indifference,
Which people say tamps out all flames.
And yet I burn. Like yesterday.
Like the day before.

I gave up the bubble which people say
Is folly incarnate.

Yet only the days of madness spent
In that cocoon feel tangible to me.

I wanted to file your name away in the gallery of oblivion, in
The hall of ice that never melts,
I flirted with enchanting tomorrows,
I yearned for obsolescence.
Yet nothing has withered.

I blotted out the best of us to feed
On the worst, which people say speeds the healing process.
Yet I
Am far from convalescence.

This walk to Canossa has taken its toll,
Writing all this.
Not doing it would take a greater toll,
Like a final breath before oblivion.

I miss our stubborn quarrels
I miss our silences
I miss our shouting matches
I miss our laughter
I miss our intellectual jousting
I miss our games of seduction
I miss your lips, your arms, the way you alone
Look longingly at me.
I even miss hearing you call me
a selfish little prick . . .

One day you said: I want you to be
A part of my life, I can't imagine you not being
A part of it, I want to travel the world with you,
Eat dinner with you, wake up by your side,
Be kidnapped by you from time to time.
See, I even miss

Our broken promises.
I've paid my tribute to pride.
I won't pay one to apathy.
I owe some debts to passion.

But I'll give it all up for reason. If that's the answer I
Receive once more in return.

The cold man with indifferent eyes she'd met in Tashun's office, the man she'd stood up to, the man at whom she'd lobbed the famous "I'm out," had fled. Because he saw in her something that she'd never been: a nurse for his future hopes. Despite his age, his experience, and his failed marriages, Aleksandre wanted to turn this parenthetical into a whole chapter, a daytrip into a long journey. It wasn't that she was reading the page right-side up and he upside down, it was quite simply that they weren't on the same page at all. Her heart heavy, she hadn't replied.

To take communion, she would have to walk up the aisle on the right, passing Aleksandre's row. She decided against it. No body of Christ for her today.

Her mother's coffin descended into the marble grave. Holy water, incense, prayers, singing, they closed the vault. During the meal, which Aleksandre didn't attend, Katmé laughed excessively, drawing reproachful glances from Tashun. When the last guests had left, Katmé stretched. The tension of the last few months was finally easing. The ceremony was over. Samy had been released from prison.

The next morning, she took Sennke to the train station. When she got home, Tashun found her. Ety was on the line, it was urgent. She picked up the receiver in the hallway.

21

Five teenage boys armed with wood-and-rubber slingshots had the pigeons in their sights. Pigeon meat was popular in Fènn and would fetch a good price. From the window of the idling bus, Katmé's eyes darted from the birds to the teens, from the teens to the birds, from the birds to the teens, from the teens to the birds, from the birds to the teens. The boys coordinated their efforts, catapulting their stones in a single volley. The projectiles hit four pigeons in the head, as well as an unfortunate robin who caught a stray pellet. The uninjured birds flapped their wings and disappeared in seconds. The pigeons that fell to the ground weren't dead, so the teens snapped their necks before tossing their bodies into the raffia bags they carried across their chests. The robin was of no use to them. It lay suffering in the dirt until it was crushed to death by the station foot traffic. Katmé squeezed her hands between her thighs to keep them from shaking.

She had climbed aboard the first bus to Akriba that seemed to be ready for departure. "Just three more customers and we'll be on our way," said the driver of the good ship *Haters Gonna Hate,* revving the engine. Katmé bought all three tickets, but the bus hadn't budged. The engine kept running. The past ten years free from the trials of public transportation had dulled her most basic reflexes. Fake passengers were sitting on the bus to hide the real number of empty seats. Every time a ticket was sold, a fake traveler got off the bus. Katmé could be waiting for ten minutes or three hours with no way of knowing who was really traveling or when they'd leave. She tried to buy more tickets, but one of the driver's impostors stopped her. "There's no point, my sister. Even if you buy every seat and he leaves with an empty bus, he'll stop as soon as he sees a passenger on the side of the road, slowing you down even more. Keep your money and wait. Where are you running to anyway? People come to an end, time goes on. Be patient, my sister." As she watched the fake passengers leave one by one, she realized she had been the first paying customer. Tashun had refused to let her take the car. "My money paid for that car, so keep your hands off it." So she'd decided to take a bus to get back to Akriba on the double. She leaned back against the seat and closed her eyes.

At the Hommes Capables Hospital, Sita Félicie stood in the doorway to keep Katmé out of the morgue. "You can't see him, Katmé. No one can. Thanks to you and your husband, we have more than our share of misfortune. Thank you for having his body transferred here. We'll manage to pay for it ourselves. I don't want any more of your money, just forget about us. Kizito is all I have left, so please, forget about him too. Now, please, go."

"And . . . the funeral?"

"You won't be there, Katmé."

"I can't come to Samy's funeral?"

"No, you can't. You've done quite enough already. Because of you and your husband, his name has been dragged through the mud, the name his father gave him. You're the reason he's dead, they used him to get to you, and you know what, I'll never forgive you for that. Never, do you hear me? It's all your fault! You're the one who encouraged his nonsense, told him he could be an artist when he had a real job, well look where your money led. If it hadn't been for that miserable show, this never would have happened; he died without seeing anything through—not his career as an artist or his profession as a teacher, no family; he saw misfortune through to the end, that much is certain. All those awful months in prison and now this torture, the things the people from this terrible neighborhood where you paid his rent did to him. Please, just go!"

Two days earlier, at her mother's dilapidated grave, Katmé swore to herself she'd never cry again. She'd dropped Sennke off at the train station, hugging her sister so close she couldn't breathe, and she hadn't cried. She'd spoken to Ety and called the director of the Hommes Capables Hospital to tell him Samuel—or rather Samuel's body—was on its way, and she hadn't cried. She'd seen Aleksandre again at the unveiling ceremony for the highway, he'd shaken her hand, smiled at her, and something in her had quivered, but no tears came. Outside the health center, once the speeches were over, the ribbon cut, congratulations given, and champagne glasses filled, Tashun had berated her when she announced that she was returning to the capital, saying, "You can't blow me off on the first day of the campaign, there's the meeting with your father and the whole team this afternoon. If you leave, I'll beat the shit out of you, I swear I will, Katmé," and her eyes remained dry, she hadn't cried. Even when her father, Innocent Patong, said, "You're going to ditch us for that loser? Now that he's dead, what difference does it make whether you go now or in a year?" she hadn't cried. She'd simply noticed that life had saddled her with a dual misfortune: her mother's absence and her father's presence. So she evicted the latter from her heart the way you extract a chigger from the sole of your foot, the way you drive away a starving rabid dog. And Sita Félicie? She could blame Katmé all she wanted, she could banish and curse her, even exclude her from Samy's funeral, but Katmé wouldn't cry. Samy was dead and there was nothing left to hope for. Why cry?

22

Tomorrow, yes, tomorrow she'd do it, get out of bed, leave her room; after all, one day she'd be buried too, everyone would be buried one day, everyone would be dead. Tomorrow the myriad aches and the harsh white fog exhausting her would begin to diminish, retreat, and fade. There's no cure for the grief of losing a loved one, not even the thought of your own mortality. She was amazed that a human heart could bear the weight of such sorrow without fragmenting. Confined to her inner world after her mother's death, confined to her room since Sita Félicie kicked her out of the morgue—Katmé was surprised to find herself back in familiar territory. Hidden away in her room, she proudly bore the standard of misfortune draped over her shoulders; she wrapped herself in it like a cape fashioned from the scattered spores of a hallucination. Her thoughts, moving, liquid coils, flitted around her head as intense and mercurial as white flowers in the morning dew. She would jump out of bed, rush to the window, lift a corner of the curtain, and get lost in deep contemplation of the jacarandas and wrought-iron ladybug sculptures—Samy's early works, before he moved on to clay. All that was left of him was this small area outside the window, and pictures, of course—memories frozen in a joyful eternity. But happy memories can't be bottled. You can't sniff them like essential oils to get through hard days.

Mama Récia and Sokjou helped the steward tend to daily affairs at the residence. Bambili took Axelle and Alix to school and picked them up afterward. The guards sent away visitors. Katmé's bedroom stayed dark. Motto didn't go anywhere near the recalcitrant curtains and stopped changing the sheets. With his colleagues, he would complain, "Ah, *tété* wives, the money really does their heads in. They don't do anything like the rest of us. When that motorcycle killed my brother, the next morning, and I mean the very next morning, when the sun was still low-low in the sky, his wife went to sell puff-puff at the market, and then again that evening, she sold puff-puff. If she stayed hidden away in her room, lying in bed all day because her husband was dead, who would feed her children? Goodness! Someone who's not even family dies and you go and act like it's the end of the world!" In the afternoon, Mama Récia and Sokjou would go into the room, pull back the curtains, change the sheets if needed, and deliver a tray of food: toast spread with sweetened condensed milk. Katmé would eat the toast. In the evening, Axelle and Alix would visit. They would sit on the edge of the bed and tell her about their day at school, then ask when she'd be better. They knew their mother had been ill since Uncle Samy's death; they'd been unable to learn how and why he died, but they seemed to be coming around to the idea that their godfather, whom their father now praised, was gone. Thanks to Mama Récia and her implacable rhetoric about the Lord Jesus Christ and His heavenly will, the girls were taking the death of their godfather better than their mother. Balbine regularly delivered mail that had been sent to the prefecture. Tashun would open it on his rare visits. The campaign took up most of his time; he came home to kiss the girls and spend the night when he could, sleeping in the neighboring bedroom. In the days after Samuel's death, he would force himself on Katmé, using his saliva to make up for her lack of enthusiasm. As soon as he pulled out, the woman he'd once called his Fènn ice cube and his coldblooded animal, the woman he'd speculated was born without tear ducts, the woman he'd always respected because she never played the sentimental trump card used by most women he did business with in order to force his hand and squeeze him for more money—that woman would cry. "Mama's dead, Samy's dead, Mama's dead, Samy's dead, Mama's dead, Samy's dead." Tashun couldn't take the refrain anymore. Of course Mama's dead! Has been for over twenty years, in fact! Took long enough for her to notice. He thought he was doing a good deed getting Samy released, since they were so insistent, all to help out the Pankeus, but now! They'd wanted to circumvent the legal system, this was the result. Whose fault was that? The investigation? We can't lock up an entire neighborhood, damn it! The campaign was exhausting by day, and Katmé was ruining his nights. "Mama's dead, Samy's dead." He was tired of feeling like a third ghost, two was more than enough for her, he'd sleep in the next room.

At night, her eyes open for empty hours, Katmé would pore over *Emancipation,* rereading the statement from the police report on the accident that took place at sculptor Samuel Pankeu's studio:

> We went to get water from the well before school, on the way home we saw him, he was on his knees cutting purple flowers and talking too. At first we thought he was talking to someone next to him that we couldn't see, but he was talking to the purple flowers, that's what set us off. He plants flowers in our neighborhood, in our neighborhood there aren't any flowers, only at his place. We told him that girls plant flowers, not boys. He said, I'm in my yard, in my own home, I can do what I please. He got angry, but in the beginning we were the ones who were angry. The whole neighborhood knows what he's done, he's tainted our neighborhood. The buckets of water on our heads were heavy, we had to get home quick to eat our puff-puff before school, but we didn't like the way he was talking to us. He put his hands on his hips and told us that it was his yard, that he could do as he pleased. That annoyed us, a boy who's not really a boy telling us that, it annoyed us. And his hands on his hips and his big tadpole head. So I said, With your big fat head like a tadpole, and he said, Why are you calling me names ****, so I put down my bucket and the others did the same. We stepped over the gutter that separates his yard from the street and we pushed him so he'd take his hands off his hips, because he looked just like a girl, we just didn't want him planting any more purple flowers in our neighborhood. In the newspaper and on television they said the Aquatics neighborhood wasn't a good neighborhood, and our friends from other neighborhoods made fun of us, saying that in our neighborhood boys are like girls, when he doesn't even live here, but he talks about our neighborhood in his photos, and now everyone says he lives in our neighborhood, and he's the one bringing shame on us, and he took the photos to make fun of us, to say we're poor, that the Aquatics swim in the rain, that

we swim in dirty water, so we were angry. We pushed him, just a little, and we tripped him, and he fell in slow motion like a leaf, I'm sure he did it on purpose, who falls in slow motion? It looked like his foot slipped on the big iron thing in the yard, the one we soldered with him on neighborhood clean-up day, we'd soldered it with him using the rusty metal we'd picked up for him all over the neighborhood and at the little market over there. He fell and his head went thunk! He stayed down on the ground. We got scared and took off running. We ran and ran, and **** said we'd forgotten the buckets and our remés would kill us if we came home without them, so we went back for them. When we came back to get the buckets, he said he was going to press charges, that our parents are getting a summons to go to the police station and that the police are giving our parents a free ride, he wasn't even hurt but he wanted to make charges with the police! His clothes were dirty and a little ripped, that's all, we swear. We took our buckets and we left, but on the way, **** said, Revenge! Revenge! He said we should ruin his stupid purple flowers and the studio too. That way he gets scared and won't tell our parents, and he'll leave our neighborhood, because if our friends in other neighborhoods find out he got out of Central and is back in our neighborhood, the shame alone will kill us at school. We came back and he was talking to his dumb flowers, saying, Sorry, my beauties, Papa will take care of you now, Papa missed you. He was talking to the flowers like he was crazy or something. **** picked up a rock in the gutter and threw it, it hurt his ear. I threw the fourth rock, I know because **** said, give him gift number four. We were yelling, get out, get out of our neighborhood, girly boy, go away and don't ever say our names again girly boy. He covered his head and said, ****, why are you doing this to me? ****, what have I ever done to you? ****, why are you doing this to me? ****, ****, ****, why, why? He ran to hide in the studio while we were throwing stones, he ran away, a coward, what kind of adult runs away like that? It annoyed us that he ran off, it made us really, really mad, it set us off, he tried to close the studio door but he didn't have time. **** put his foot in the doorway, and all six of us pushed the door, we pushed and pushed as hard as we could until he backed away and let us in. We tripped him, he fell again, I was so ashamed, what kind of grown man falls down from a little pushing? He just kept begging, Leave me alone, leave me alone, get out of here, leave me alone, I won't say a thing to your parents, ****, ****, ****, ****, ****, ****, ****, please, have mercy, just leave me alone. We didn't have mercy for him because girly boys aren't like us real boys. My mother says that girly boys are the anti . . . anti . . . God? Anti . . . Jesus? Antichrist, you mean? Yes, that's it, Antichrist! And God doesn't love Antichrists. **** kicked him like a rotten cocoyam, we picked something up off the floor, like a part of a panther, it was heavy, **** helped me, he understood what I wanted to do, it pissed us off to hear a grown man begging like that, we dropped it on his willy. Thud, the blood came out! He was crying like a girl, like a baby! Like my little sister the day hot water spilled on her foot and she cried. We were laughing, a grown man crying like that. He was wearing white shorts which turned bright red in front, we took off his shorts to see. **** said that if he was a real boy then sperm would be pouring out of his willy along with the blood, but there was only blood. We thought it was funny to see that he had a real willy because my mama says that when boys act like girls, their willy disappears, he still had his willy and his willy was so full of blood. He was screaming, we were afraid someone outside would hear. We go to the well at five thirty in the morning to get water for our families so we can wash before school. Maybe it was already around six thirty. Since he was screaming so much, we said, be quiet, but he kept screaming. We locked the door to the studio, we know the studio well, we know where he keeps his dirty rags, we put two rags in his mouth, he kept opening his big frog eyes to look at us but with the rags we couldn't hear his voice anymore. Well, when I saw the rags, it made me feel strange and it scared me a little too, we used those rags to wipe our hands when he was showing us how to make terracotta jugs. I was scared because the rags reminded me of the jugs, we use to sell the jugs and make money off it, but when the police van came to give him his free ride, we stopped making jugs to sell at the market and our parents were mad. Afterward, **** said we were going to be late for school, that we had to go. I thought about the jugs too, and it made me a little sad. I used to come here and stay to watch him work in the studio. Well my father said that if he touched me he'll cut off his willy and shove it in his mouth so he can eat it, but I told my father that he never touched me. Well, it didn't make me sad because he's a bad man, a half-devil. He's bad even if he did teach us to make clay jugs, my mother says that girly boys do bad things at night when respectable people are sleeping. That's when someone started banging on the door, saying open up! Open up! Open up! We started to get scared. I recognized my father's voice, we opened the door, and he was there with other fathers and mothers, it was already eight o'clock in the morning! We were late for school. They headed to the well to look for us since we hadn't come home around six thirty as usual, and on the way they saw our water buckets next to the gutter in front of the studio. They didn't know that he was back to the neighborhood, because he came back in the night, no one knew he was back in the studio, my father got really, really mad, and said: You dare come back here, you disgusting pervert? You dare come back? We'll give you what you're asking for then, nasty beast! You came back to ruin our children? What's wrong with this country? They let you out? They set you free? We'll give you what you're asking for! One of our fathers took the rags out of his mouth and pulled him outside, he kept screaming and crying, lots and lots of blood was streaming from his willy. Outside he screamed so loud and so much that the whole neighborhood came out. A man took a tool from the studio, a ri . . . What did he say it was called again? A riddler? It looks like a strange knife, like a file. The riffler! You always forget everything he taught us, it's called a riffler, that's what he told us the day we made the clay vase with him, the one with lots of drawings on it, don't you remember? My mother went into the studio too and picked up a lot of tools he uses in his work, when she came out, a man said: Excellent, my sister, we'll get to work on him with that! Well, my mother went back to our house since it's not far, and she came back with her shoe, the one with the suuuuuper pointy heel, like thiiiiiiiiiiiis long. They took off his shorts and everyone was hitting, hitting, hitting. He rolled himself into a ball like a baby in his mama's belly. Well, I live with my aunt, and she went home to plug in the iron. He was lying on the road, everyone could see his crushed willy, and we were shouting, Pervert! Pervert! Pervert! The shop owner said good work children, very good work, you punished him precisely where he sinned, good work! Other people were spitting on him or kicking him. ****'s aunt came back with the hot iron and started ironing him, the skin peeled off, he wasn't crying anymore, just gasping, gasping, panting so, so hard. My father gave tools to whoever wanted them. I know the names of all the tools, unlike ****, so I said: this is a turning tool, who wants the turning tool? Here's a throwing stick, who'll take the throwing stick? And the ribbon tool, who should we give it to? After that, he talked some more, we couldn't hear very well but he said, have mercy, for the love of God, mercy for the love of God. My mother said, you dare call out to God?! Child of Satan! The person who had taken the ri . . . the riffler stabbed it into his eyes, his eyes burst, he screamed and screamed, it was like a signal because afterward everyone and all the tools struck his body, his body kept moving, moving, like, like a breakdancer, ****'s mama hit his head with the heel of her shoe. Then a man came and said, What are you doing? Dear Lord, what are you doing? You're monsters! What has this man ever done to you? Stop! I'm calling the police, you murderers! My father said, you want to defend this filthy faggot? Do you know who this man is? He's not even a man, are you willing to let someone who's worth less than a dog, less than a mouse, breathe the same air as you? Then children started crying, some people said the mamas should take them home but others said, no, why hide the truth from them, they have to learn life's lessons, what we did we did it for their benefit, they need to know where to draw the line between good and evil. Then someone said, Don't let that man leave, he'll betray us, maybe he's a girly boy too, catch him! Then the man shouted, Let go of me, murderers, I have a Mass to lead this morning, damn all your souls, you murderers! I'm the Saint-Michel parish priest. When he said he was a priest, a woman said it was true, that he'd just joined the neighborhood church. We locked the priest up in the studio, when the men lifted him up, his feet didn't reach the ground, his legs bicycled in the air and he said, I'll report you, I'll report every one of you, I swear it, even if it costs me my life, I'll report every one of you butchers! Butchers! His blood will spill onto you and your children for four generations. We laughed at the priest's feet bicycling in the air. After we locked up the priest, he was still on the ground, still breakdancing, the woman with the iron started ironing him again, she would touch him with the iron and as soon as she lifted it up his skin peeled off, he looked like a skinned pig, an albino. When the iron cooled, the woman ran home on the double to heat it up again, but when she came back, he wasn't moving anymore. Someone said, he's not moving anymore. My mama stopped hitting his head with the heel of her shoe. Then someone else said, he's not dead, he's pretending to be dead so we'll leave him alone, you'll see, tomorrow he'll be crowing through the neighborhood for all to see. He went to get the thing they use to seal septic tanks, it was heavy, three men carried it together, they dropped it on his head, his head went crunch! Cracked right open! We stepped back because there was blood everywhere, but we were so happy to see his head cracked open. He didn't even scream. Someone said, he's dead, some women crossed themselves, then someone said, we have to get to work, it's late, almost ten o'clock. Someone else said, What? Ten o'clock? He wasted two hours of our time?! He was a real tough nut, we don't even have time to necklace him, my boss is waiting for me at the brick plant, that bastard's lucky we don't have time to light up the tire, he would've roasted up real nice. Then, gesturing toward the ground, someone else said, what do we do with this? It was awful the way he lay like an albino on the ground, like a skinned pig. I don't like when they burn people in our neighborhood, when they burn thieves, I'm scared at night because they keep burning for so, so long, it's like roasted meat after a while and you can smell it everywhere in the neighborhood for days and days. Yeah, me too, when they burn a thief in the neighborhood I can go ten days without eating meat. Then we heard a voice shouting behind us, we couldn't see because the whole neighborhood was there in a closed circle. The woman's voice shouted, what's going on here, what's going on, what are you doing at my son's studio? She cut through the crowd, pushing everyone out of the way, she reached the center, next to us, his mama, she fell to her knees next to him, his head still under the septic tank cover, we couldn't see his face, how did she know it was her son? It's okay to kill a girly boy, right? A girly boy who talks to flowers like a crazy person isn't really a person, right? Are you going to arrest us? You won't arrest the people from the neighborhood, will you? In my class at school the teacher said what we had rendered a service to our community, I didn't understand what that meant, but he didn't punish me for missing class. Yeah, me too, my teacher asked the whole class to give me a round of applause. Well, in my class, ****, my archenemy, had to clap for me. But the principal threw up, he threw up a lot, and then he cried, and afterward he said, I'm taking these children down to the station, inform their parents. What does it mean to render a service to the community?

Despite his wife's absence at rallies, the articles—sometimes contradictory—which blamed Tashun for the release and death of sculptor Samuel Pankeu, despite the incumbent opposition governor's obstinacy in fighting his colon cancer while running for office again at the age of sixty-nine, despite the vengeful, obese Mama Caramel Two-for-Ten who sent marabouts to pour castrated sheep's blood on the ground right outside the residence gate just after midnight, despite accusations of voter fraud for handing thousand-franc bills and ground-beef sandwiches dripping with tomato sauce to every person who came out of the voting booth holding his adversaries' ballots, despite proof of collusion with the representatives of opposition parties present at polling stations, despite the ballot boxes deemed void because their seals were already broken by the time they reached the vote-counting station, despite the obvious forgery of official reports, digital scheming, and contestation from his opponents who claimed voter registrations had been tampered with, Tashun was elected and Katmé forced to emerge from her reclusion.

They were moving.

23

Katmé tore her eyes from the jacarandas and iron sculptures, dropped the curtain, turned around, and realized she'd said aloud what she'd been thinking. She also realized that every second she'd spent in her bedroom for the past month had been preparing her for this moment, which she knew—without really knowing—was inescapable. Inside her chest, she heard the muffled groan of a heart rusted by the rough waters of life. When had she gone under? When had the oxidation taken hold? She'd been withering since the day she received the letter from the town hall. Now the process had reached its zenith—she was like a thin, frayed raffia vine—and she had finally realized what was happening.

With her hands balled into fists in the pockets of her satin robe, she repeated, "I won't go."

"What's this nonsense again? What do you mean, you won't go? My patience is wearing thin, really, very thin!"

Standing tall, both feet planted firmly, she tugged hard on the belt around her waist. "I want to pick up my life where I left it twelve years ago."

"I see your brain is still on the fritz. Where exactly did you leave it? In a locker at the train station? Go find it then! Everyone told me no good would come of being too understanding with my wife, but I didn't listen. I let you get away with too much. Take care of the move, Mrs. Abbia, that will get your head straight!"

Katmé pushed through the door to the kitchen where a white neon light had replaced the orange bulb in the ceiling fixture. "Mama!" Axelle and Alix exclaimed as they threw themselves into her arms. "Are you cured, Mama? Are you better? We prayed and prayed to God, Grandma Récia taught us lots of payers, lots and lots, we prayed for you and now you're healed! Oh, Mama!" While they prepared the smoked fish folong and half-ripe plantains, the loquacious twins coaxed distracted smiles out of their mother. Relieved to see her cousin emerge from her lethargy, Sokjou fussed over Katmé. As did

Bambili. Only Mama Récia glanced worriedly in her direction, noticing how absent she seemed.

Where would she live with no money and no job? It would take at least six months to get a new job in a high school, where she'd earn less than a night guard at an expatriate compound. Who would pay Mama Récia's rent? Her bills? Should she take the girls? Where? To what home? What lifestyle? The vault in Fènn had been built on land Tashun owned, would she have to plan a third funeral elsewhere? Who would help a woman who had left her husband, the former prefect of the capital and current governor of Haut-Fènn, of her own free will? Who would understand why she'd climbed so high only to fall so low? "When you eat with four pieces of silverware on either side of your plate, you don't rise up in revolution," Keuna had teased her. Aleksandre had suggested they start over. Together. Aleksandre who was in love and generous with his early-days promises. Promises that could lead—whatever he might say—to the sense that she was in some way his. One thing was sure: if she left Tashun, never again would she live under the same roof as the man with whom she shared her life.

She'd gotten married to escape the suffocating atmosphere at Mama Récia's house and to ensure she was entitled—though it seemed ridiculous now—to a married woman's funeral. She married Tashun so her corpse would be spared the shame of being buried with scarcely more care than a pet. To ensure her children, if she ever had any, would be spared the dishonor of watching their mother be buried outside their father's family plot. To be someone's wife, so no one would call her a loose woman, an immoral woman like her mother. She wanted the crown of a married woman, which turned every adult woman of reproductive age in the country into *a real woman,* so how could she now imagine, if only for a moment, casting it aside? How do you return to living when you've spent the last twelve years in an incubator? The other option: carry on. Keep spreading her legs and allowing that brutal to-and-fro inside her, keep accepting the drops of sweat that landed on her face and chest, counting the seconds, putting up with his panting, feeling nothing, pursing her lips, closing her eyes, enduring the presence of the sticky liquid inside her no matter how loath was her vagina, putting on a fulfilled smile and nodding her head to the question "good, right?" patting his chest, sleeping, dreaming of another, waking up, noticing the abominable liquid on her panty liner, watching it drip down her thighs. When she dreamed about Aleksandre, he was always wearing jeans and a T-shirt. He'd returned to Fènn heavier than before. Her lips would tickle his harelip scar, her fingers would flutter beneath his shirt, roaming across his familiar skin. She liked it when he wore a T-shirt in her dreams. She'd never managed to slip her hands beneath his tailored, monastic abacost. The other option? Become. Become Mama Governor. Cocktails, dinners, Masses, grand openings. The other option? Forget. Forget that for the life they took from Samy there would be no arrest, no trial, that no one would be held without bail at Central. "We can't lock up an entire neighborhood, damn it! You want to send ten- and twelve-year-old kids to jail? The Aquatics are savages, he shouldn't have opened his studio there. What good would it do to stir things up? It's behind us. God has sent us trials, we've overcome them, we're starting over." Starting over. The residents of the Enseignants neighborhood and the Aquatics were starting over. *Tropics Daily* was starting over. Mama Caramel-Two-for-Ten was starting over. The party's Central Committee was starting over. Were Kizito and Sita Félicie starting over too? Forget the *accident that took place at sculptor Samuel Pankeu's studio.* An accident at the studio, she knew what that was. Samy had explained it, she'd seen them, experienced them with him. A piece that cracks or shatters; overworked clay that rebels, refusing to take on the shape you give it, clay you can get nothing more out of, or miscalculating the amount of material to remove—*those* are accidents at the studio. Samy's death, his horrific death, pelted with rocks as he lay beside his African violets, stoned by his *pro bono publico* apprentices—Paul, Blaise, Kouankeu, Little Paul, Emmanuel and Chrysostome; Samy ironed, shucked like corn, flattened beneath a slab of concrete, *that* was not an accident at the studio. Living life as a sellout; not that you could call a series of compromises a life . . . Was standing up for what she believed in finally a possibility?

Axelle and Alix snuggled into her arms and Katmé laughed, running her hand over their unkempt cornrows. "Moïndjamoto, your hair needs washing."

"Mama, will you braid our hair?" asked Axelle.

24

The semester was over at the University of Haut-Fènn. The peddlers' wooden crates filled with office supplies and academic forms had disappeared along with the grills for roasting corn, plantains, and safous, replaced by a carpet of drenched, dark-pink flame trees. Katmé zipped her cardigan up all the way, opened the car door, and sunk her suede loafers into the spongy earth. She'd left Akriba at dawn, as though army ants had been biting her beneath the sheets, and hadn't thought to bring an umbrella, much less season-appropriate shoes. The storm had hit while she was navigating the many potholes on the steep path that led from the paved road up to the university. She'd parked in front of the dilapidated, austere buildings perched at the top of the mountain whose flanks were a sea of rusty corrugated iron roofs like so many red cankers. She looked at her shoes. She couldn't save them. She inhaled greedily, relishing the scent of the wet Fènn earth after a morning storm, with its hints of kaolin and soaked spruce.

Kizito didn't take time off between semesters. He used the break to write articles commissioned by foreign publications and local newspapers or prepare the menus for future issues of *Counterpoint.* Did the editor-in-chief's words still interest readers, and in particular his former base, since candidate Tashun Abbia's broad smile had made the journal's cover? Katmé headed instinctively toward the building she thought was the law school. She'd only been there once before. With Samy. Their first trip to Fènn together. He was still working on *Ante Mortem,* the FZC had yet to vote to take the orphaned children from Vita to visit the exhibition and studio, and Mama Caramel Two-for-Ten hadn't turned Samy into a javelin to hurl at Tashun. She could still see Samy shielding his eyes from the sun as he looked up at the tiny dormer windows in the offices. His cell at Central didn't have a window. A few months earlier, they'd been here together, taking in the depressingly identical buildings. Just a few short months . . . She asked a summer-school student for directions. She wasn't in the right wing, she couldn't trust the writing on the wooden arrows, she needed to turn left, she'd see a sign for the political science department, after that she'd need to walk along the side of the building to the back where she'd find a third building with a sign for the communications department, which was also wrong—that's where she'd find the law school and Kizito's office, on the fifth floor at the end of the hallway after the stairs, on the right. A few yards later, Katmé was perplexed; she hadn't retained a thing the student had said. She asked for directions a second time, and the woman's face lit up. Her Excellency Madam Governor! The chemistry professor felt it was her duty to escort her. The deserted hallway, the locked office doors, the muddy paint on the walls, the dirty, broken windowpanes, the wide cracks in the cement floor, the gaping hole in the ceiling caused by the storm through which she caught a glimpse of a white sky flecked with bluish spots, the pond she had to step around underneath it; she'd walked down this hallway with Samy. The floor had been dry that day.

The office door was ajar, Kizito absent. Katmé's guide offered to locate him, but Madam Governor dissuaded her by plunging her hand into her purse to pull out a five-thousand-franc bill. "For your children's yogurt. Thanks so much for your help. You can go. I'll wait." The professor hesitated, then held out her hand to accept the banknote. She kept it in her balled fist rather than putting it in her bag. After a moment, she spread her fingers, looked thoughtfully at the money, took hold of Katmé's wrist, opened her palm and placed the bill back in her hand. "I was only showing you the way, Madam Governor. Have a nice day." She smiled and backed away at first, then turned and strode off quickly. As Katmé watched her back shrink in the distance, she could hear Samy's sardonic laugh. "There's something desperate about your inability to keep your money in your bag, truly desperate." She unzipped her sweater and tied it around her waist, over her white pants.

The professor—now an evanescent dot in the empty, silent hallway—slowed as a person at least two heads taller drew closer. Katmé saw Samuel's lanky, suit-and-tie-clad shadow coming toward her, his steps seemingly muffled by thick slippers. The white light of day dripped down through the skylight, outlining the silhouette and its swaying gait from behind. The resemblance between the two brothers had never seemed so striking before. Kizito didn't appear surprised to find her waiting; someone must have informed him she was looking for him. He pushed through the door and gestured with his head for her to follow. In the tiny room he called an office, nothing had moved since her last visit with Samy. The Formica desk piled high with binders of every shade; the wooden chair with studded velvet upholstery; the pleather armchair; the bookshelf buckling from the weight of academic journals and volumes on law, communications, and political science, and a hefty dose of dust. On the wall, two strips of glass the width of a piece of a standard sheet of paper let air into the tight space and provided a view of the sky above, and a corn and groundnut field below. Without a word, without asking as he often did, "So, how is my brother's sister?" Kizito began paging through the colorful binders. My brother's sister, that's what he used to call her. Before. He opened a file, then closed it, opened another, and read a few pages. Nothing has moved, but everything has changed, thought Katmé. She'd steeled herself against the possibility he might be unpleasant. And he was. She was convinced that Kizito was just buying time before deciding the fate of their relationship: save the friendship or opt for enmity.

The sound of the cardboard files grating against one another annoyed her after a while. "Are you looking for something?" she asked.

He shut the folder he'd just opened. "What are you doing here?" His tone was hostile.

Enmity then.

"I want to visit Samy's grave."

Kizito pinched his nose between his index finger and thumb, then pulled. The same aquiline nose as Samy.

"You didn't come to his funeral and now you have the nerve to ask to visit his grave? You think I'm going to let you visit his grave?"

"Your mother forbade me to come!"

Kizito's upper lip curled into a snarl. "Mama had just lost her son in circumstances so violent, so atrocious that even someone like me, someone who knows just how far people will go when they unleash their inner beast, couldn't have imagined them. She was as devastated as any mother would be in her shoes, and you—a smart woman, almost a member of the family—you're saying you just took her words at face value? Where's Katmé? Isn't Mrs. Abbia here? Everyone wondered where you were at the funeral! And you have the nerve to show up here and demand to visit his grave? Who do you think you are? Ah, I see! Mama Governor can do as she pleases?"

Katmé took her face in her hands. The Pankeus couldn't refuse her this . . .

"How could I have come?" she shouted, her voice laden with tears. "Sita Félicie told me—"

"Oh, that's enough! Blaming my mother is the easy way out. I called your house every day for a week, left messages, asked for you to call me back. Nothing. Madam isn't home. Madam is out. Yes, we'll tell her you called. Madam will return your call. Madam never returned my call."

"You . . . You called me?"

"Yes, Kat. I called you. Mama regretted what she had said to you. I got angry, we wanted to apologize, to tell you that you would always be welcome in our family. You never called me back, not once. Then Ety took over, he called you too . . ."

She could have been at Samy's wake with Sita Félicie, been near him for a few more days, maybe even touched him, talked to him, swept the ground in his house nine days after his funeral, been there when they opened his room after the sweeping, his bedroom where they'd built and deconstructed the world together, eased her grief a little with those who had loved him. "Will you be there for me whatever happens?" he would ask when he was in prison. Mama Récia, Sokjou, and Bambili had stolen her mourning period—on Tashun's orders, of course.

Katmé pushed her chair back, moved behind it, left her sweater on the seat, stepped back, then stood in the doorway, arms open. "Look at me, Kizito." She submitted to his inspection: dirty braids, wan face, glassy eyes, protruding collar bones beneath her tailored striped blouse, loose white crepe pants with muddy hems, loafers caked in earth. "I haven't left my house since I spoke to your mother at the morgue. I left my room last night and the house this morning. I came straight from Akriba."

He examined her from top to bottom. Avoided meeting her eyes. Katmé sat back down on top of her sweater.

Head hung low as he fiddled with a pen, Kizito finally asked, "Were you . . . de . . . depressed?" displaying the circumspection of a person for whom even the word, much less the condition, was quite foreign.

Katmé smiled weakly. "I don't know. I didn't have the strength to do anything at all. Every time I closed my eyes it all came flooding back, again and again . . . I remembered so many things. After seeing your mother at the morgue, I just wanted to sleep, just sleep, sleep, sleep, and never wake up."

Kizito ran his hand over his head several times as if trying to order his thoughts. "And now? Are you . . . better?"

"I still don't want to wake up. But life before death is already just a long sleep, I suppose."

"We are all tempted to never open our eyes to this nightmare again. I was twelve years old when Sam was born, and I remember thinking, when my parents came home from the hospital with him in the bassinet, that I would never be lonely again, that I would never be alone. Our age difference and Papa's death made us more like father and son than big brother and little brother, but you already know all that. When he was held back after attempting his final year of high school with a scientific focus, he came to tell me that he wanted to try a literary focus instead. Our father was willing to let Sam rot away a hundred years in his final year of high school if that's what it took for him to graduate with a science focus. When Sam failed the second time, I finally managed to convince our father. It wasn't easy. When you came into Sam's life, he became a new person, more open, less introverted, I was sure the two of you would get married one day, he was so attached to you, I thought you were in love. And then you got married; he told me how unhappy your marriage made him, though it wasn't for the reasons I imagined."

Kizito paused as a muscle in his cheek spasmed. The vibrant warmth Katmé was accustomed to in his voice had returned. He reached up and grabbed a volume from a shelf six inches above his head—a volume Katmé had assumed was an encyclopedia due to its rigid, black cover and bare spine. He handed her the somber tome.

Katmé's eyelids began to twitch.

"I keep the album here and Mama cooks for him. Every day. Termites, grubs, or grasshoppers depending on what she finds at the market. I've spent all my weekends in Akriba since the accident. I bring the children. She stuffs us with them at lunch and dinner. Now the kids don't want to go anymore. She serves us and makes sure we clean our plates. She doesn't even taste it herself. She asks the children, 'Enough salt? What about chili pepper? And garlic?' The children nod and she adds, 'Little one likes it good and spicy, and salty too, I don't grate the garlic, I cut it up into big pieces and add them at the end, when the rest is all cooked.' I'm sure you know she always called him 'little one' when he was a baby. 'Little one likes the garlic to be firm between his teeth. Go on, eat, eat it all up, I put some aside for him in the fridge. He'll eat when he gets back from the studio.' The refrigerator and freezer are full of plastic containers and packages wrapped in aluminum foil. Little one's share. There's no point telling her she's scaring the children. 'Mamie Félicie is losing it,' they tell their mother when we get home."

It was an album of photos from Samy's funeral. A plain, unfinished casket, completely sealed, of course, no glass rectangle to provide a glimpse of the body. Flowers, no jacarandas or African violets—his favorites. Not even Ety had thought to order them. Sita Félicie dressed in white. Kizito, his wife, and children in black. The students from his fine arts classes at Félix Éboué Middle School in uniform, the principal in a black suit with a red tie—the color code for the funeral of a person who had died in an accident. Gabrielle and Khadidiatou from the FZC, Gabrielle's Norma Desmond beauty mark even darker than usual. Aleksandre in a black abacost. Aleksandre. An orchestra, artists, Emile—the painter who had given Samy *The Double Life of Véronique,* lots of people, unknown faces, fewer than for her mother's second funeral, but they'd come to say a final farewell to Samy with no designs, expecting nothing in return. So very many people at Samy's funeral, but not her, not his better half.

"Who are these people wearing orange badges on their chests?"

"Look at the rest of the pictures. There's a photo where one of them is holding a spray of flowers."

Katmé flipped through the pages and spotted the spray. Birds of paradise and torch ginger, and a neon-orange banner bearing the message:

Rest in Peace, Vice President
The DC Society

"The DC Society?"

"DC for decriminalization."

She closed her eyes for a moment, opened them again. "I didn't know he was the vice president of a society, or that such a society even existed."

Hands joined beneath his chin and elbows propped on the desk, Kizito watched her closely. She swallowed hard and returned her gaze to the album. The pictures grew blurry. Samy was the vice president of the DC Society. He hadn't even mentioned it to her. Why? "Your relationship is too exclusive, you're too close to one another, it's not healthy," Tashun always said. Now it seemed he'd been wrong. Yes, she shared every aspect of her life with Samy, held nothing back, but he had excluded her from a part of his. Why? Because she didn't know what it was like to be in his shoes? He lived something that remained abstract for her, lived it in his flesh, his entire being. She could flinch in the deepest parts of herself when anyone touched Samy, but she didn't know what it was like to risk spending the rest of her life in prison, to be lynched by preteen neighbors and their parents, to be someone who spends their adolescence and adulthood, their entire existence, controlling themselves, hiding themselves from others, wearing a mask to move through society. Samy had seen a speech therapist to deepen his voice and make it sound more virile, had taken body-language classes. Katmé had paid for both, though she hadn't known such things even existed. The young men and women wearing the orange badge knew what it was like to be in his shoes, not her. Not her. She had told him she couldn't care less about homosexuals in Zambuena or anywhere else on earth for that matter, "I don't give a shit," she'd shouted. For her, he was the only thing that mattered, *because he was him.* She'd never wondered what it meant for Samy, *ontologically speaking,* to be homosexual in a country where homosexuality can lead to life in prison. Whatever Samy's reasons, however valid, he hadn't told her, and it hurt.

"Sam is buried in the yard behind the house, next to Papa. I know he would have liked for you to visit him. Màma and I were caught off guard to meet so many of Samy's rather peculiar friends . . . My mother might ask you . . . She never believed what the papers wrote about him. Neither did I, in fact. Ms. Bessonguè informed me after the funeral. How long have you known?"

Katmé looked up from the album. "What does it matter?"

"It matters because I wouldn't have written those articles, or at least not in the same tone, if I had suspected the truth."

"He told me in high school."

"My little brother was a homosexual beginning in high school?!"

"You don't need a diploma, you know . . ."

"The two of you really took me for a ride! Do you know if . . . Did Sam . . ." Kizito stammered, kneading the folds between his fingers. "In concrete terms, beyond being attracted to . . . uh . . . Did Sam, I mean, did he really—"

"Did he have a boyfriend? Did he really sleep with men?"

"Basically, yes."

"What do you think?"

"One man in particular?"

Katmé nodded.

"Do I know him?"

She nodded again.

"Who is it?"

"You know him."

Kizito lifted his elbows off the desk and ran his palm over his scalp. His eyes went wide. "It can't be . . . Ety?"

He read the truth in Katmé's eyes.

"I really am stupid," he said with a shake of his head. "It must have been so difficult for him. All those lies, so many secrets."

"What should I tell Sita Félicie if she asks?"

"Tell her no, of course. No. Tell her and anyone else who asks: no. Even if you told her the truth, my mother wouldn't believe you, and that's for the best. She's troubled enough as it is."

Kizito, Katmé thought, was still firmly rooted in the realities of Zambuena. A wife, six children, a fragile mother, colleagues. Brother of the murdered fag—there were titles easier to bear.

He pushed his chair back and pulled open one of the four drawers in his desk. "The owner refused to take the rent we paid him after Sam's accident." Katmé heard the jingling of metal. Her heart began to race. "You'll know your way around better than us. The police rushed the investigation and gave us the keys back after a week. Bring anything you don't want to keep to Mama's house. She cleaned up the blood and tidied up. You won't see any traces of the accident."

"It wasn't an accident, Kizito. It was a murder. We have to reopen the investigation. Samy was killed. The Aquatics have to be arrested and tried."

"We're all Aquatics, Katmé. All of us. What about the role played by Mama Caramel Two-for-Ten and the APM conspirators? By your husband? What about your own silence? My refusal to see Sam for who he really was? If Sam were to come back to us, how would I handle having a gay little brother? Would I ask him to keep hiding it to spare the rest of us? The parents and children of the Cité des Enseignants felt they had every right to take Sam's life because they knew that the community, the justice system, and the self-righteous multitudes in this country implicitly authorized them to purge this evil from society. Exposed, stripped naked, and put to death. Fate decided to take Samy's Ring of Gyges away. That's just the way it is."

"His ring of what?"

"Never mind. Here, take these," Kizito said as he handed her the keys to the studio.

"I won't accept your fatalism. Even if you're right, we can't simply say, that's just the way it is, nothing to be done! Bessonguè was right. We have to try, we have to reopen the investigation, change the damn law! We can't give up! I can't give up, Kizito!"

"I don't have the strength, Katmé," he replied, defeated. "Even though your husband only featured on the cover of a single issue, since Samuel's death put an end to that debased alliance, *Counterpoint* lost all its foreign sponsors and I lost all of the freelance work I used to do for other papers. On the first day of the campaign, all my tires were slashed and my rear windshield shattered. The locals see me as a sellout, just like the former mayor who was elected as part of your husband's team. The university is all I have left, I can't risk it."

Kizito took a tissue from the upper left pocket of his army-green blazer to pat at his forehead and eyes. He was crying.

The conical roof of the vault on the mountainside seemed to be reaching toward the azure sky. The dwarf pines had grown, the eucalyptus grove seemed denser, the sun shone brightly, warming the earth. Katmé poured a demijohn of raffia wine, two pounds of salt, and a bottle of palm oil on the marble tomb, then placed a loaf of koki corn, macabo leaf cornbread, her mother's favorite, atop it. With bare feet and a broom in hand, she climbed onto a stool to clear the cobwebs from every corner of the ceiling.

She returned to the car, opened the trunk, removed a bottle of perfume from a plastic bag, and made her way back to the vault. She spritzed a hundred milliliters of *Poison* by Dior, the only perfume she'd ever known her mother to wear, on the walls, moldings, cornices, baseboards, plaster ceiling, and corners, then in the air. She kissed the cold marble and whispered, "Mama, Mama, Mama . . . What would you do? What should I do, Mama? Take care of Samy, Mama, take care of him. Has he told you about how much he loves jacarandas and African violets? Tell him that Keuna will take care of his pieces, and so will I. We'll take care of his work."

On the way back to Akriba, she stopped the RAV4, made a U-turn, and sped back to the University of Haut-Fènn. Kizito was grading papers. He didn't seem to have left his chair since their visit a few hours earlier. Katmé stood tall in the doorway. "I'm just asking for your blessing, Kizito. Nothing more. When I have enough money, I'll have the investigation reopened. Tell me you won't fight it, that's all. I'm begging you . . ."

"Katmé . . ." he said with a sigh, "you're even dirtier than before. Come here."

He took her to the faculty restroom and used the key he kept on his belt to open the door for her. She took off her shoes, opened the faucet, and ran the outside of her loafers under the trickle of water, removing clumps of dried mud from the suede. Kizito waited with his back against the door frame holding a box of tissues.

"I'm going to ask for my teaching job back," she announced. "I'm staying in Akriba."

"What about Tashun?" he asked, coming closer.

"He'll be here, in the governor's palace, I guess," she replied with a shrug.

Kizito's expression of disbelief made him look exactly like Samuel. "He's repudiating you?"

Repudiation, like in biblical times. Even for someone like Kizito, a woman making such a decision was unthinkable.

"I'm leaving *him.*"

"That won't bring Samy back! You can't get divorced! You have two children!"

"I'm not married to my children."

"You don't just wake up one morning and decide to get divorced. What happened with Sam is awful, but don't add to the drama. You have two children to raise."

She placed the shoe she was holding in her hand on the mosaic of tiny tiles on the restroom floor and mindlessly wiped her hands on her white pants, leaving behind reddish stains. Kizito handed her the box of tissues and looked deep into her eyes. "Why do you want to leave? It's Fortès, isn't it. It's him?"

Katmé put on a neutral expression, accepted the tissues, took her time wiping her fingers one after another.

"Katmé, I was blind with Sam. But that's not always the case . . . You must know that Fortès resigned from the highway project and left Mival after what happened."

She looked up at Kizito, meeting his gaze. "I didn't."

"He came to tell me goodbye before he left."

"He has nothing to do with my decision. I lived under my mother's rules, then my aunt's, and finally my husband's. I just want to live my life. I'm not ten years old. I don't want to have to explain myself to anyone anymore. And I'm sure of one thing: I don't love Tashun anymore."

"You don't love Tashun anymore?" Kizito asked with great hilarity. "Come on, Katmé, what does love have to do with marriage? People get married because it's the done thing, period. I mean, people get married for lots of reasons, and those are the same reasons people stay, no matter what, they stay together and raise their children. I can guess why you want to leave, maybe I even approve, but given the state of the country, if you leave your husband, no one will have mercy on you, don't kid yourself. If your husband leaves you, people criticize you and say you didn't know how to keep him, but at least you get to be a victim. That status has advantages in the context we live in. Don't be a fool, little sis, if *you* leave *him* you're putting your head on the guillotine block, and the executioner is everyone. I'm sure you know all this. Think hard, sis. Think hard, you have two children."

He walked with her back to the car and hugged her close. "I'll call Mama and let her know you'll be stopping by. She'll be happy to see you." A rainbow suddenly appeared overhead. They shielded their eyes with their hands to look up at it.

Katmé got in the car and lowered the window. Kizito hunched over, lowering his face to the opening, then exhaled at length, emptying his lungs as if completing a deep breathing exercise. "I promised myself I wouldn't bring it up," he said, "but . . . I think . . . Well, I have his contact information, if you want it . . ."

The back of Katmé's neck tingled. She stared at the windshield and the hideous building that contained Kizito's office and those of his faculty colleagues.

"It seems he's struggling to turn the page on Zambuena, Fènn, you."

She nodded perfunctorily.

"My brother's sister, I'm here if you need me . . ."

Katmé gave him an uncertain smile and turned the key in the ignition. Kizito backed away and straightened up.

As the distance between them grew, she thought of the rainbow. Kizito had once told her and Samy that rainbows were rare in Haut-Fènn, even after a rainstorm.

25

The expression on Tashun's face betrayed his belief that his wife had completely lost her mind. The four of them were having dinner in the beige dining room. Above the percale tablecloth adorned with horses galloping through a cornfield, their manes blowing in the wind, he abruptly announced to Axelle and Alix that their mother wanted to pick her life up where she'd left off twelve years earlier, in other words, before they were born, without them, without him. The girls, who had been babbling about their day at Saint-Christophe, went silent. It was as though their voices had been seized by the beige dining room walls, the beige shades on the brass sconces, the beige upholstery on the chairs. Alix set down her fork and knife beside her plate. Axelle reached for the water pitcher, which slipped from her hand. The handle chipped upon impact with the big serving dish full of shredded macabo. The water spilled onto the tablecloth, the laps of the twins and their parents, and the floor. Bambili was standing behind the double swing doors to the kitchen to ensure the meal went smoothly. She scooped the sponges from the dishwashing basin, kitchen towels from the sideboard, and a mop from the broom closet, then rushed help. The meal was cut short.

Later, sitting on a bed in the girls' room, Katmé said, "*Moïndjamoto,* earlier, when Papa . . ." The girls pulled their covers up to their chins and exchanged a glance. They hadn't dared ask any questions at dinner. In fact, they hadn't said anything at all after the announcement.

"We're tired," said Alix.

"We want to go to sleep," added Axelle.

Katmé ignored the glacial gust that hit her in the face and asked, "What time should I wake you up tomorrow?"

"Whenever you want," Axelle answered weakly.

Katmé kissed the girls on their foreheads and returned to her room, a corset of indecision and fear squeezing her midsection.

Tashun was lying on the bedspread, hands behind his head, staring up at the ceiling as he waited. "I gave you your ticket . . . You took my name. And now you want to humiliate me?" he asked, propped up on his elbows. "Do you really think I'll let you humiliate me? Since when do women file for divorce in this country? Since when?! And the girls, what about them? You, you, you! You'll leave if I say you can, Mrs. Abbia! Only if I say you can!"

Since in Zambuena marriage was less about two people committing to a single fate and more about two families coming together, less about two individuals than about two communities coming together to create one, with the dowry and religious ceremony consecrating supposedly inalterable, binding ties, Tashun turned to Djama for help.

"You think filing for divorce is an act of bravery? Believe me, staying married is the real feat. Like my father always said, when they're carried off by the river's current, some people think the raindrops are what's getting them wet. You want to go back to work? Bad luck! Maybe if you had a real job! A home economics teacher, that's no job! What about a stable home for the girls? If you're feeling the itch, find an A and keep a low profile. Where would you go? And you'll be thrown out of the FZC, have you thought of that? You can't give your feet over to the chiggers and later claim God doesn't love you. Bad luck!"

Then Tashun summoned Mama Récia. "You were married in the church, dear. If you do this, it's eternal damnation. True love, eternal love can only be found in heaven. Living with my husband was like a stay on Calvary hill, but I didn't leave. In a marriage, you learn to live together, you put up with one another. That's what marriage is. If you leave this marriage, what will happen to us? How will we live? With what money?"

Next Tashun's secretary, Balbine Kempé, tried her hand. "All couples have problems, Madam Katmé. The roof and walls hide it all. It's not easy to find a husband like His Excellency the Prefect . . . the Governor. Time heals all ills, you'll see."

Even Motto, the valet, mentioned the situation one morning as he opened the curtains. "You have enough to eat, Madam, you're not hungry, that's why you want to leave. A full belly can't think straight. Don't leave, Mama Governor. You're making a mistake."

One evening, a letter from Sennke appeared on her dressing table, as if left there by the Holy Spirit. "Jesus performed his first miracle at the wedding at Cana, *blah blah blah* . . . He changed water into wine, *blah blah blah* . . . What God has joined together, *blah blah blah* . . . Marriage, *blah blah blah* . . . The children, *blah blah blah* . . . Your life together *blah blah blah* . . . Divine grace *blah blah blah* . . ." Katmé went directly to the end of the letter. "Whatever you decide, I'll be there for you. When will you come visit?"

Katmé tried to introduce herself. "I know who you are," Cécile Bessonguè said, cutting her off. "You were my client, more or less, weren't you?" she asked, her shrewd eyes studying Katmé from behind round glasses. Samuel Pankeu had told her who was paying her fees. The lawyer pushed a box of tissues toward Katmé. It was raining and Tashun had taken back the RAV4. She'd waited for a taxi on the side of the road for quite some time. She patted at her face and arms. Her soaked blouse clung to her skin as the drizzle continued to fall outside in tight, regular formation.

Once she'd worked up the courage to face the woman who had taken Samy's side from the beginning, Katmé blurted, "I have to warn you, I won't be able to pay you."

After leaving Bessonguè's office, she went to pick up her girls from school. Once they were inside the taxi she'd reserved for an hour—the driver waited outside with his back against the door—Katmé did her best to tame her pounding heart and painstakingly utter the words she had to tell them.

"Are you going to go live with another husband, Mama?" Alix asked when Katmé had finished.

"No, *Moïndjamoto,* I'm going to go live with myself. And if my lawyer's any good, with the two of you from time to time."

"Be gone, Asmodeus!"

"Be gone, Asmodeus!"

"The choir of angels and sainted archangels will purify you!"

Mama Récia and her daughters were chanting. Katmé's aunt was tracing the shape of a cross on her forehead and spritzing her face, ears, and crotch with Ash Wednesday ashes from the previous year mixed with holy water from the Jordan River and holy oil from Jerusalem, which she'd purchased at the Procure shop near the cathedral. Rosine, whose breasts were pressing into the high back of the chair Katmé was sitting on, had wrapped her arms around her cousin's upper body, imprisoning her torso and limbs. At her feet, Sokjou lay on her side with her hands wrapped around Katmé's ankles and her head pressing against her left leg like a treasure she'd never let go.

"Jesus's blood washes away your sins!"

"The virgin and her crown of twelve stars wash away your sins!"

"There can be no divorced women in a blessed family!"

"No divorce among the children of Jesus Christ!"

Whenever Katmé protested—peacefully at first, "What were you thinking, what is this nonsense, come on, stop it!" then less politely, "You demonic fuckers, if God does exist, I hope he makes sure Satan fucks you in the ass for all of eternity"—her aunt sprayed the mixture into her open mouth, between her teeth, on her tongue, and Katmé's final words were strangled. She might as well have said nothing since Mama Récia, given over entirely to her soul-saving mission, credited her niece's rude words to the Devil and pretended not to notice the flames burning in her eyes. "Holy water whores! Jezebels! Ladies of the night! Green bitches! Mothers of half-caste babies! *You're* the Asmodeus here!" Katmé's spicy repertoire would have shaken any Christian woman with less favor from the Holy Spirit than her aunt. "Don't give up, pray, it's Asmodeus speaking through her, Asmodeus who feels threatened, it's his voice, he's possessed Katmé, we have to set her free . . ." A lot was at stake for Mama Récia. Her own financial future and that of some of her children were on the line.

Katmé's aunt had called her the day before, suggesting she come over for some sanga. Katmé had chosen a dress her aunt liked to see her in: floral wax-print fabric, short sleeves, modestly low-cut V neckline, fitted at the waist, and loose on her hips. With help from a ruse rooted in biblical rhetoric, thirty minutes after they'd finished the sanga, Mama Récia had locked the front door, closed the windows, and shut out the upbeat, late-morning light to shroud the living room in artificial darkness lessened only by fluorescent tubes and lamps. Both her cousins had thrown themselves at her, binding her to the chair like an evildoer they had to exorcise before the police arrived. While huge dark clouds gathered outside and rain and thunder eclipsed the sun, inside Mama Récia was trying to eradicate in Katmé the desire to "put asunder what God hath joined together," and to free her from Asmodeus, "the demon of lust that pushes women to leave their husbands." Tashun, her son-in-law-sent-by-God-himself-in-his-immeasurable-bounty, didn't deserve such betrayal.

"You don't have to follow in your mother's footsteps. Money for hand, back for ground doesn't have to be handed down from mother to daughter," Rosine mumbled in Katmé's neck.

"You dare talk about my—"

Psht to the face!

"About my mother? You green bitch!"

Psht to the face!

The greasy water from the spray bottle had started to clog Katmé's ears; it was dripping down her face, neck, back, breasts, and inner thighs.

"Be gone, Asmodeus!"

"Be gone, Asmodeus!"

"God our Father, save her soul, save her marriage!"

"Free her from Asmodeus!"

"Free her from original sin!"

"Deliver your servant!"

With her strong arms wrapped around Katmé's ankles like handcuffs, Sokjou scolded her cousin. "God took pity on you and gave you a husband, you didn't become a whore like your mother, and now you want to hurt Tashun? *Megde!*"

The taste of chloroquine flooded Katmé's mouth. Blind with rage, she knew she would never see her aunt or her brood ever again. Free, yes, she was free. Her mother had finally been laid to rest for good.

Over the next few days, Katmé looked for a studio apartment to rent. With no money to pay the six-month deposit, she ended up spending a few days at Ety's until Keuna offered to house her and give her a part-time job at the gallery while she waited to return to teaching. She received a cool reception when she attended a DC Society meeting. Ety had failed to persuade her to skip it. DC didn't accept heterosexuals.

Heterosexuals would sign up for the Society and protest alongside them, but then those who managed to get a visa and pay for plane tickets flew off to Europe or North America, where they claimed they had been persecuted in their home country and received asylum, to the detriment of real homosexuals.

The day Ms. Bessonguè had Tashun served with divorce papers, Katmé got a phone call from Djama at Bubinga Project. "You've signed your social death certificate. Now you're a Z, Katmé. A zero. A nobody. A single hand can't close a bag, as my father always said, and you'll soon find that out for yourself. I've heard that in addition to leaving your husband, you want to reopen the investigation into the death of that young man with that lady lawyer? Bad luck! You're on the road to ruin, believe me. We'll help you get there too. You're no longer a member of the FZC. You're never to set foot at another meeting. Just look where your stupidity has left you."

Katmé's ears were hot to the touch. "Djama, Djama, Djama," she said without raising her voice. "First of all, do me a favor, would you? I'd really appreciate it. Be a dear and shove your FZC right up your ass, okay? And your threats can join it up there, okay? Stupid bitch!"

Gabrielle, Faith, and Khadidiatou were clearly surprised to see her working as Keuna's assistant at a vernissage at Bubinga Project one night. Gabrielle grabbed Katmé's arm as she was handing out flyers. "Wait a second, you're Katmé Abbia, you used to be big!" Katmé put on a broad smile, pulled her shoulders back, narrowed her eyes, raised her eyebrows, and slightly lifted her chin. With the arrogance of Norma Desmond in her voice, she replied, "I *am* big. It's my old life that got small."

26

When she got out of the taxi, by the gutter, she looked for signs—in the puddles, on the faces watching her, in the roar of the corn mill motor, in the smell of adulterated gasoline coming from motorcycle exhaust pipes, in the eyes of the women selling safous and plantains, the voices of innocent children playing soccer, men chuckling as they played checkers, young women in pagnes, the second-hand book salesman, the swarms of mosquitos and flies hovering over the murky water in the gutter, in the clear sky and the cool, dry air. She was looking for proof, anything to prove that an inalterable bolt of lightning had zigzagged across the rainy, brown sky the day Samy had been erased from the face of the earth right there.

Her hands shook. The beds of African violets were gone. Her hands shook, and she didn't remember how the lock on the front door worked. Her hands shook; Samy wouldn't be behind the door, at his desk, in his purple smock, kneading clay, his face as dark as night dotted with gray spots, his eyes full of good-natured mischief, his teeth sparkling white. Her hands shook; this was the last time she'd ever be here.

As she stepped into the studio, she knew that the sketches, drawings, unfinished pieces, forgotten, abandoned, and neglected tools, idle and covered in dust, would whisper that Samy was gone. And they did. The door would open and Samy would come in, preceded by his contagious laugh, his hands white with clay and heavy with the weight of a new sculpture; he'd introduce her to his newest creation like an elated new father. He'd say, "Here's the newest edition, Katinétou, what do you think?" He wouldn't be pleased to find her there in the studio without him. "Mbindi, you know you're not allowed in here without me." She was breaking Samy's rule. Alone in his studio without him. Even while he was in prison, she'd stayed away.

The former warehouse felt monstrous.

Samy and the objects in the studio were a single entity. Separated from him, the terracotta jugs he helped Little Paul, Emmanuel, Kounakeu and the others make, the cot where he spent more time sweating than sleeping, the photographs, the basin of water clouded with clay, his sandals, the dirty smocks piled up in the laundry basin, and the failed sculptures were all waiting quietly, impassively for someone to decide their fate.

Katmé took in the jugs which would never be painted by children with Samy's guidance. How could she reconcile the busy little hands eagerly working the clay, the concentrated, attentive faces, the happy, curious faces she'd seen, with the way they had relentlessly stamped out Samy's skin, body, face, and smile?

On the top shelf of the wicker bookcase, alongside volumes on sculpture, there was a big, spiral notebook of sorts containing alternating sheets of paper and plastic sleeves. On the pages, Samuel had glued analyses of his work that had been published in the press, in chronological order, with the most recent articles first. The plastic sleeves contained photographs of his pieces and shows. On the shelf immediately beneath it, a shoebox bearing the word "Friends" in black marker drew her attention. Here Samuel had collected negative critiques of his work. She found a folded copy of the issue of *Tropics Daily* that had sparked the Samuel Pankeu Affair, as well as a few other virulent attacks—"The Work of Samuel Pankeu: An Ode to Uselessness"; "The Art of Sculpting Emptiness"; "Samuel Pankeu, or the Professionalization of Mediocrity"; "How to Go from Mediocre Amateur to Mediocre Professional"—and Tashun's interview in *The Voice of Zambuena* where he was very clear about his opinion of the show. The first nail Tashun drove into Samy's coffin, not long after the havoc wreaked by Mama Caramel's twisted mind. "We're all Aquatics," Kizito had said.

The stone, the clay, all the inert, inanimate objects Samy had devoted his days to, sacrificed his nights to, all of it could as easily end up on the scrapheap as live on indefinitely. In single combat, *mano a mano,* a rag dropped carelessly on the corner of the cluttered table, a rag covered in all sorts of stains, a rag Samy had held between his fingers, a rag whose life expectancy, though hard to know for sure, was undoubtedly quite brief, had triumphed over the artist Samuel Pankeu, who was gone, dead, buried, returned to the earth, to the worms, to nothingness. The toilet paper, toothbrush, socks, pencils, underwear, bathmat, walls, corrugated iron roof, pajamas, plates, and teapot—everything in the studio, all of these breakable, crushable, buyable, givable, disposable things, all of these lifeless but potentially enduring things, had secured victory over a funny, smart young man, full of wit, a walking dictionary of Latin quotes, an unrivaled godfather, a talented artist. The simplistic, ridiculous realization of everyone who ever experiences the death of a loved one humiliated Katmé in her grief. Rag: 1, Samuel Pankeu: 0.

Nothing could have prepared her for seeing Samy again without Samy.

She looked for a place to sit down, rejecting the tall bamboo chairs she'd so often sat on to watch Samuel work. There was dust everywhere. Mold fought with cobwebs for dominion over the corners of the room. Her vision blurred by tears, she opted for the cot, where she pulled back the Scottish wool blanket, lay down diagonally on the wrinkled yellow sheets, and curled her body into the fetal position.

Mama's funeral Mass in Fènn. The casket in the pavilion, Samy sitting next to Mama Caramel Two-for-Ten and Uncle Lollipop, the panther with blue paws singing near the altar. The publisher from *Tropics Daily* dressed up as an archbishop was hopping around in his purple cassock, while the other priests clapped their hands. Tashun, in his undertaker's suit, kept farting again and again; everyone plugged their nose. Samy left his pew, bowed quickly before me, and invited me to dance. The panther with blue paws serenaded us:

You asked to see me, so here I am,
Look at me! Zimanto!
I'm the panther who falls on his right side,
I'm the panther who falls on his left side,
I'm the panther who raises his paws,
Here I am! Zimanto!

With his hand on my waist, Samy whispered, "You want to reopen the investigation into my death, Mbindi? You want to challenge the law? Watch the panther dance. It keeps dancing and dancing. The more I have this dream, the realer the nightmare ahead becomes."

"Katmé, Kat? Are you here?" I woke up with a start. Someone was pounding on the door. The cot, the studio, his *pro bono publico* work, the panther, Zimanto the blue panther, the Aquatics. I was scared all of a sudden. It took a few seconds for me to pull myself together and remember that I'd called Ety the night before to ask him to join me at the studio. I'd also asked the landlord to come by so I could pay the three months of back rent. Keuna was supposed to stop by as well. There was so much to sort through, so many pieces to save.

I ran to unlock the door.

Acknowledgments

To David Mignot, the artisan behind a radiant dawn.

To Henri Jobbé-Duval, for "a room of my own" in Rotheneuf.

To Annick Piers, Catherine Feuillet, Elisabeth Marliangeas, Xavier Carniaux, for their friendship and patient readings.

To Yannick Lewat, Virginie Pandja, Annice Nana, Diane Lewat, Chrislin Nana. Yann and grandmother, thank you for all the delicious food. Vicho, you were, as always, my better half.

To Stéphane Tchakam, who now travels the other shore, a companion on the roads to enlightenment, who will always be with us.

To Julie Trassard-Donatien, for knowing what to say when I was full of doubt, and for bringing the radiant Isaée into my life.

Last but not least, to Etienne Fiatte. For everything and more, I'm proud to be your Mbindi réssé.

Coffee House Press began as a small letterpress operation in 1972 and has grown into an internationally renowned nonprofit publisher of literary fiction, essay, poetry, and other work that doesn't fit neatly into genre categories.

LITERATURE
is not the same thing as
PUBLISHING

Funder Acknowledgments

Coffee House Press is an internationally renowned independent book publisher and arts nonprofit based in Minneapolis, MN; through its literary publications, Coffee House acts as a catalyst and connector—between authors and readers, ideas and resources, creativity and community, inspiration and action.

Coffee House Press books are made possible through the generous support of grants and donations from corporations, state and federal grant programs, family foundations, and the many individuals who believe in the transformational power of literature. This activity is made possible by the voters of Minnesota through a Minnesota State Arts Board Operating Support grant, thanks to the legislative appropriation from the Arts and Cultural Heritage Fund. Coffee House also receives major operating support from the Amazon Literary Partnership, McKnight Foundation, and the National Endowment for the Arts (NEA). To find out more about how NEA grants impact individuals and communities, visit www.arts.gov.

Coffee House Press receives additional support from Bookmobile; Dorsey & Whitney LLP; and the Schwab Charitable Fund.

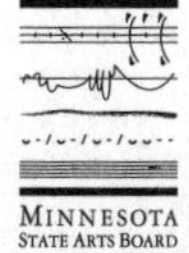

McKNIGHT FOUNDATION

The Publisher's Circle of Coffee House Press

Publisher's Circle members make significant contributions to Coffee House Press's annual giving campaign. Understanding that a strong financial base is necessary for the press to meet the challenges and opportunities that arise each year, this group plays a crucial part in the success of Coffee House's mission.

Recent Publisher's Circle members include many anonymous donors, Patricia A. Beithon, Robin Chemers Neustein, Kelli Cloutier, Theodore Cornwell, Jane Dalrymple-Hollo, Jeremy M. Davies, Mary Ebert and Paul Stembler, Kamilah Foreman, Eva Galiber, Bryan Garrett, Roger Hale and Nor Hall, William Hardacker, Randy Hartten and Ron Lotz, Carl and Heidi Horsch, Amy L. Hubbard and Geoffrey J. Kehoe Fund of the St. Paul & Minnesota Foundation, Hyde Family Charitable Fund, Kenneth & Susan Kahn, the Kenneth Koch Literary Estate, Cinda Kornblum, the Lenfestey Family Foundation, Carol and Aaron Mack, Gillian McCain, Mary and Malcolm McDermid, Daniel N. Smith III and Maureen Millea Smith, Vance Opperman, Mr. Pancks' Fund in memory of Graham Kimpton, Alan Polsky, Robin Preble, Ronald Restrepo and Candace S. Baggett, Elizabeth Schnieders, Steve Smith, Jeffrey Sugerman and Sarah Schultz, Paul Thissen, Allyson Tucker, Grant Wood, Margaret Wurtele, Aptara Inc., The Buckley Charitable Fund, and Dorsey and Whitney Foundation.

For more information about the Publisher's Circle and other ways to support Coffee House Press books, authors, and activities, please visit www.coffeehousepress.org/pages/donate or contact us at info@coffeehousepress.org.

OSVALDE LEWAT is a Cameroonian author. Osvalde is a renowned documentary filmmaker whose work has been awarded the prestigious Peabody Award. Her debut novel, *The Aquatics,* won the Pan-African Prize for Literature, the French Academy Literature Prize, and the Kourouma Prize.

MAREN BAUDET-LACKNER is an American literary translator from the French who is passionate about bringing exceptional works of literature by traditionally underrepresented authors to English-speaking readers. She has published over a dozen titles with major imprints in the United Kingdom and United States and is the recipient of a 2023 PEN Presents Award and a 2024 PEN Translates Award. She also received Albertine Translation grants for her work in 2023 and 2024. Maren holds advanced degrees from Yale and the Sorbonne and lives near Paris with her family.

The Aquatics was designed by Bookmobile Design & Digital Publisher Services. Text is set in Warnock Pro.